air head

Being Nikki

Praise for *Airhead*

'*Airhead* is packed with romance, adventure and stardom, the perfect recipe for a girly read'
Independent on Sunday

'It's the secret dream of most girls, and this book is the first of a trilogy that promises to be huge fun'
Daily Telegraph

'Gives you a fun look into what can happen when you're suddenly no longer yourself. This hysterical book will have you wondering whether you really want to trade lives with a celebrity after all'
Seventeen.com

Books by Meg Cabot

The Princess Diaries series

The Mediator series

All American Girl
All American Girl: Ready or Not

Airhead
Airhead: Being Nikki
Avalon High
Avalon High manga: The Merlin Prophecy
Teen Idol
How to Be Popular
Jinx
Tommy Sullivan Is a Freak
Nicola and the Viscount
Victoria and the Rogue

For younger readers
The Allie Finkle series

For older readers
The Guy Next Door
Boy Meets Girl
Every Boy's Got One
Queen of Babble series
The Heather Wells series

Also available in audio

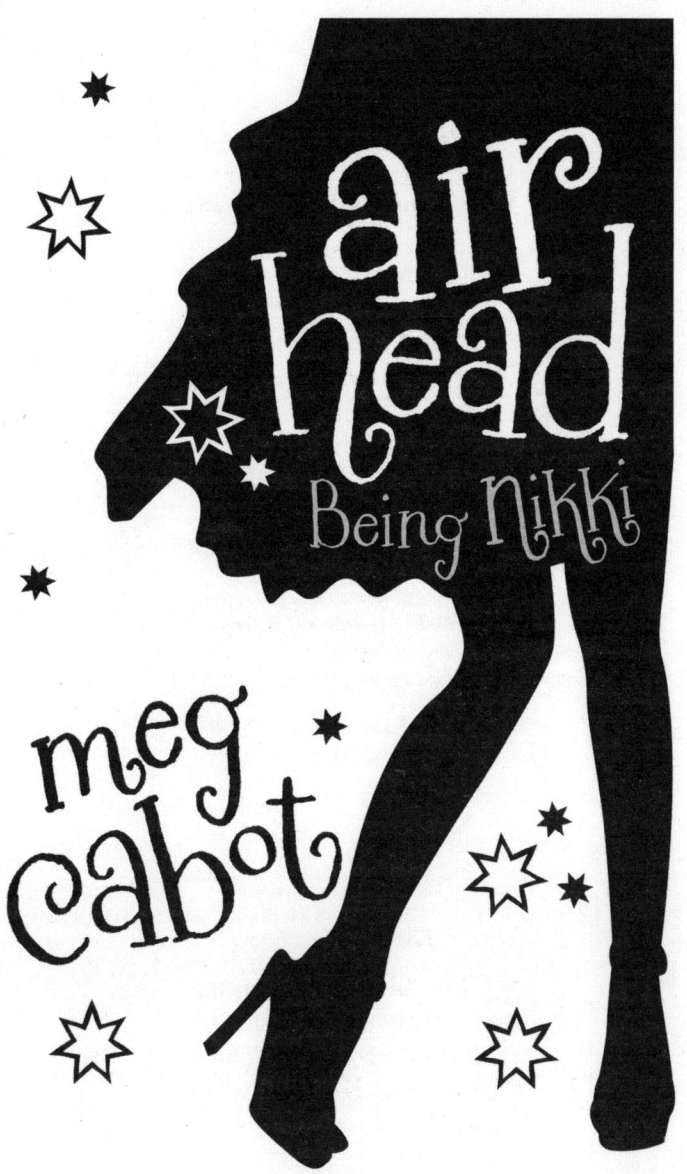

air head

head

Being Nikki

meg cabot

MACMILLAN

First published 2009 by Macmillan Children's Books
a division of Macmillan Publishers Limited
20 New Wharf Road, London N1 9RR
Basingstoke and Oxford
Associated companies throughout the world
www.panmacmillan.com

ISBN 978-0-230-73937-6

1 3 5 7 9 8 6 4 2

A CIP catalogue record for this book is available from
the British Library.

Typeset by Nigel Hazle
Printed and bound in the UK by CPI Mackays, Chatham ME5 8TD

For Benjamin

Special thanks to Beth Ader, Jennifer Brown, Michele Jaffe, Laura Langlie, Abigail McAden and especially Benjamin Egnatz

One

I'm cold.

I'm freezing, actually.

The waves are crashing against the backs of my legs, and the water, which this afternoon had been a warm turquoise, has turned an icy black. The rocks to which I'm clinging are cutting into my fingertips and the bottoms of my feet. They're slippery as a glacier, but I can't let go or I'll fall into that frigid water – in which, no exaggeration, sharks are swarming – beneath me.

And since I'm wearing nothing but an extremely small white bikini and a thigh holder for the dagger I've got clenched between my teeth, I haven't got anything to protect me from their razor-sharp teeth. I just have to hang on, or else face possible limb amputation or, at the very least, excruciating pain – worse than the pain I'm already experiencing even. I've got to complete my mission, deliver the package to the mansion perched on the cliff above me . . .

Or I'll have to listen to André, the bitchy art director, go on about it all night.

'No, no, no,' André yelled on the boat from which he was directing the shoot. 'Viv, adjust the gel on that spot over there. No, that one over *there*.'

Seriously. I should have just fallen backwards into the

water and let the sharks eat me. I was fairly certain the sharks *wanted* to eat me, despite what Dom, the guy Stark Enterprises rented the boat from, told us. He said they were nurse sharks, perfectly harmless, and more scared of us than we were of them. He kept insisting they were attracted to the bright lights Francesco, the photographer, had set up, and weren't hanging around because they wanted me for a snack.

But really, how did he know? They'd probably never tasted supermodel before. I'm betting they'd find me delicious.

'Nik?' Brandon Stark called from the boat. 'How you doing?'

Like he even cared. Well, I mean, I guess he *cared*.

But it wasn't as if he was even here for any reason other than that he wanted to snag a ride on the corporate jet, so he could spend the day cruising around the island of St John on a jet ski. He was solicitous now entirely because it was expected of him.

Or because he thought it was going to help him get into my pants later. Like that's ever worked.

Lately, anyway.

'Oh, I'm great,' I called back. Only you couldn't tell what I was saying, because of the dagger stuck in my mouth. Which I couldn't remove, because my hands were clinging to the rocks, keeping me from becoming a shark snack. There was spit pooling at the sides of my lips. Nice.

'We just need a few more shots, Nikki,' André called.

2

'You're doing great.' Someone said something, and he added, 'Can you try to stop trembling?'

'I'm not trembling,' I pointed out. 'I'm shaking. With cold.'

'What did she say?' André asked Brandon. No one could understand a word coming out of my mouth because of the dagger.

'How should I know?' Brandon said to André. 'Nikki,' he called to me. 'What did you say?'

'I said I'm *cold*,' I yelled. The waves were getting bigger, wetting the bottom of my suit now. My butt was numb. Great. I couldn't feel my butt.

Why was I doing this again? Was it for a Stark-brand perfume? Or a cellphone? I couldn't even remember any more.

And Lulu had said how lucky I was, getting to go to the Virgin Islands in December, when every other New Yorker would be – to quote her directly – freezing their butt off.

If only she knew the truth. I *was* freezing my butt off. Literally.

'I don't know what she said,' I heard Brandon telling André.

'Never mind, just shoot, Francesco,' André said to the photographer. 'Nikki, we're shooting again!'

I couldn't tell what was happening, because the boat was behind me. But flashes started going off. I strained my neck, looking up the side of the cliff, trying to stay in my part. I tried not to think about the fact that I was in a way too skimpy white bikini. Instead, I pictured myself in body armour. I wasn't me, Em Watts, at all. I was Lenneth Valkyrie, recruiting souls of fallen warriors and leading them to Valhalla. I could do it. I could do *anything*.

Except that it wasn't Valhalla at the top of the cliff, just a road that tourists took on their way to the airport with some scrubby weeds growing along it.

I could have done with some body armour. It made no sense, really, that a trained assassin – which is what I was apparently supposed to be – would climb a cliff barefoot in a bikini, without even a pocket where she'd be able to keep a cellphone. Except possibly in her knife-holder. Maybe that's why I was holding the knife in my mouth instead of where it would make sense – *in the holder*?

But then, I'd noticed that role-playing-game designers – or art directors – never considered practicality when outfitting their characters and models.

You know what else would have made sense? Photographing me in a nice warm studio back in New York and then computer-imposing the image of the cliff and the waves and the moonlight around me.

But Francesco wanted to inject realism into his shots. That's why Stark hired him. Only the best for Stark Enterprises.

The sharks that were swarming below me, waiting to eat me when I fell off the stupid cliff face, were super-realistic.

'You're doing great, Nikki,' Francesco called, clicking

away. 'I can really see the grim determination on your face –'

I vowed that when I got off this cliff I was going to take the knife and plunge it into one of Francesco's eyeballs.

Except that the knife blade was made out of plastic.

But I bet it'd still do the job just fine.

'– the sheer desperation of a girl reduced by circumstances to her most fundamental self,' Francesco went on, 'as she struggles for survival in a world where everyone and everything seems to be pitted against her –'

The funny thing was, Francesco had basically just described my daily existence.

'I think she's supposed to be happy, actually,' André said, sounding concerned. 'Because she knows she's wearing Stark-brand deodorant, and that gives girls the confidence they need to get the job done.'

Oh. So this was a deodorant ad.

'Happy, Nikki,' André called. 'Be happy! We're in the islands! You should be having a good time with this!'

I knew André was right. I *should* have been having a good time with this. What did I have to be so unhappy about anyway? I had everything a girl my age could want: I had a great career as the Face of Stark Enterprises, for which I was more than well compensated. I had my own two-bedroom loft in a landmark building in downtown Manhattan, which I shared with the most adorable miniature poodle in the history of time, plus a hilarious – though I'm not sure she means to be – celebutante room-mate who routinely gets us into all the best party spots in town.

I was rich. I had a designer wardrobe in my overstuffed closets, and Frette sheets on my king-sized bed, an en-suite master bath with a jacuzzi tub, a gourmet chef's kitchen with black granite counters and all Sub-Zero appliances, and a full-time housekeeper slash masseuse who also, I recently discovered, knows how to give (almost) painless waxes.

I was even still doing pretty well in school (despite the late nights and oh-so-painful early mornings, thanks to that celebutante room-mate).

And, OK, my straight-A average was pretty much shot due to the fact that my employer kept ripping me out of class periodically to send me to some tropical island to wave my butt over a bunch of sharks so he could have my picture taken in the dark.

But if I spent every spare minute of my time studying, I could maybe graduate on time with the rest of my class. Not too shabby for a girl who had spent a month of this past semester in a coma.

So why was I so freaking depressed?

'Make her look happy,' I heard André say to Brandon, who obliged by calling out, 'Hey, Nik! This is just like that time you and I were in Mustique together last year, remember? And you were doing that shoot for British *Vogue,* and we had that private cabana? And we drank all that Goldschläger? Then we went skinny-dipping? God, we had the best time . . .'

That was when I remembered. Why I was so depressed, I mean.

That was also when I let go of the cliff-face.

It was just that suddenly, being eaten by sharks seemed preferable to hearing the rest of Brandon's story.

Because I'd heard a lot of similar stories over the past month – not just from Brandon, but from guys all over Manhattan – and I had a pretty good idea how it was going to turn out. For a seventeen-year-old – and one who was allegedly going out with her employer's only son – Nikki Howard had certainly had a lot of male companions.

I heard screams from the boat. But a part of me didn't even care. I hit the water backwards. It was even colder than I'd imagined it would be. All the breath was sucked from my body, and the shock was so intense, for a second I wondered if a shark had bitten me in half. I knew from a documentary Christopher and I had once watched that a shark's teeth were so sharp, their victims didn't even feel that first, initial crunch. They often weren't aware they'd been injured . . . not until they were surrounded by the warm current of their own blood.

Bone-chilling cold wasn't the only thing I experienced as I hit the water, though. I was also plunged into darkness. At least at first. Until my vision adjusted to the murky water, and I saw that the lights from the boat had lit up the ocean around me. That was when I knew I hadn't been bitten in half. There weren't any swirling clouds of blood around me. Just dark blobs I realized were nurse sharks, swimming frantically to get away from me. I guess Dom had been right – they *were* more scared of us than we were of them. I could also see my own hair, swaying like golden seaweed around me. They'd rowed me over to the cliff so carefully in a rubber dinghy just forty-five minutes earlier to keep my hair – and the swimsuit – from getting wet.

And now I'd ruined everything. Vanessa, the stylist who'd worked for nearly an hour to get my blonde tresses perfect, was going to be annoyed when I resurfaced, wet as a mermaid.

If I resurfaced.

Except . . . well, the truth was, it was kind of nice down there. Cold, yeah. But peaceful. Quiet. Mermaids had the right idea. What was Ariel thinking, wanting to live on land, anyway?

It was totally amazing, and for a second or two, I forgot about how cold and miserable I was, and that I couldn't feel my butt. Oh, and that I couldn't breathe and was probably drowning.

But then, what did I have to live for anyway? Sure, it was great, I guess, having access to the Stark Enterprises private plane and not having to do my own dishes and getting all the free lipgloss I could ever want.

But I'd never actually cared about lipgloss.

The fact was, I was being forced to work for a corporation I was pretty sure was responsible for turning America into one endless, soulless strip mall.

And the guy I liked didn't know I was alive. Literally.

And if I told him I wasn't dead, Stark Enterprises, that I was pretty sure was spying on me every chance it got, was going to throw my parents in jail.

And, oh yeah: my brain has been removed from my body and put into someone else's.

So what was the point of living? I mean, really?

I figured I'd just stay down there. It was less stressful, in a lot of ways, than my real life. And that was no exaggeration.

The next thing I knew, though, there was an enormous splash beside me. And suddenly Brandon, fully clothed, was swimming towards me, and had grabbed me, and was pulling me – gasping and choking – to the surface, and then to the boat.

I was a little angry. And also shivering uncontrollably.

OK, I guess I didn't really want to live on the bottom of the ocean.

But I didn't need to be rescued either. I wasn't *really* going to stay under there until my lungs filled and I choked to death on brackish seawater.

I don't think.

When I looked past Brandon's taut arm muscles as he towed me back to the boat, I saw my agent's assistant peering at me worriedly from the bow.

'Oh my God, Nikki, are you OK?' Shauna cried. Cosabella, who she was clutching in her arms, was barking hysterically. Cosabella. I'd forgotten about Cosabella. How could I have been so selfish? Who'd have taken care of Cosabella? Lulu isn't responsible enough. She forgets to feed herself half the time (except for mojitos and popcorn). No way would she remember to feed a tiny dog.

Shauna had asked a good question. *Was* I OK? That was something I'd been asking myself for a while now.

Sometimes I wondered if I'd ever be OK again.

'Nikki,' I heard Francesco call out from the boat, 'thank God. It's all right. I got the shot.'

Great. Not: *Nikki, thank God.* You're *all right.* But: *Nikki, thank God.* It's *all right: I got the shot.*

God forbid he might not have.

Because Stark Enterprises would never have let any of us go home otherwise.

Not until we got the shot.

Two

I was alone in my hotel room (well, alone except for Cosabella, who wouldn't stop licking the salt water from my face), attempting to defrost in my balcony's private hot tub. I had the jets on full, hoping to ease the cuts on my hands and feet caused by hanging on to the cliff-face. Being a model, I was learning, could be painful, and sometimes even life-threatening. Brandon and the rest of the people from the photo shoot had gone off for another one of their thousand-dollar sashimi dinners – expensed to Brandon's father, billionaire Robert Stark, of course – at the hotel restaurant downstairs. I'd declined joining them in favour of the hot tub, a burger from room service, and a few rounds of *Journeyquest* in front of my MacBook Air. Listening to gossip about the Olsen twins and then dancing to techno-pop, which I knew would follow, didn't seem all that appealing after what I'd been through.

Actually, it never seemed all that appealing to me . . . although Brandon had stood outside my door, begging me to reconsider, for a long time while I'd shivered.

Which was why, when Nikki's cellphone played the first few bars of Fergie's 'Barracuda', I was sure it was him calling.

It's embarrassing to have 'Barracuda' as a ringtone. But I'd never gotten around to changing it. Actually, since

I'd never gotten over my suspicion that Nikki's Stark-brand cellphone was bugged (her Stark-brand PC had had tracking software on it – why wouldn't Stark be listening in on her phone calls too?), I'd just never bothered to take the time to figure out how to work her phone beyond hitting the delete button. I simply avoided using it most of the time, preferring to make my personal calls on the iPhone I'd bought with one of Nikki's credit cards instead.

I checked the caller ID (I'd totally learned not to pick up unless I recognized the name. Otherwise I'd find myself at the receiving end of a long harangue about why I hadn't called in so long and how much someone with a name like Eduardo was just dying to fly to Paris with me again) and was surprised to see that it wasn't Brandon at all, but Lulu.

'What?' I said. We stopped being polite with each other the night she and Brandon had kidnapped me from the hospital after my surgery in a misguided attempt to 'rescue' me.

'Um,' Lulu said, 'there was a guy here to see you.'

'Lulu.' In the short time that I'd lived with Lulu, I'd come to love her like a sister. So I'd be the first person to admit she's short of a few brain cells. 'There's *always* a guy there to see me.'

It was sad, but true. The loft we shared was like guy central. The only guy who'd never stopped by our loft to see me was the one guy I actually longed to have there.

And he didn't seem to have made up his mind about whether or not he liked me yet. At least if the weird looks

12

he kept throwing me in first period Public Speaking were any indication.

Then again, lately he was always throwing McKayla Donofrio weird looks in class all the time too, so this might have meant nothing.

'This one was different,' Lulu said.

That piece of information caused me to sit up straighter in the hot tub.

'No kidding?' I'd gotten a bit pruny from having been in the hot tub so long. Plus my hands were wet, so I almost dropped the cellphone. 'What did he want?'

'Duh. To talk to you.'

'I know,' I said with forced patience. You needed a lot of patience when dealing with Lulu. It was like dealing with a five-year-old. 'But what about? I mean, did he say what he wanted?'

Lulu was chewing gum. Loudly. In my ear. 'He just said you'd know. And that it was important and that he needed to see you and that he'd be back. He didn't leave his name.'

My shoulders slumped with disappointment. It wasn't Christopher. I mean, Christopher would have left his name. He was like that.

Which meant it could only have been another one of *them*.

Seriously, you'd think they'd give up. Just how long were these scam artists going to keep at it? Really, announce on the news that a wealthy celebrity had amnesia and you wouldn't believe what kind of scum crawled out of the bowels of the F-train tunnel, claiming to be a close friend, or even a relation. It was unbelievable how many first cousins Nikki Howard apparently had.

'He said you'd know what it was about,' Lulu informed me.

'How am I supposed to know what it's about if I don't even know his name?' I asked.

'I don't know,' Lulu said, 'but Karl showed me what the guy looked like on the security camera. And he wasn't like all the other ones. This one was young. And kinda hot. And he didn't have any visible neck tattoos.'

My heart skipped a beat. And not because I'd been in the hot tub longer than the twenty minutes recommended on the sign posted beside the timer on the balcony wall, either.

'Young?' I didn't want to get my hopes up. I mean, they'd already been dashed so many times before when Christopher had glanced my way in Public Speaking, only to turn out to be looking at the clock, or some homeless guy out the window, or McKayla Donofrio. 'Wait, Lulu . . . was this guy blond?'

There was a pause as Lulu appeared to be trying to remember. 'Yeah. Blond-ish, anyway.'

Good enough. 'Was he tall?' I asked.

'Uh-huh,' Lulu said.

I thought I must be having a heart attack, which the hot tub regulations explicitly warned could happen. At least in the pregnant or elderly, of which I was neither.

But I had had major surgery a couple months ago, so

you never know. Beside me, Cosabella was licking my cheek eagerly where some of the water from the hot tub had splashed on to my face.

'Was he built?' I asked. I'd started scrambling to get out of the hot tub. I didn't need to die of a heart attack just when my dream was finally about to come true. And OK, I knew an hour ago I'd been seriously considering permanent residence under the sea. But not really. It had been pretty cold down there.

Also, I did kind of want to see what happened in *Realms*, the newest version of *Journeyquest*. The only problem was, in an exclusive deal with the game's designer, you could only get *Realms* if you bought Stark Quark, the new PC Stark Enterprises was unveiling for the holidays. *Journeyquest* fans hadn't been *too* mad about that. Much. 'Like, not *built*-built, but . . . fit?'

'It was hard to tell on the security camera,' Lulu said. 'But I wouldn't kick him out of the loft, let's put it that way.'

'Oh my God.' I snatched a towel off the balcony railing. My heart was racing like I'd just gotten off the treadmill (which was something I had to do regularly now, in order to stay in shape. But it was OK, because Nikki's body enjoyed working out, unlike my old one, which despised it). I couldn't believe it. After all this time – weeks now, I'd been waiting – Christopher was finally coming around.

And I had to be in the Virgin Islands when it happened!

'Lulu. *Lulu*. That was Christopher! It has to be!'

Now that I was out of the hot tub, I'd stopped feeling like I was going to have a heart attack. My heart was still slamming into the back of my ribs, but it was doing it in a happy, anticipatory way. Like, *Bang-bang, Christopher wants to see you! Bang-bang, Christopher finally gets it!* I had gone out of my way these past few weeks to subtly convince him that while on the outside I might seem like the perfect face of a soulless corporation intent on sucking the lifeblood from small businesses everywhere, on the inside I was still his cool, video-game loving, soulless-corporation-hating best friend, Em.

Without actually saying so, of course, or I might have invoked the full wrath of Robert Stark and his high-powered legal team. While I was positive I could trust Christopher with the truth, and that he'd never tell – if I could even get him to believe me, which was a whole other story – what I couldn't do was trust that my telling him wouldn't be overheard somehow by Stark. Sometimes they even seemed to know what I was *thinking*. Don't ask me how.

Still, it hadn't been easy, trying to get Christopher to see that I was Em behind Nikki Howard's perfect blue eyes, especially what with McKayla Donofrio constantly trying to interrupt me every five seconds (what was with her new crush on Christopher? He cut his hair and suddenly even the head of Tribeca Alternative's Business Club thought he was hot) and my having to refer to *Journeyquest* almost constantly in order to hold his attention.

Was that what had lured him to the loft? It had to be.

Either Christopher was finally catching on that I was his old friend Em Watts in Nikki Howard's body, or he was starting to think I was stalking him. Maybe he'd stopped by to tell me he was dating McKayla and to gently recommend I seek counselling.

Wait. No. I refused to stoop to such negative thinking.

'Can you just ask the doorman to tell him that I'm coming home?' I said to Lulu. 'Christopher, I mean. If he comes back. That I'll be home as soon as I possibly can.'

'Sure,' Lulu said, with a yawn. 'I mean, I guess. But I don't see why you can't just call him and tell him yourself. Invite him to the holiday party –'

Lulu had been planning this huge holiday party for weeks. Apparently, she and Nikki had been famous for it, and their over-the-top entertaining in general. The annual party had always been a huge success (the two years the girls had had it so far), with paparazzi showing up and photos from it appearing in *Page Six* and even in *Vogue*, and their friends loved it. Lulu herself hadn't been able to concentrate on anything else since December the first, much to the chagrin of her agent and manager, who were trying to get her to finish her album, which was supposed to drop sometime in the spring.

There was just one little problem with Lulu's holiday party this year, a problem that she didn't know about yet: I wasn't going to be there.

I didn't know quite how I was going to break this news to her. Basically, Lulu didn't have any family except for me (or, rather, Nikki), since her parents were divorced and seemingly completely uninterested in her. I felt terrible leaving her alone for the holidays, especially for her big blowout party.

But what was I supposed to do? I had a previous commitment.

In reply to her question about Christopher, 'I'm not supposed to know his number,' I reminded her. 'Remember? I wonder how he found out where I live.'

'It's not hard,' Lulu said. 'All anybody has to do is look for the lines of depressed-looking Eurotrash hipsters hanging around outside, wanting to know why you won't give them the time of day . . . or the money they want you to think you owe them because they're your long-lost unemployed cousin.'

I'd towelled off and was throwing on a pair of jeans and a cami over my bra and panties – no easy feat while clutching a cellphone and trying not to step on an excited miniature poodle.

But you'd be surprised how fast you learn to get dressed in all kinds of conditions when people are constantly stripping you with absolutely no privacy whatsoever.

'Lulu,' I said, 'do we have to talk about my faux relatives right now?'

'Whatever,' Lulu said. 'That one dude was kind of hot, in a greasy way.'

'He was my *fake* cousin,' I reminded her. 'Seriously, Lulu, what am I going to do? Brandon wants to take me jet-skiing tomorrow.'

'What?' Lulu sounded confused. 'Brandon wants to what?'

'Take me jet-skiing,' I repeated. 'He says he thinks I'm wound too tight.'

'Wound too tight?' Now Lulu sounded incredulous. 'Why would he think *that*? The spirit-transfer thing again?'

'Uh . . .' Poor Lulu was still convinced her former roommate Nikki and I had swapped souls, not that my brain had been transplanted into her body. I didn't want to tell her the truth – the part about Brandon having recently dragged me up from the ocean floor, after my having made no attempt to save myself from drowning. It was too weird. Plus, since we were talking over Nikki's Stark-brand phone, which I was sure was bugged, and there was every chance someone from Brandon's dad's office was probably listening in on our conversation, it was a bad idea to have been talking about any of this – especially my 'spirit transfer' – anyway. So I just said, 'Yeah. I guess so.'

'But you got the shot, right?'

'Of course we got the shot,' I said.

'Then,' Lulu said, 'whatever. You're Nikki Howard. What you say goes. Just tell him the jet leaves tomorrow, or else.' Stark Enterprises flies its employees, including me, around on one of several private jets, a move that's time efficient for them but hardly friendly towards the environment. My carbon footprint is now huge. I've had to donate large amounts of Nikki's money in an attempt to offset it.

Still, even though the jet said Stark Enterprises on it, Brandon considered it his personal property.

'But technically it's *Brandon's* jet,' I reminded her. 'Or his dad's, really, but whatever. How do I talk him into leaving early?'

'You don't *talk* him into leaving early,' Lulu said. 'You *tell* him you have to leave tomorrow, and to make sure the plane is ready. Then you do that thing you do with your tongue—'

'Oh, my God,' I interrupted, quickly. This was definitely not a conversation for Stark legal, or whoever might be listening in on Nikki Howard's phone calls – if, indeed, anyone was – to overhear. 'Lulu!'

'Or you could just get back together with him,' Lulu said, sounding as if the idea had just occurred to her. 'I mean, you know that's what he wants. He's been a wreck ever since the two of you broke up. But I don't see how getting back together with him would work, since you like another guy—'

'OK, Lulu,' I said. She'd obviously been eating way too much microwave popcorn again. Some days when I wasn't around, that's all she ate, because she couldn't cook. 'I have to go now . . .'

'Too bad you can't just leave tonight,' Lulu said, with a sigh. 'But that would mean flying *commercial*.'

She uttered the words 'flying *commercial*' in the same revolted tone my sister Frida would say 'wearing non-designer jeans'.

'Ooooh,' Lulu squealed in my ear, having apparently

just thought of something else. 'I'm getting the caterer to serve Oysters Rockefeller at the party, and you know what oysters are? An aphrodisiac, that's what. Once Christopher has one, he won't be able to resist you!'

This wasn't the time or place to break it to her that I wasn't going to be around for the holidays (also, oysters, so not my thing), so I just said of course, and hung up. Then I grabbed my room key and headed out to look for Brandon, Cosabella trotting along after me.

I found him – or rather, Cosabella did – sitting on one of the thickly cushioned chairs on the empty moonlit deck outside the hotel bar with his face buried in the cleavage of the restaurant hostess.

'Excuse me,' I said, torn between mortification and amusement.

Brandon dropped the hostess in surprise. She fell off the deckchair, landing on the hard terrazzo deck with an '*Oof!*'.

I gasped and said, 'Oh, I'm so sorry!' Cosy barked excitedly as the hostess – her name tag read Rhonda – rubbed her backside and glared at me from the ground.

'Nikki.' Brandon stood up and stepped over Rhonda as if she wasn't even there. 'Are you all right? What are you doing here? I thought you said you were going to bed.'

'I am,' I said. 'Or at least, I'm going to soon. Are you all right?' I asked Rhonda, since Brandon seemed to have forgotten her existence.

'I'm fine,' Rhonda said, giving Brandon a withering glance he didn't even notice.

'Is there something wrong?' Brandon wanted to know. Only he was asking me, not the woman whose backside he'd nearly just broken in the process of dropping her. 'Can I get you something? Dinner? Are you hungry?'

'No,' I said. 'I'm fine. I just to needed to ask you something—'

'Anything.' Brandon looked eager. 'What is it?'

'Um,' I said, bending down and scooping Cosy up to give Rhonda a chance to escape, since the dog kept trying to lick the hostess's face as she tried to climb to her feet. 'It can wait . . .'

'No, really.' Brandon didn't seem to care at all about Rhonda any more, or her efforts to become vertical. 'What?'

Behind him, Rhonda had gotten up, smoothed out her tight black skirt, and lifted the tray on which she'd been serving Brandon his after-dinner drink when things had apparently gotten . . . well, cosy between them. As she walked away, her head held high, I got a hint of her perfume as it wafted back towards us on the warm tropical breeze.

It was 'Nikki', now available at a special holiday rate of forty-nine ninety-nine at any Stark Megastore. It costs Stark a couple of dollars a bottle to make (in China, of course), less than that to ship, and smells so cloying I wouldn't actually wear it in a million years.

'It's just that I know you mentioned wanting to leave the day after tomorrow,' I said. 'But I was wondering if we could leave a little earlier instead.'

'Earlier?' Brandon seemed confused. Whatever it was he'd apparently been expecting me to ask, it wasn't this. I had a suspicion Lulu had been right, and that he'd been hoping I was going to ask him if he wanted to get back together. It was a hope he'd been harbouring for some time. Sadly, it was never going to come true . . . Brandon might have been Nikki's type, but he just wasn't mine. At least, not while there was still hope that Christopher might some day come around. 'How much earlier?'

'Oh, not too much,' I said. 'I was thinking, say, tomorrow morning, around nine.'

'But that's when Dad had us originally scheduled to leave,' Brandon said, looking astonished. 'I was going to blow that off and take you on a jet-ski tour of the island instead.'

During which, I was sure, he'd been hoping I'd fall head over heels in love with him again.

'Yeah,' I said. 'And that's so sweet of you. But something's come up, and I really need to get back to town—'

'And snorkelling,' Brandon said. 'I was thinking we could go snorkelling tomorrow after lunch.'

Well, I had shown a certain affinity for being underwater.

'That sounds so fun,' I said. 'But I really need to get home.'

'Why?' Brandon asked. His dark eyebrows had lowered in a manner that, if I hadn't known better, I might have described as menacing. Except that Brandon didn't have a menacing bone in his body.

'It's personal,' I said. I wasn't about to elaborate further.

'But . . . I don't want to leave early.' Brandon flopped back down into the deckchair he'd popped out of, and reached for his drink. It was clear from his attitude that he was ready to argue. And that, unless I was ready to be his girlfriend, he wasn't going anywhere.

Great. I should have known it would come to this.

No way, however, was I doing the thing with my tongue, whatever it was.

I slipped on to the deckchair beside Brandon's and leaned forward, even though I knew my cami gapped in the front when I did this. I was wearing a bra, of course, so it wasn't like he was seeing anything he hadn't been seeing a few hours earlier when I was in my bikini.

Still, he couldn't seem to make himself *not* look. It really was true . . . the power of the cami was not to be underestimated, something Frida had tried to drill into my head years before, but I would never listen, insisting that, as a feminist, I wouldn't wear garments that objectified the female form. Lulu was the one who'd pointed out that camis don't objectify, but *enhance* the parts all women should be proud of, no matter what their size.

'Does your father know you're keeping the corporate jet an extra twenty-four hours, Brandon?' I asked sweetly.

Brandon went right on looking.

'Who cares what my dad thinks?' he asked a little sullenly. 'It's not like we don't have other jets he can use if he needs one . . .'

'Don't you feel guilty about all the money this is costing your father, when we've already got the shot? Especially when it's just so you can go snorkelling and jet-skiing?' I asked.

'No,' Brandon said, watching as I traced a little circle on his knee – a trick I'd seen Lulu perform numerous times on guys who'd bought her drinks at the nightclub Cave. Did I feel bad performing it on Brandon? A little. Did I hope it worked? Totally. 'My dad and I aren't exactly close, you know.'

'I know,' I said sympathetically.

'My mom left years ago for that ashram, and I've barely seen her since,' Brandon went on, slurring his words a little. I could tell he'd had too much to drink. As usual.

'I know,' I said again. I actually didn't know this personally. But I'd read an article about it once in a *People* magazine Frida left lying around. 'Look, I can't speak for everyone else, but personally I'd prefer it if we left tomorrow as scheduled. If we don't –' I took my hand away from his knee and leaned back abruptly, taking away his pleasant view down my shirt. This was another strategy Lulu had taught me. Giveth a little, then taketh away. But you have to time it just right. – 'I'm going to leave on the first commercial flight I can get on.'

'Commercial?' Like Lulu, Brandon seemed horrified at the idea of my flying commercial. So horrified that he caught up my hand and, with a quick movement, tugged me towards him. Hard.

'Now what's so important back in New York that you, Nikki Howard, would fly *commercial*?' he demanded.

Um . . . oops. I always seemed to forget – maybe because he so wasn't my type, with his frat-boy good looks and apparent lack of interest in anything but Bacardi and the latest hip-hop artist he was promoting – that Brandon was Nikki Howard's ex. Also that the two of them – according to the tabloid clippings I'd found in Nikki's room (she'd saved every article ever printed about her in a drawer at the bottom of her nightstand) – had been hot and heavy for at least a year. The last thing I needed was Brandon getting jealous that the reason I wanted to get back to Manhattan so badly was because the guy I'm in love with might finally be coming around.

'Nothing,' I said innocently. 'I just have to get back to school. Remember? I'm still in school? I have finals this week.'

Brandon's grip on my hand got a little looser. Instead of clinging possessively, he started sliding his fingers up my arm.

'Oh, sure. School,' he echoed. 'Finals.'

As soon as his fingers reached the back of my neck and curled into the heavy damp tangles of my hair, I realized we were going to have a problem. I won't deny it: it felt good, having his fingers there. That was the problem, and Brandon knew it. This was one of the many issues I had with what Stark Enterprises had done to me, putting my brain inside Nikki Howard's body. I didn't like Brandon Stark – at least, not in *that* way.

26

But Nikki Howard liked Brandon Stark . . . or at least her body did. My eyes drifted closed – totally against my will – as Brandon began to gently knead the place where my skull met my spine.

This was so wrong! Brandon knew Nikki Howard was defenceless in the face of a good neck massage. Her entire body, I'd discovered shortly after a hairstylist first tried it on me, went limp when anyone started kneading the place where her spine met the back of her neck.

Brandon obviously knew that, and was taking unfair advantage of the situation.

'It seems like school is all you ever think about now,' he went on. 'That and this Stark-Enterprises-is-ruining-the-country crap.'

'It's not crap,' I murmured as his fingers went on kneading. 'Your dad's company is contributing to global warming as well as to the decay of small-town America—'

'Man, it's sexy when you talk all revolutionary like that,' Brandon murmured back.

His voice sounded so close, I opened my eyes. I was surprised to find his face directly in front of mine, his lips just a inch from my mouth.

Oh no. It was happening again. I could feel myself leaning towards him, my body swaying closer to his as if pushed by some unseen force . . . even though kissing Brandon Stark was the last thing I wanted to do just then. Intellectually, I mean.

The thing was, it wasn't *me*. *I* had no control over it. It was Nikki. She was just boy-crazy like that.

Not that there's anything wrong with a woman who enjoys kissing guys. Kissing guys is fantastic. In fact, I can't believe I spent so much of my life pre-being Nikki *not* kissing guys.

The problem with Nikki was that she seemed to have spent so much of her life before my brain was inside her kissing the *wrong* guys. So much time, in fact, that kissing the wrong guys had become a habit too hard to break, and was now something her body did on automatic, without my being able to stop it.

Like right then, for instance. Before I could do anything, my mouth was on Brandon's, and we were full-on making out in the exact spot where just minutes before he'd been hooking up with Rhonda the hostess.

And I could see why Rhonda had been so into him too. Brandon's lips were so soft, his hand cradling the back of my head as his mouth moved insistently against mine.

And I could feel that *thing* happening, that *thing* that always started happening whenever a guy started kissing Nikki, whether I liked him or not – which was how I'd almost ended up ruining my relationship with Lulu a month or two earlier, by making out with her boyfriend. It was horrible, but I honestly couldn't seem to stop myself – er, Nikki, rather. My body began arching towards Brandon's as if of its own accord, my hands reaching up until they were slipping along his strong, sinewy arms, then wrapping around his neck, clinging to him.

The thing was, I *knew* it was happening, that I was about

to get lost, sucked under, just like when I'd fallen into the water. I knew it was happening . . .

. . . and yet I couldn't stop myself, any more than I could keep my head upright when someone was giving me a neck massage.

Because it wasn't me. I swear it wasn't me.

And how could I control someone else's body, someone I wasn't? At least, someone I wasn't yet. Not entirely.

And then Brandon moved his hand, his fingers brushing the still-sensitive raised scar along the back of my head. Little needles of pain shot through me. I jerked my face from his.

'Ow!' I cried.

'What?' Brandon's expression had turned from one of desire to one of confusion. 'What'd I do? Hey, what *is* that on your head? You have . . . Are those *hair extensions?*'

'It's not . . . it's . . . never mind.' I leaned back in my chair, my lips still throbbing a little from where he'd pressed them against his. I felt a myriad of emotions, but the primary one was relief. I had never been so grateful for my scar. What was I *doing*? Making out with *Brandon*? Oh my God. Lulu had said to do the tongue thing, but seriously, I hadn't meant to take her *literally*. 'J-just another reason why it would be better for us to leave tomorrow, *as scheduled.*'

My voice wasn't as steady as I might have hoped, considering the fact that I was in love with someone else. The truth was, while I was grateful to Stark Enterprises for giving me the chance to live, I sometimes wished they'd found someone else's body to slip my brain into . . . someone not quite so . . . *excitable* as Nikki.

'Fine,' Brandon said, looking down at his own hand, as if he was expecting to see it covered in blood.

Which was ridiculous. I'd had my stitches out weeks ago.

Only he didn't know that.

'You know, Nik, I just don't get you lately,' Brandon went on, eyeing me from his deckchair.

'I know,' I said. 'I'm sorry about that. I have . . . some issues. I'm working on them. But I really do like you, Brandon.'

He raised one of those dark eyebrows. 'Yeah?' he said. 'How much? Enough to want to get back together? Because I gotta tell you –' There was no mistaking his tone – 'I'd be up for it.'

I swallowed, feeling panic rise. This was so *not* what I needed . . . and exactly what I deserved for flirting with the boss's son. Why had I ever thought I had the slightest idea what I was doing, playing with Brandon's emotions the way I just had? I haven't been Nikki long enough to know how to play the game as she apparently used to.

'Um, that is so sweet of you, Brandon,' I said quickly. 'But I think it's probably better I stay single for now, while I work out those issues I mentioned.'

Of course, if things went the way I hoped they would when I got home, and Christopher and I got together, Brandon was going to be mad when he found out I was lying to him about the wanting to stay single thing.

But I'd cross that bridge when I came to it.

Brandon glared at me, almost as if he'd been reading my thoughts. 'You've never been single a minute of your life,' he said. 'Who's the guy?'

'There's no guy,' I assured him with a laugh. I hoped the laugh didn't sound as shaky to him as it did to me. 'Honest. I'm just taking some me time right now.' I'd heard that on *Oprah* the other day. Would he fall for it? Maybe if I nagged him a little to do the same. 'You might want to try it as well. And I think there are things you could be doing to help convince your dad to make his company more globally responsible.'

Brandon looked away. 'My dad and I have some issues of our own,' he said tonelessly.

'Oh,' I said. 'Right.' I remembered the conversation we'd had about his dad at a photo shoot a month or two earlier. *He doesn't speak to the talent*, Brandon had said. *Or to me.*

'I guess I'll call the pilot, then, if leaving early is all you want.' Brandon fumbled in the pocket of his shorts for his cellphone. He looked a little – there was no other way to describe it – angry.

And why wouldn't he? It couldn't be easy, growing up in a billionaire's shadow. Sure, he had everything a guy could want.

Except his dad's approval.

And Nikki Howard to make out with, apparently.

'Thanks, Bran,' I said, and cleared my throat. 'You're a great guy.'

'Yeah,' Brandon said, looking everywhere but at me. 'That's what they all say.'

It was amazing, I thought to myself as I walked back to my suite, Cosabella trotting along at my heels. Thanks to the gigantic scar along the back of my head, I'd been saved from making a pretty colossal mistake. Well, probably. I doubt Brandon and I would really have gotten it on right there, outside Sea Breezes, the hotel bar.

But if it hadn't been for the surgery, I wouldn't have been in this situation in the first place.

Instead I'd be dead.

Maybe, I thought, as I noticed how the full moon was shining down on the cold, dark water that a few hours before, I'd been immersed in over my head, it was time to stop feeling sorry for myself and start appreciating the fact that I was alive. Sure, my new life wasn't perfect.

But things were starting to look up.

Funny how, at the time, I really did believe that.

As it turned out, however, I couldn't have been more wrong.

Three

The best thing about travelling on private jets is that you don't have to do the getting-to-the-airport-two-hours-before-your-flight-is-scheduled-to-leave thing. You show up five minutes before your flight is supposed to take off, and you don't even have to go through security. They open a special gate and let your limo drive straight up to the plane, so you can just hop out with your bag (and dog, which you don't even have to put in a carrying case, because it's your plane . . . or your boss's plane, but whatever) and go right up the steps to your seat. No one checks your ticket, or your ID, or anything. They just go, 'Good morning, Miss Howard,' and offer you a glass of champagne (or, if you're under age, orange juice).

Then, five minutes later, you take off. No safety demonstrations. No screaming babies. No waiting in line to use the cramped bathroom. Nothing like that.

Instead you've got luxurious leather seats, shiny mahogany tables, Wi-Fi (oh, yes: that thing about how you can't use Wi-Fi or cellphones in the air? Total bull. You completely can, when you fly Stark Air), fresh-cut flowers, your own window and your own personal DVD player if you want it, with a vast library of newly released movies to choose from.

A girl could get used to this kind of lifestyle. And have

difficulty going back to commercial travel. Am I a huge hypocrite hating Stark Enterprises for what they did to me (and thousands of small-business owners, not to mention the environment), while choosing to fly on Robert Stark's private jet instead of flying commercially?

Yeah.

But if it was going to get me home to Christopher – and my new, happy life, when the two of us started dating – eight hours earlier than if I took a commercial flight, I didn't care.

Sooner than I would have thought possible, the Manhattan skyline came into view beneath us, shrouded in dreary grey rain clouds. But somehow the sight of this island, sticking out of the brackish black water of the Hudson and East rivers like a middle finger, thrilled me much more than the white-beached tropical island we'd just left.

I was straining my neck to see if I could catch a glimpse of Washington Square Park and my family's apartment building when I got a text on my non-Stark-brand cellphone.

SOS, Frida wrote. **Call ASAP.**

I was dialling her cell number before I even considered that it was my sister Frida, and to her an emergency is Sephora running out of eyeliner. All I could think was, *Dad. Heart attack.* He was, after all, a middle-aged white male who worked too hard, living in New Haven most of the week so he could teach at Yale. We only saw him at weekends. I knew perfectly well what he ate most of the time. Dunkin'

Donuts Munchkins and day-old coffee. I'd never once seen him exercise. Or consume a piece of fruit.

'Frida?' I said as soon as she picked up. I noticed Brandon, across the aisle, open an irritated eye at the frantic tone of my voice. He'd slept the whole way. Or pretended to sleep. He'd been treating me a little distantly all morning. I don't think he'd quite gotten over what had happened between us the night before – my turning down his offer to become boyfriend/girlfriend again, I mean.

He closed the single bloodshot eye he'd opened as soon as he realized I was just on the phone and not speaking to him.

'What is it?' I asked Frida urgently, keeping my voice low so as not to disturb my boss's hungover son. 'Is it Dad? Is everything all right?'

'What? No, it's not Dad.' Frida, on the other end of the phone, sounded upset. 'And no, everything's not all right. It's Mom.'

'What about Mom?' *Mom?* Mom was the epitome of good health. She swam laps every morning at the student gym. She ate nothing but salads and chicken with the skin pulled off. It was almost disgusting how healthy she was. 'Is she all right?'

'She's fine,' Frida said. '*Physically*. Mentally is question-able. She found out about cheerleading, and now she's trying to get me kicked off the squad.'

I slumped back in my leather seat. My relief was so great, I couldn't even speak. Also, I wanted to kill Frida for scaring me like that.

'Em,' Frida was saying, 'you have to come over right away and try to reason with her. She says I can't go to cheerleading camp.'

'I'm on a plane at the moment,' I said, looking out the window at the Hudson river coldly winking back at me. 'I was just in the Virgin Islands, remember? So coming over isn't really an option.' Plus, I had something a little more important I needed to be doing than refereeing fights between my mother and my sister. True, the likelihood of Christopher stopping by again wasn't great – although it *was* Sunday, so it wasn't like he had anything better to do. I knew all Christopher ever did on Sunday was play *Journeyquest*, or maybe hang around the video-game stores, to see if they'd got in anything new on Saturday. Still, I intended to sit home all day, just in case.

'And isn't it a little early to be worrying about cheerleading camp now?' I asked her. 'It's December. You have months until summer to wear her down.' And possibly lose interest in cheerleading and develop an interest in something more cerebrally challenging, such as rocket science, I thought, but didn't add, aloud.

'This is a week-long cheer camp to perfect our routine over winter break,' Frida explained. 'In Florida. Everybody on the team goes. Only Mom's saying over her dead body will she let her daughter go to something called cheer camp.'

'Aren't we going to Grandma's for winter break?' I asked as Cosabella, who loved riding in planes almost as much as she loved riding in cars, decided the view from my lap wasn't exciting enough and bounded across the aisle to see what was going on outside Brandon's window, severely racking him with her claws and also waking him up again in a manner I would have to call not very pleasant. I mouthed *Sorry* to him, but he only gave me an aggrieved look.

There was an uncomfortable silence over the phone. I thought we'd hit a patch of no-service until Frida said, 'Well, yeah. We are. Cheer camp doesn't start until after the holidays. But, Em—'

'Problem solved, then,' I said. 'Look, I'll give Mom a call. She should be happy you're making friends, staying physically fit, and doing something extra-curricular that will look good on your college apps. I guess. And OK, soccer or lacrosse might have been preferable, but—'

'Calling her isn't good enough,' Frida interrupted. 'You have to come over. She has to hear it from you in person. Otherwise she's never going to let me go—'

'Fine,' I said. 'I'll be over after I drop off all my stuff. I have presents for you guys anyway.' Holiday shopping had taken on a whole new level now that I actually had money to spend. Being able to buy my family the kind of gifts I knew they'd always longed for but were never able to afford was awesome. It truly was better to give than to receive. I couldn't wait to see Frida's face when she opened the tiny black velvet box I was giving her.

Frida was silent again.

It could have been that she was just so overwhelmed with gratitude, she didn't know what to say.

Yeah. Right.

I hung up and went to fish my dog out of Nikki Howard's ex-boyfriend's lap.

Brandon didn't look very grateful. I couldn't blame him. Cosabella really needed some obedience training.

Although it was hard being cooped up in a plane, as Cosy illustrated when the first thing she did after we disembarked was pee all over the tarmac. She did the same thing when Karl, the doorman, opened the door of the limo that brought me home from Teterboro, the private airport where Robert Stark keeps his jets. Cosy popped out and trotted over to the planters outside 240 Centre Street. It was embarrassing, but where else was she going to do it?

'Welcome back, Miss Howard,' Karl said as I stepped out into the freezing drizzle that was coming down from the leaden sky overhead. It was a far cry from the balmy breezes of the Virgin Islands, and no one was exactly rushing over to give me a pina colada like they did at the hotel back in St John. 'I hope you had a nice time while you were away.'

'It was great,' I said automatically. I was freaking out, as always, about the dog. Karl must have been able to tell, because he said, 'Oh, I'll clean that up, Miss Howard. You just hurry on inside, where it's warm. Oh, I think you should know . . . you have a visitor waiting in the lobby. I wasn't sure if . . . well, you'll see.'

My heart did that flip-floppy thing, even though I told myself it couldn't be him. I mean, Christopher was not the type to sit in the lobby of a girl's apartment building and wait for her to come home.

Still, when I walked into the lobby and saw a flash of short blond hair, I couldn't help thinking, *It's him! Oh God, it's him!*

And then I practically started shaking, I was suddenly so nervous.

Which was ridiculous. I mean, I'd been best friends with the guy since forever. I'd had burping contests with him, for God's sake. And OK, that was in the seventh grade, but still. Why was I getting nervous now? I was the one in a new body, and he hadn't even figured it out yet, despite my once leaving him a very obvious clue. He was still so busy missing the old me – the one he'd never even noticed until it was too late – that he hadn't realized (until now, apparently) that reports of my death had been greatly exaggerated.

So why was I the one turning to Jell-O?

But I couldn't even bring myself to look his way. Instead, because I couldn't deal with the situation and was trying to play it cool like Lulu had once advised me to do, I pretended not to notice him, and moved towards the elevator, trying to sashay like Nikki Howard but knowing I was more likely stumbling like Em Watts, Cosabella scampering at my heels, until I heard a masculine voice call out, 'Nikki.'

I didn't want to look too eager. Guys hate that (according to Lulu, my resident expert on all things guy). I had to let him take the lead. I had to let him think coming here was all his idea (which it was, actually). I had to –

'Nikki.'

Wait a minute. That wasn't him.

That's not Christopher's voice.

I looked around. There was a tall blond guy standing in the lobby of my building, it was true. He was built, just like Lulu had said on the phone. And he was looking right at me.

But he was dressed in US Navy fatigues.

Christopher would never join the military, considering his father, the Commander, a political science professor at NYU, had drilled into his son a deep-rooted mistrust of all authority figures. And seeing as how he was only in eleventh grade like me, Christopher couldn't join the navy even if he wanted to.

On the blond guy's face was an expression of extreme dislike.

The dislike appeared to be for me. There was no one else around at whom it could be directed.

Great. What had I ever done to Blondie? I'd never even seen him before.

'Um,' I said, quickly stabbing the Up button for the elevator, 'I'm sorry. Are you speaking to me?'

The expression of dislike on Blondie's face deepened. He looked as if he was twenty, maybe a little older. There were a lot of insignias on his uniform. But I was too transfixed by the dislike on his face to drag my gaze away from it to read what they said.

'Cut the act, Nik,' he said, stalking towards me. His voice was deep. I noticed a very faint twinge of southern accent in it. 'That amnesia thing may work on all your fashionable friends, but it's not going to work on me.'

I blinked at him, then glanced towards the building's front doors. Karl was still outside cleaning up Cosabella's mess. Which was unfortunate, because it was his job to prevent unpleasant scenes like this. I will admit that Blondie didn't look like the usual ponytailed hipsters who showed up, demanding money from me or they'd go to the *Star* with their story of our torrid night in Vegas or wherever.

But why else was he here?

'I'm sorry,' I said, preparing to swing into the speech I'd had to say so many times over the past few weeks when I'd run into Nikki's so-called friends and relatives who'd confronted me in the exact same way, 'but because of my amnesia, which I can assure you really is real, I don't remember who you are. You're going to have to introduce yourself. Your name is?'

Blondie's blue eyes – which were pretty cold to start out with and got even colder as he stared at me – reminded me of someone. Only who?

'Seriously,' he said. 'That's what you're going to go with? The amnesia thing? You really think that's going to work on me? *Me?*'

He said 'the amnesia thing' like it was some kind of lie Nikki had tried on him before. And apparently it hadn't worked the first time.

'It's not a thing,' I said, sticking out my chin. Although, of course, it was. Considering I didn't have amnesia. I just wasn't Nikki Howard. Except legally. 'I really don't have any idea who you are. If you choose not to believe that, I suggest you leave before I have to do something we're both going to regret.'

'Like what?' he asked. 'Call the cops?'

Since that was exactly what I was going to have Karl do – although it seemed like a shame to have to do that to a member of the US military services – I didn't say anything.

Blondie stared at me some more.

'My God,' he said after a minute, incredulity slowly dawning across his handsome if somewhat tired-looking face. 'You'd really do it, wouldn't you? Call the cops on me.'

'I told you,' I said. The elevator, to my relief, had finally come. 'I don't have the slightest idea who you are. Now if you don't mind, I just got home from a shoot, and I'm really tired, and I still have to unpack—'

To my total surprise, he reached out and grabbed my arm. His grip was hard. There was no way I could break it if I tried. And I wasn't about to try, because I wanted to keep all my limbs in one piece.

Now I was starting to get scared. The lobby was empty, unusual for a Sunday afternoon when the rest of the tenants of our upwardly mobile $10,000-a-month-rent condo building tended to be running off to their workouts or to Starbucks for their latte fixes. Who was this creepy guy, with his cold-eyed stare and military uniform?

'I said to cut the act, Nik,' he said in a voice as hard as his grip. Cosabella, down at my feet, was beginning to sense something was wrong, and was whining nervously. Blondie ignored her. 'You're embarrassed to admit you know me? Fine. You always were. But how could you do what you did to her? She disappears and you don't even care? You know I couldn't keep tabs on her while I was in a submarine. And now she's gone. No one even knows where she is, not even her best friends, Leanne and Mary Beth. They haven't heard from her. Don't even try to make out like any of this isn't your fault.'

He stared at me accusingly, but I honestly had no idea what he was talking about. Everything he was saying sounded like gibberish to me. Leanne? Mary Beth? And who was gone? Who was *she*?

Whoever she was, she seemed very important to him. So important that his gaze no longer looked cold, but was shining with emotion.

An emotion that looked to me a lot like hate.

For me.

'Whoa,' I said, holding up a single hand – the one not attached to the arm he was cutting off all the circulation to with his death grip. 'Slow down. I have no idea what you're talking about. Who's Leanne? Who's Mary Beth? Who are *you*? And who is this missing woman you're talking about?'

The last question seemed to slam him like a fist. He was so shocked he actually dropped my arm and took a step back, staring at me like I was some sort of strange and not particularly attractive breed of animal that had just been unveiled at the zoo. Maybe in the reptile house.

'*She* is your mother,' he said finally, pointing to one of the insignias on his chest, which I now saw, belatedly, read *Howard*. 'And I'm your big brother, Steven. *Now* do you remember me, Nikki?'

Four

Well, that did kind of explain the nasty looks he kept giving me.

And continued to give me, now that I'd brought him up to the loft. Not that I blamed him. It wasn't like I knew what to say to him exactly, and I was nervously buzzing around, making him an espresso from our deluxe cappuccino/espresso maker, which Lulu had only recently showed me how to work. I wasn't sure what else to do really, other than offer him coffee. I mean, I'd never had a big brother before. Let alone a big brother who was really mad at me for losing our mother.

He didn't seem too enthused about the espresso, but at least he'd finally accepted the amnesia explanation. Sort of. Lulu was a big help. She'd come staggering out of her room (wearing nothing but a shiny peach-coloured camisole and a pair of tap pants, with her hair doing something crazy because she had evidently just woken up, even though it was two in the afternoon – early for her, really) while I was trying to get the cappuccino maker to work. Lulu took one look at the uniformed man taking up so much space in our living room (not that he was fat or anything. He was just tall and muscular and . . . well, the kind of guy who took up a lot of space), and went, 'Well, hell-ooooo there,' with this big smile on her face.

I wanted to go, *Not now, Lulu*, because I knew exactly what she was up to. Lulu was getting ready to make Steven fall in love with her, the way she did every cute guy she encountered. Making cute guys fall in love with her is Lulu's hobby, besides shopping, drinking mojitos, and occasionally recording songs for her record album, which never seems to get finished.

But I needn't have worried. Because Steven – Nikki's brother – just went, 'Hi,' to Lulu in this totally uninterested way and kept right on saying what he'd been saying the whole time we were coming up in the elevator together, which was, 'Amnesia? Like people get on soap operas?'

'Not exactly,' I assured him. Even though, from what I understand, there isn't such a thing really. Well, there is, but not the way Nikki Howard was supposed to have it. People don't conk their head and just selectively forget some stuff when they get amnesia. They forget *everything*. Like their own names and the country they live in. Sometimes they even forget how to tie their shoes.

'And you're telling me you don't remember,' Steven went on, completely ignoring Lulu, who was now sauntering past him in her shiny get-up, which she'd accessorized with a pair of matching feathered mules, 'that you promised to look after Mom while I was gone, make sure she was paying her rent on time, and that things were running smoothly with the dog-grooming kennel?'

Dog-grooming kennel? Nikki Howard's mom owned a *dog-grooming kennel*? This was information it might have been helpful for someone to have shared with me – along with the fact that Nikki had a brother in the navy – earlier than oh, say, now. All anyone had ever said to me was that Nikki was an emancipated minor who hadn't gotten along with her family.

For this reason I shot Lulu a dirty look as she hopped up on to one of the kitchen-counter stools – careful to cross her spray-tanned legs so that Steven had as full a view of them as possible. But Lulu completely ignored me, all her attention being focused on the handsome blond man in the uniform standing in the middle of our living room.

'Um,' I said, fumbling with the espresso machine. Better to concentrate on the coffee maker than on what was happening in the living room, which was precisely what it looked like: trouble. Nice of Nikki, by the way, to have a whole drawer of press clippings about herself and not a single photo of her own family. 'Up until you told me, I didn't even know I had a brother. So, the answer is no, I don't remember telling you that. Or about Mom and her dog-grooming business either, for that matter.'

'So what rank are you?' Lulu wanted to know, her gaze raking Steven's buff form as he stood with his arms crossed, consequently making his biceps bulge a little beneath his uniform. Lulu couldn't seem to keep her foot from jiggling, and this was causing one of her feathered mules to bobble up and down in a very distracting manner. She was doing this on purpose of course, to get Steven to look at her recently waxed legs.

Steven continued to ignore her.

'And what about all the messages I left you,' he asked me. 'You just thought it was better to ignore those?'

'I get a ton of messages from guys I don't know,' I explained. This was excruciating. 'They all say they're related to me and that I owe them money for something. I stopped listening to Nikki's – I mean, my – messages a long time ago.'

'Great,' Steven said. He turned away, running a hand through his hair . . . the exact same colour and texture of the hair that sprouted from my own head, I realized. Only his hadn't been treated to some golden-honey highlights. 'That's just fantastic. Do you still have them? Those messages. Maybe Mom tried to reach you, left you a message or something, telling you where she's gone.'

'Are you, like, an officer?' Lulu asked Steven, her foot still bobbing like mad. I noticed she'd had a pedicure – Ballet Slipper Pink. Don't ask me how I know these things, when three months ago I wouldn't have been able to tell the different nail polish colours apart if you'd held a gun to my head. 'Do you give people orders all day? I love taking orders from a man. It's so *sexy*.'

'Sorry,' I said, apologizing both for my room-mate and what I was about to tell him. Because I really was sorry. For both. 'I deleted all Nikki's – I mean, my messages. But –' I slipped a tiny espresso cup under the appropriate spout and pressed the button with a small cup on it – 'I'm sure she'll call back. Right?'

Steven shook his head, looking more exhausted than ever, and slid on to one of the kitchen-counter stools like he couldn't support his own weight any more. Lulu looked delighted, because the seat he'd chosen was only two stools down from hers. Apparently she didn't get the subtle message that he'd chosen the stool *furthest away* from her. She immediately straightened up to show her chest area to better advantage and gave him a dazzling smile, which he ignored.

'You really *do* have amnesia,' he said to me. His face was a mask of misery. I felt so sorry for him, my heart twisted. 'Mom never calls back. She's always been one and done. Why do you think I'm here checking to see if she's been in touch with you instead of waiting to hear from her back in Gasper?'

Lulu completely forgot about making Steven fall in love with her and choked on some of her own saliva. 'Did you say G-Gasper?' she gasped between coughs.

Steven actually looked at her for a second, then back at me. 'You never told her?' he said. It was more of a statement than a question, and it caused me to pause as I slid the espresso I'd made in front of him.

'Um . . . apparently not,' I said. I had no idea what he was talking about either, of course, since I wasn't actually his sister. His sister was dead. Or at least, her brain was sitting in formaldehyde in a jar somewhere in the bowels of the Stark Institute for Neurology and Neurosurgery, even if the rest of her might have been walking around with my brain inside it, using her credit cards and making her brother espressos.

Which made her dead enough.

I just couldn't tell her brother that.

Steven was looking at me over his steaming espresso like he couldn't quite believe what he'd heard.

'Wait,' he said, his blue-eyed gaze incredulous. 'You don't remember home either?'

Hesitantly I shook my head. I didn't want to hurt him. The truth was, he looked like he'd been hurt enough.

But I couldn't outright lie to him either, no matter how much Stark Enterprises might expect me to.

And now I knew where I'd seen those eyes before: in the mirror, every time I glanced at my new reflection. They were Nikki's eyes.

Only without Chanel Inimitable Multi-Dimensional mascara in Noir-Black on the lashes.

Steven folded his arms, leaned against the back of his stool, and stared at the ceiling. For a second, I wondered if he was noticing the same thing I'd come home and noticed the other day . . . the two round holes, no bigger than pennies, on either side of the sunken halogen lamps. They hadn't been there before, and had obviously been filled in, but rapidly and badly, as if someone had been placing something in there and gotten the news that one of the loft's occupants was coming home early.

What were those holes for? They were too high up for me to ever climb up there and check myself – the ceilings were twenty feet high at least.

But they couldn't possibly serve any purpose – other than a nefarious Stark-related one. Maybe I was just being paranoid. When I asked Karl about the holes, he consulted a maintenance schedule and told me it looked like a routine wiring check.

Wiring my butt.

'Routine wiring' was not the reason why the RF transmitter – or bug – detector I bought at one of the surveillance-gear stores downtown, shortly after I noticed the holes in the ceiling and my paranoia got the better of me, went crazy every time I turned it on inside the loft. The place was either loaded with listening devices, or the detector itself was a total scam (but for the money I paid, it ought to have been genuine). Besides, it didn't go off anywhere else – school, for instance.

But Steven, it appeared, hadn't noticed the holes. Instead, it looked as if he was staring at the ceiling because he might be trying to hold back tears. Tears over his missing mom, and the fact that I didn't even remember the hometown we shared in common.

I threw a panicky glance at Lulu, who dropped her vamp act for a millisecond and looked just as alarmed as I was. *What do we do?* our gazes seemed to ask as we stared at one another. We had a big strong military man in our girly loft . . . and he was crying! Over his lost mother!

Oh, this was awful. How could Stark Enterprises have put me in a position like this? It was one thing when I just had to fool make-up artists and Nikki's mostly heinous ex-boyfriends that I was her and not me.

But this was different! Poor guy. I was such a loser. I mean, here I was in all these AP classes at one of the best high schools in Manhattan – I was more capable of using a bug detector, diagramming a complex sentence and writing a simple string processor than anyone at Tribeca Alternative.

But help Nikki Howard's brother find his mom? My hands were tied thanks to the confidentiality clause Stark had my parents sign. I couldn't say a word – especially not here in the loft, which was electronically bugged.

Then I heard a sound come from Nikki's brother. For one breathless moment, I thought it must have been a sob. A single glance at Lulu revealed she felt the same way I did – like crying too. It really was just the sweetest thing, this big strong guy, crying over his mom.

It took us a second or two to realize Steven wasn't crying at all. He was laughing.

Not like someone who found something genuinely funny though.

'You are a piece of work, Nik,' he finally said when he looked away from the ceiling. There were tears in his eyes all right. But they were tears of amusement. 'You're so ashamed of where you come from, you never even told anyone the name of the town you were born in? Not even your best friend?'

I blinked at him in confusion.

'Wait.' Lulu leaned forward on her stool. 'You're laughing?'

'Hell, yeah,' Steven said. 'How can you not? Did you know this girl used to tell people she was from New York, New York, when we were growing up? That's how ashamed

she was to say she was from Gasper. I'm not surpr\
never told you.'

Lulu looked over at me. 'Really, Nikki?' she asked. 'You used to tell people you were from here?'

'How would I know?' I asked. 'I have amnesia, remember?'

'Yes, she did,' Steven said in reply to Lulu's question. Now, instead of ignoring Lulu, he was ignoring me. 'Are you saying she never even told you she had a brother?'

Lulu shook her head, delighted he was paying attention to her. Her brown eyes were enormous, thanks to last night's make-up being sexily smudged around her lashes. She looked, as always, adorable, like a doll.

'Noooo,' she said. She leaned an elbow on the counter and cupped her pointed chin in her hand so she could peer up at him. 'I'd have remembered if she'd mentioned having someone like *you* around while she was growing up.'

Steven snorted and threw a disgusted look at me. *Typical*, the look seemed to say.

Great. Now my room-mate and brother were ganging up on me.

Which was so unfair. I was getting blamed for something I didn't even do. Nikki did it!

Or had she?

'Look, I don't mean to be rude, or anything . . .' I said. Which I know was a horrible way to start a sentence, because of course whenever you say *I don't mean to be rude*, whatever you're about to say is going to be rude. That was something the mean girls at school, who I thought of as the Walking Dead, and especially Whitney Robertson, had taught me, since she used to preface all her most tactless barbs with *I don't mean to be rude, but*.

So: 'I don't mean to be rude, Em, but have you ever thought about going on a diet? Your butt is so big, it's almost impossible to pass you in the hallway. Maybe you need to put a sign on your ass that says Wide Load.'

Or: 'I don't mean to be rude, Em, but have you ever considered wearing a bra during PE? Those things are flopping around so much, you're going to put someone's eye out.'

And: 'I don't mean to be rude, Em, but has it ever occurred to you that your harping on about how not enough women are entering the sciences might be one of the reasons none of them wants to? Maybe they don't want to hang around with girls like you.'

Still, even though Whitney's *I don't mean to be rude*'s had stung me so many times, I found myself saying the exact same words – and to my own brother, of all people. Well, Nikki's brother.

'. . . but how do I even know for sure you're who you say you are?' I asked.

The difference between me and Whitney, though, was that I felt awful for my *I don't mean to be rude*. I really did.

At the same time, how *did* I know Steven really was Nikki's brother? I mean, he seemed sincere, and yeah, he looked a lot like the reflection I saw every day in the mirror (and in magazines and, on billboards, and on the sides of buses, and OK, just about everywhere).

But there'd been guys (and even some women) showing up in our lobby for weeks now with stories saying they were related to me. How did I know this one was legit?

And, I mean, I knew from the way everyone (except Brandon) reacted to me that Nikki must have been pretty awful back in the day.

But I had a hard time believing she'd cut her own big brother out of her life . . . not to mention never having said a word about him to her best friend. Who, by the way, was shooting me an astonished look over my *I don't mean to be rude.*

'Nikki!' Lulu cried. 'Of course Steven is who he says he is! How could you even ask such a thing?'

'Well,' I said. I felt bad for having to ask. I really did. If Nikki had kept a family photo instead of press clippings of herself anywhere in the loft, I wouldn't have had to. But none of this was *my* fault. 'I'm sorry. But you have to admit, Lu, there've been a lot of guys lately with kind of similar stories, and I'm just trying to . . .'

My voice trailed off. This was because Steven had reached around to his back pocket, pulled out a wallet, opened it and unveiled a school photo of a smiling young blonde girl in pigtails and braces. He held the wallet, photo dangling forward, in front of me.

Wait. What was *this*?

Five

This turned out to be a photo of Nikki Howard. Which in and of itself wouldn't have been that extraordinary. There were hundreds – no, thousands – of photos of Nikki Howard all over the place.

But this one was of Nikki Howard in that extremely awkward phase all of us go through when we're thirteen, just turning fourteen. What Britney Spears called 'not a girl, not yet a woman'.

I'd never have guessed Nikki Howard had gone through *that* phase . . . or anything that could remotely be called awkward . . . let alone have allowed anyone to take a picture while she was going through it. From what I could tell, Nikki was nothing if not ruthless about having all photos in which she looked the slightest bit bad destroyed.

But she'd missed this one.

'Oooooh,' Lulu cooed, as she leaned forward to peer at the photo. 'Look at you, Nik! You had braces! And were you using Sun-In back then? My God, I'm surprised you have a hair left on your head.'

'Flip to the next photo,' Steven said to me.

Obediently, I flipped to the next photo.

It was of Nikki in the same hairdo and braces beside a slightly younger version of Steven, hosing down a poodle that was not unlike Cosabella, only with black fur, in a doggie-grooming parlour. Both siblings – and they looked even more alike in this photo, recognizably related – were grinning, although Nikki's grin seemed strained. It was what I've come to recognize (having seen endless Polaroids of my new face during photo shoots) as her hurry-up-and-take-the-photo, I'm-sick-of-this smile.

'That,' Steven said, about the photo of the two of us, 'was taken about a year before you decided you were embarrassed to be seen with me. And Mom. Before that talent-agent lady's car broke down outside town and she saw you at the Stop 'n Shop and asked you if you'd ever thought of modelling, and the next thing we knew, she was signing you up to be the new Face of Stark. Next time I saw you, it was on the cover of some magazine.'

I nodded. I believed him now. This sounded too much like the Nikki I knew – the one who kept only photos of (and press clippings about) herself lying around – not to be true.

'OK,' I said softly, handing the wallet back to Steven, 'I'm sorry. Of course you're really my brother. I . . . I'm not saying I didn't believe you.' Even though I hadn't believed him. 'I just . . . I mean, I had to check. There've been a lot of creeps who've shown up saying all kinds of crazy things. So . . . what have you found out so far? About, um, Mom?'

'That no one's seen or heard from her since shortly after your "accident".' He said the word *accident* like there were quotes around it . . . or like he didn't believe there'd ever been one. 'She hasn't used any of her credit cards since then either. Or paid any of her bills.'

Lulu gasped. 'Oh my gosh!' she cried. 'I saw an episode of *Law & Order* like this once! Did anyone call the police?'

I shot her a warning look. I mean, this was the guy's mother we were talking about, not some TV show. I didn't want him getting upset. Or more upset than he already was.

'Well,' Lulu said, noticing my look but evidently not registering why what she was saying might be upsetting to anyone. 'What if there's been foul play? On the *Law & Order* episode I saw, where this woman disappeared, everyone thought she'd run off with her boyfriend, but really she was inside the couch the whole time because the boyfriend had conked her on the head and hidden her dead body there! Your mom could be inside the couch. Did anyone look?'

'Lulu,' I said severely.

'I notified the local police when I got home and found her gone,' Steven said. I realize the reason he wasn't offended by Lulu was because he was ignoring her again. 'I tried calling you to see if you'd heard from her, but you wouldn't return my calls. So I had to come here in person to see if you'd heard from her.'

I bit my lower lip. But what could I say? His call was just one of thousands I'd ignored on Nikki's cell. Thankfully, Steven went on without seeming to expect a comment from me.

'The cops said there's nothing they can do. A woman not

using her credit cards or refusing to answer her cellphone and leaving her apartment and business in the lurch isn't a crime. It's more like she went on vacation without telling anybody. And took her dogs with her.'

'Well,' I said hopefully, 'maybe she did just that.'

'You think Mom just took off,' Steven said, 'on vacation, without letting any of her customers know she was going? She didn't cancel any of her grooming appointments. She hasn't paid up the rent on either her apartment or the kennel. You really think that's something a dedicated business owner like Mom would have done – left for a fun-filled vacation without finding someone to take over her appointments first?'

'So,' Lulu said, looking wide-eyed, 'you really think your mom's . . . missing? No one knows *anything* about where she could be?'

'No one I've talked to,' Steven said. 'Nikki was my last hope. But –' He glanced down at the espresso in front of him, which by now had gone cold – 'I guess that was a waste of time.'

'Maybe I can get a printout or something of the incoming calls I've had,' I offered. I desperately wanted to do something – anything – to help him. He just looked so tired and sad. 'And see if any of them were from your – I mean, our – mom. Then maybe we can see if the phone company can figure out where she was when she made them.'

'They can triangulate her position through the position of the cell towers,' Lulu said. When we both glanced at her, she said, 'I saw that on an episode of *Law & Order* too.' Then she added, 'Oh, and you can hire a private detective, Nikki! My dad used to hire those to follow my mom around when he thought she was cheating on him.' She gave Steven a brilliant smile. 'I come from a broken home.'

I'm sure, if he'd ever seen a single episode of *Entertainment Tonight*, he already knew this. But Steven wasn't paying any attention to her.

'I don't want Nikki to do anything she doesn't feel comfortable doing,' he said stiffly.

'It's no problem,' I said. 'I'll hire a private investigator to find . . . Mom. Maybe you can recommend some good ones, Lulu, since you seem to have so much experience with them.'

'Oh, yeah,' Lulu said, twinkling. No, really. She twinkled as she said it, like freaking Tinkerbell. 'Mind you, detectives aren't cheap.'

'That shouldn't be a problem,' Steven said with a smile in my direction. 'Nikki can afford it.'

I smiled sweetly back at him, but all I could think was, I am so dead. And not even literally, for once. I couldn't hire a detective. A detective was only going to uncover stuff related to my brain transplant and blow this Stark thing sky-high, and next thing I knew, it'd be on CNN and I'd be on the run from Brandon's dad's armed gunmen.

And don't even try to tell me Robert Stark doesn't have them.

OK, just calm down and smile at the nice sailor.

'Fine then,' I said. 'So, I'll start calling private eyes first thing in the morning.' Seriously. This was my life now? Well, why not. I'd already had a brain transplant and have to wear mascara every single day. So why not this?

'And in the meantime –' Lulu twinkled some more in Steven's direction. – 'you have to stay here with us. Because we're having this holiday party, and we want you to be the guest of honour.'

I threw Lulu another warning look, because having Nikki's brother stay with us didn't exactly seem like a good idea to me. For one thing, we only had the two bedrooms, so where was he going to sleep ... on the couch? And for another, how long was it going to take him to catch on that I wasn't calling private detectives like I said I would ... oh, and that I wasn't his sister at all, but another girl living in his sister's body?

Plus there was the whole thing about him being the guest of honour at a party at which I wasn't even going to be in attendance, except I hadn't quite worked up the courage to tell the hostess yet ...

And then there was that thing about our loft possibly – OK, probably – being bugged by parties unknown (even though I was pretty sure who was responsible).

'Uh,' Steven said, looking uncomfortable. Who could blame him? I was a virtual stranger to him (in more ways than he knew). 'Thanks for the invitation, but I grabbed a hotel room uptown—'

Lulu looked horrified.

'A hotel room!' she cried. 'No! You're family! Stay here. That'll give you and Nikki a chance to reconnect. Right, Nikki?'

'Sure,' I said, hoping Steven didn't sense my reluctance. 'Although we do only have the two bedrooms—'

'He can sleep in my room,' Lulu volunteered. Then, looking a little embarrassed – a first for Lulu – she explained, 'What I mean is, Nikki has this huge king-sized bed. I can sleep with her and, Steven, you can have my room.'

'No,' Steven said, not unkindly. There was warmth in his voice, and in his expression – real, human warmth – the first I'd seen him show since meeting him downstairs in the lobby. I felt bad about the fact that I had no intention of helping to look for his mother. Wait. I *did* intend to help him look for his mom. I just didn't intend to hire a detective to do it.

Only how do you find a missing woman on your own?

'Thanks, that's really nice of you,' Steven continued. 'But I wouldn't want to put you out—'

'Stay,' I heard myself saying.

I don't know what came over me. I mean, I needed Nikki Howard's brother hanging around the loft like I needed a(nother) hole in my head.

But I knew from something I'd seen in the photo he'd shown me – the one of him and Nikki washing the dog – that Steven Howard loved his mother. I was pretty sure she'd been the one taking the picture that he had in his wallet. The look in his eyes as he gazed at the person holding the camera had been one of pure – if slightly irritated – affection.

I knew what I had to do. And that was everything I could to help him find her. It was the least I could do to make up for Nikki having been such a horrible sister and daughter. So horrible she had never even kept a picture of either her brother or mother in her room or wallet.

'Really,' I said when he turned his astonished gaze towards me. 'You have to. I insist.'

'You insist?' He gave me a strange look. I didn't know if it was because I'd used the word insist, and that's not the kind of thing Nikki ordinarily would have said, or because he was the older one, and he wasn't used to Nikki bossing him around.

Whatever the reason, my insisting did the trick. He shrugged and said, 'Well, if you insist. I'll just go back uptown then and get my gear.'

Then, without another word, he slid off the kitchen stool and headed for the elevator.

He stepped inside and looked at us for a second.

'See you in a few,' he said. And then the door closed and he was gone.

Six

OK, so things were bad. But they still weren't *that* bad. Nikki Howard's brother might been moving in, and her mom might have been missing, and I might have put myself in charge of finding her.

But at least Nikki *had* a brother and mom, whereas a few hours ago, I'd thought of her as a siblingless orphan. Well, practically. Some family was always better than none, right?

Of course, it was a little annoying that every five seconds my room-mate kept going, 'Do you think he liked me?'

That was all Lulu could ask.

And ask.

And ask again.

I'd never seen Lulu like this over a guy. Granted, I hadn't known her all that long.

But even if I didn't know her at all, I'd have been able to tell: she had the hots (and that was putting it mildly) for Nikki Howard's big brother.

Which was sad, because I was pretty sure the feeling wasn't mutual.

In fact, I'm fairly certain that was *why* Lulu liked Steven Howard so much. He was the first straight guy she'd ever met who wasn't a hundred or something who didn't like her back.

'He had to like me a little bit,' Lulu was saying as she lay sprawled out across my bed, still in her silky pyjamas. 'I mean, I'm cute, right?'

'You're so cute,' I assured her, jamming my feet into a pair of Stark-brand imitation Uggs. I seriously never thought I'd be caught dead – *ha ha* – in a pair of these, since every girl I knew at Tribeca Alternative had a pair of the real things, including my own sister. I wouldn't wear them at all if I wasn't *required* to by my employer. Stark-brand Ugg knockoffs were the hot new thing . . . half the price of the real ones. Although, believe it or not, they were the most comfortable things you could put on if the bottoms of your feet were raw from having been clinging to a cliff-face the night before. Also if you'd spent an hour pacing the length of your apartment while calling your cell service provider, begging them to give you a printout of all the calls you'd received – not made – on it for the past two months.

'I *am* cute,' Lulu said firmly as she rubbed Cosabella's ears, breaking into my reflections. 'I'm totally cute! He just doesn't know me yet. Every guy who gets to know me agrees – Lulu Collins is cute! And anyway, Steven's all bummed out from the awful way you've treated him over the years. I mean, no wonder he's all tortured and moody and stuff.'

'Hey,' I said, shooting her a wounded look. I was still completely guilt-stricken over the fact that I hadn't recognized my own brother. Well, Nikki's brother. Now I was going to have to get to the bottom of his mother's disappearance and find her myself if it was the last thing I did. Even though I didn't know how.

'Oh, right,' Lulu said. 'I forgot. The old you was the one that was mean to Steven. Sorry. Still. How could you have treated him that way? He's so hot. I've never met a guy that hot. Did you see those *arms*? I mean,' Lulu went on, bunching one of my pillows beneath her head, and staring dreamily up at my ceiling, 'he looked strong enough that if he lifted me, he could do it with just *one hand*. Did you notice that?'

'Uh,' I said, slipping on a fitted leather jacket, then snapping my fingers for Cosabella to come to me. 'He's my brother, Lulu. I wasn't exactly checking out his arms. Because, ew. Look, if anyone calls, I'm just going to take Cosy for a walk for an hour or so. I'll be back soon. OK?'

'Mrs Captain Steven Howard,' Lulu breathed, still staring up at the ceiling. 'No – Mrs Major Steven Howard!'

Lulu had totally lost it. It was sad really, what a uniform could do to a girl. I hoped she'd be feeling more like herself when I got home. Or that she'd at least have brushed her teeth.

In the meantime, I had places to be. I left my room, threw on a scarf and gloves and woolly cap and sunglasses (even though it was still grey and dismal outside. But I didn't need anyone recognizing me. Until I started walking around in a celebrity's body, I had no idea what they had to go through, with people grabbing them and screaming and trying to get them to talk on their cellphones to their friends in Pasadena just to prove they'd really met them). Then I grabbed Cosy's leash and a dog coat for her (because dogs get cold and wet exactly like we do; Cosabella actually shivered like a person when she got cold), my tote of gifts for my family, and finally left the building, heading across town towards Washington Square Park.

It wasn't somewhere I was supposed to be. In fact, my 'handlers' at Stark had subtly been encouraging me not to go home to visit my parents since the first time I went there in my new body (and brought Lulu). It wasn't hard to imagine how they knew we'd been there . . . not once I saw the holes in the ceiling in the loft when we got back. I just tried to make sure none of my family took any Stark-brand electronic products home, even promotional gifts given to us by Stark.

But there was nothing I could do about the fact that I'm regularly followed . . . at least by paparazzi (though not today. The weather outside was horrible. It was spitting little drops of ice crystals that stung my skin wherever it was exposed, and it had to be barely thirty degrees out. Anyone sane was staying in where it was warm and dry.

Then again . . . whoever said the paparazzi were sane?).

I didn't think I was being paranoid about feeling as if I was being spied on. Pictures of me doing the most innocuous things were popping up all over the place. I could be at the corner deli, buying *toilet paper* at eleven o'clock at night, for Pete's sake, and the next day a picture of me would show up in *Page Six*, looking all pasty and strung out (because it was after a shoot and I was exhausted and had no make-up on and it was *eleven o'clock at night at the corner deli* and I was *buying toilet paper*, the toilet paper Lulu should have remembered to buy, but hadn't) and the story underneath my photo would read, *What's Nikki Howard been smoking? We'd sure like some of that!* when I had not, in fact, been smoking anything, because I don't smoke.

How had they even gotten that photo? I never saw a flash go off. There wasn't even anyone in the store with me except the clerk. It was creepy, that's what it was.

And next thing I knew, this extremely unflattering photo, in which I did, in fact, look high or stoned or whatever, was on every Internet gossip site known to man, with even less complimentary captions than *What's Nikki Howard been smoking?*

And then my mother was calling, wanting to know if we needed to 'talk' about my recreational drug use. My *mother!* It was bad enough that Gabriel Luna, hot up-and-coming British Latino heart-throb singing sensation with whom I was constantly being thrown together because he's on the Stark label, and who always seemed to see me out in clubs with Lulu and Brandon (where I drank nothing stronger than *water*, thanks very much), believed my press and thought I had chemical-dependence issues (although in Gabriel's case, he knew I'd been hospitalized a couple of months ago . . . just not for what). But my own *mother?*

Yeah. Someone was spying on me all right. For all I knew, he could be watching as I stood on the corner of Houston and Broadway at this very moment, cursing the fact that I hadn't brought along an umbrella to ward off the sleet. Although if I had, I probably wouldn't have been able to juggle it *and* Cosy's leash *and* my tote *and* Nikki Howard's cellphone, which suddenly went off. I had to fumble around in my pocket to find it instead of just letting it go to voicemail as usual, because I was afraid it might be Nikki's mom, and I'd miss her, and then I'd have even *more* to feel guilty about.

'Hello?' I said.

It wasn't Nikki's mother though. It was Nikki's agent, Rebecca. Who was exactly like a mom, if you asked me. If your mom smoked and wore four-inch heels and talked through a headset all the time and said things like, 'Ten thousand? Are they high?' or kept asking you if you'd remembered to keep your bikini-line electrolysis appointment. (Yeah. Nikki has no hair down there. Well, a strip. Talk about creepy. But it cuts down on the amount of time I have to spend getting waxed by Katerina.)

'Why are you calling me on a Sunday?' I asked her, when she said, 'Thank God you're there.'

'You know I work seven days a week,' Rebecca replied in her smoke-roughened voice.

'You're supposed to take Sundays off,' I informed her. 'Even God took Sunday off.'

'Well, if He hadn't,' Rebecca said, 'maybe the world wouldn't be such a mess. How was the shoot in St John?'

'Fine,' I said. 'Except for the part where I nearly tore off most of the skin on my fingers and toes, clinging to this cliff. Oh, and where Brandon Stark wanted to stay an extra day to take me jet-skiing. I think someone is letting money and fame go to his head.'

I'd crossed Houston, and was walking past the Stark Megastore where, ironically enough, all this happened to me.

'Brandon Stark is worth thirty million.' Rebecca sounded like she was inhaling. 'At least. A billion when his father croaks. Maybe more. Breaking up with him was a big mistake.'

'I'll keep that in mind.' I take it back about Rebecca being like a mom. No mom would give the kind of advice she does. Which reminded me. 'Rebecca, have you heard anything from Nik – I mean, my mom?'

'Why would I hear anything from that woman?' Rebecca asked. She said *that woman* like Nikki's mom wasn't someone she liked.

'Because,' I said, 'apparently she's missing. No one's heard from her in three months, and people back in, um, Gasper are starting to worry maybe something's happened to her.'

'Well,' Rebecca said, 'your mother was never the sharpest knife in the drawer. Chances are, she went to Atlantic City to play craps and got lost.'

'Oh,' I said. 'Good to know.' For some reason I didn't mention Nikki's brother. I don't know why. I just didn't.

It didn't matter, I guess, because Rebecca had already moved on.

'But about why I'm calling,' she said. 'So, listen. Are you sitting down?'

'No. I'm walking Cosabella.' I didn't tell her I was really on the way to see my family. That's the last thing I'd mention to Rebecca. Because she doesn't know about my real family. Or the real me.

'Well, I just got the call from Robert Stark himself . . . The nationally televised Stark Angels New Year's fashion show is going to be shot at the newly constructed Stark sound studios at midtown live on New Year's Eve . . . and they want *you* to be the angel wearing the ten-million-dollar diamond bra. Apparently it's just your size. Giselle dropped out due to a contract dispute. Could you die? Nikki? Nik?'

I stumbled over a grate in the sidewalk and nearly dropped my phone. A couple who were hurrying by, as anxious to get out of the rain as I was, barely gave me a second glance, even though my image was in every window of the store next to us, blown up to ten feet tall. Nikki Howard in a trench coat, Nikki Howard in a bikini, Nikki Howard in an evening gown, Nikki Howard in a summer dress, Nikki Howard on a pair of skis, Nikki Howard in riding jodhpurs, Nikki Howard in a kimono, Nikki Howard in a matching Stark Angels bra and panty lingerie set. The sunglasses and knitted cap totally worked as a disguise.

'Oh no,' I breathed into the phone. My heart felt as if it had just gone into overdrive. I thought I might throw up.

Because Stark Angels lingerie was seriously the saddest of the sad. It was Stark Enterprises' attempt to compete with Victoria's Secret for the American woman's underwear drawer. Only Stark's bras and panties cost about twenty per cent less, and itched and poked about fifty per cent more. And the Angels were a straight up ripoff of the Victoria's Secret's Angels. Only their wings were much smaller and cheaper looking. The only thing more expensive was Stark's diamond bra – ten million as opposed to Victoria's Secret's paltry million-dollar bra.

'*Oh, no.*' Rebecca sounded shocked as she echoed what I'd just said. 'What do you mean, *Oh, no?*'

'I mean,' I said, trying to keep my voice steady, 'I have to go to high school every day.' I tugged Cosabella away from someone's abandoned hot pretzel, now cold and congealed on the sidewalk, which she seemed determined to examine and then consume, even though I feed her extremely well at home. 'I'm not going to go on live national television on New Year's Eve in a pair of wings and a demi-cup bra . . . even if it is one made out of diamonds!'

'You'd be wearing panties too,' Rebecca said, sounding surprised that I hadn't realized this.

'Oh well, that just makes everything all better,' I said sarcastically.

'It would be very tasteful,' Rebecca said. 'You wouldn't be showing any more than you did in the *Sports Illustrated* bathing-suit shoot last week.'

'But this is underwear!' I wailed. 'Even worse, Stark's underwear!'

'Oh, that's a nice way to talk about your employer,' Rebecca snapped.

If only she knew about the phone tap. And the spyware

on my Stark-brand PC. And the hidden surveillance transmitters in my loft (if that's what they are). Oh, and about the brain transplant. Which did save my life, but still.

'And that was still photography,' I said. 'This is TV.'

'There's a seven-second delay,' Rebecca said. 'So if anything was to – you know, slip out, you adjust it before . . . you know.'

'That is just so reassuring,' I said.

'Nikki, honey,' Rebecca said, exhaling audibly. 'I wasn't actually asking your permission. Robert Stark called to let me know it's already settled. You're doing this. I would have thought you'd be thrilled. You're the lead angel. Do you have any idea what that means?'

Yeah. I knew. I knew, all right.

'I have to go,' I said to Rebecca. I knew I'd been wrong to think everything was going to be all right.

'Wait,' Rebecca said. 'Don't you want to know how much they're paying you for this? Because you're never going to believe what I negotiated—'

But I'd already hung up. It really didn't matter. However much it was, it would never be enough. Not for being publicly humiliated in front of everyone I knew. Specifically, Christopher.

Who, OK, wouldn't actually know it was me, his old pal Em Watts.

But we used to sit and watch the Stark Angel fashion show every year together and make merciless fun of it, and especially of the dumb angels and how many starving

Africans they could have fed with the money that had gone into making the diamond bra.

And now I was going to be the dumb angel wearing it.

Great. Just great.

Maybe I could give the money to some Africans.

Except I was probably going to need it. For therapy.

Seven

The part I was probably going to need the most therapy for was the expression I saw on Mom's face every time I let myself into the apartment.

Like just now.

It was all about the flicker – it only lasted an instant – of excitement, followed by disappointment, then resignation. She was expecting the old Em, and instead she got Nikki . . . well, outwardly, anyway. So for a split second, she was disappointed. It passed in a flash, to be replaced with her normal Oh-of-course-it's-you face.

But it was always there, every time she saw me – the disappointment.

Because the truth was, I wasn't her daughter. Not really. Not any more.

On the inside maybe. But not on the outside.

And she hadn't accepted the new me. Not completely.

And a part of me knew she never would.

I couldn't blame her really, I guess.

'Oh, Em, honey,' she said. The flicker was gone, and she recognized me, the stranger in her apartment, the tall blonde with the miniature poodle in the waterproof coat prancing at her side. I guess she'd never come to accept me – in Nikki's body – unless I got rid of the poodle, stopped washing my hair, gained fifty pounds and started wearing nothing but sweats again, like the old me. People are funny. 'I can't believe you came all the way over in this weather! Weren't you supposed to be in Aruba or something today?'

'St John,' I said, leaning down to kiss her. Before the accident, Mom had been taller than me. Now I'm nearly taller than Dad. Even in my Stark-brand imitation Uggs. 'We flew back this morning. I came over as soon as I could.' I wasn't going to tell her about the long-lost brother I found waiting for me in my lobby. She had enough problems, and I wasn't going to burden her with mine. Instead, I shrugged out of my outdoor things, which were rapidly becoming sopping wet in the over-radiated heat of the apartment. 'What's this I hear about cheerleading camp?'

Mom rolled her eyes and said, 'Don't get me started,' just as Frida burst from her bedroom, having heard me come in.

'You came!' Her eyes were wide with excitement. 'You're the awesomest! Did you bring Lulu?'

On my sister's register of all things awesome, Lulu Collins rated only slightly below Nikki Howard. The fact that both of them were now in her life on an almost daily basis had put her into a kind of teen-girl nirvana from which I feared she wouldn't emerge until college.

'Uh, Lulu's busy,' I said, deeming it unnecessary to mention that Lulu was busy staring at my ceiling, planning her wedding to Nikki Howard's estranged big brother. 'Is Dad around?'

'Dad went back to New Haven,' Frida said. 'He couldn't stand the fighting.'

'There was no fighting,' Mom corrected her. 'Fighting implies that the issue was ever negotiable, and it isn't.'

Frida threw me a 'help-me' look. 'See?' she said.

Mom glared at me. 'And I can't believe,' she added, going back to the sofa and the Sunday *Times*, which she had strewn all around her, her normal weekend habit, 'that you knew all this time, and you didn't tell me.'

'Well,' I said lamely. If she only knew the things I knew and haven't told her, 'I don't see what's wrong with it, really. Cheerleading is a sport, after all.'

Mom didn't even look up from the 'Week in Review' section. 'Name a sport you play in a miniskirt,' she said.

I almost laughed, since I'd tried the same argument on Frida when I'd first heard about her going out for the team.

'Well,' I said, 'figure-skaters wear even shorter skirts, and figure-skating is an Olympic sport. As is tennis. And so is gymnastics. And cheerleading is basically all gymnastics.'

Mom just rattled the paper. There was classical music playing softly over the music system. The whole apartment looked so cosy and warm, I almost wanted to cry. Somewhere, I knew, were bagels Dad had picked up that morning from H & H. With vegetable cream cheese (I couldn't eat bagels any more because they caused Nikki massive acid reflux. Anything doughy did).

But looks, of course, were deceiving. Cosy as the place

looked, I couldn't help suspecting it was every bit as wired as the loft was. I didn't know where the bugs were, but I was sure they were there somewhere, and that Stark was listening. Hadn't Dr Holcombe, during my last check-up, asked me if I thought it was such a good idea to introduce Lulu to my family . . . something he could only have known I'd done if Stark had been listening in that time Lulu and I dropped by my old apartment with a pizza?

And hadn't the Stark Institute for Neurology and Neurosurgery handed us all brand-new Stark-brand cellphones on which to call one another? Phones that were way more staticky than any mobile phone I'd ever owned. Clear proof – to me, anyway – that they were tapped.

It had been kind of hard after that not to believe Stark wasn't spying on us. Especially since my pocket bug detector – yes, I'd bought every gadget the Spy Store at midtown had in stock while I was there – whined like crazy every time I walked in the door. I didn't know where the bugs were – but they were there somewhere. Which was why I had encouraged my family to use the non-Stark-brand, non-staticky cellphones I'd bought them, and why I now usually kept my visits to my old home brief.

'The thing is,' Frida said to Mom, 'I *have* to go with the team to winter camp. We have all our routines down, and I'm like the most important person. I'm a base, and without me, basically all our pyramids, our stunts, anything involving a flyer, everything falls down. Furthermore, if I don't receive proper training, someone – including me – could be badly injured. Which isn't to say our coach isn't

78

magnificent, because she is, but at this week-lon
camp we learn proper techniques to avoid injuries
new stunts and routines that will blow the compe᠎ ᠎ᠵᠠ out
of the water. Besides, cheerleading is a really good extra-
curricular. It looks great on your college apps. I mean, do
you want me to look like a total loser, like Em, who has no
extra-curriculars whatsoever?'

'Hey,' I said, coming to my own defence.

'Sorry,' Frida said, throwing me an apologetic look, 'but
it's true. Until your surgery, you never did anything after
school, except boring computer stuff with Christopher.
Now at least you go to tropical islands for swimsuit shoots
and stuff.'

'I do not like,' Mom said, finally lowering her paper,
'the tone that this conversation has taken. I do not want
my daughters' extra-curricular activities to be swimsuit
shoots and being the base supports of human pyramids.'

'Mom,' Frida said, going to sit on the couch beside her.
'It's so much more than that. I'm learning teamwork and
physics and making new friends, while at the same time
getting physically fit and staying healthy—'

I brightened up a little. The truth was, I'd been feeling
a little depressed since this afternoon, coming home and
finding Steven Howard, not Christopher, waiting for me in
my lobby, then getting the news about Nikki's mom. That,
followed by the information that I was now a Stark Angel,
hadn't really done much to cheer me up since the whole
sitting-at-the-bottom-of-the-ocean thing.

But seeing how much Frida had matured over the past

couple of months? That was doing the trick. I mean, she wasn't half the whiny, self-centred kid she'd been before my accident, always insisting on getting her way. Not any more.

'That's why it's so important you let me go to this cheerleading camp over break,' Frida went on. 'I swear I won't do anything to make you regret it, Mom. Because, the best part is, the camp is in Miami, which is really close to where Grandma lives in Boca Raton. We're going there anyway for winter break. So, I can still be with you guys at night, and during the day I can go to camp with everybody else. I don't even have to stay in the hotel with the rest of the team.'

See? Frida had learned how to compromise and see things from other people's point of view. This was something she'd rarely, if ever, done before. I couldn't believe how my little sister had grown. She was practically a mature young woman now! Never mind that she was wearing a pair of trousers that said 'Juicy' on the butt.

'That sounds totally reasonable,' I said. 'We can all fly down together and stay at Grandma's, and then Frida can go off to cheerleading camp with her friends, and, Mom, you and Dad and I can hang with Gran. Won't that be fun?'

Before the words were fully out of my mouth though, I noticed both Mom and Frida were staring at me with odd looks on their faces. I couldn't figure out why. I mean, we always went to Grandma's in Boca for the holidays. Mom's Jewish and Dad's not, so in our house we'd always

celebrated both Christmas (the secular, Santa
and Hanukkah. Gran was always fine with that, and
nice to spend Christmas Day at the beach, getting a   ιe
sun after enduring half a New York winter.

Was this year going to be different somehow? That's
what Mom and Frida's looks seemed to imply.

'Em, honey,' Mom said after a tense silence. 'You
weren't thinking . . . I know we never discussed it, but I just
assumed . . . I mean, you know you can't go to Grandma's
this year. Or any year. Stark would never allow it. You know
you're not supposed to be seen with us. How would they
explain it if the paparazzi snapped a picture of you with us
on the beach in Florida over the holidays?'

I blinked at her.

Oh. Right. Stark. My employer. The contract. The
people bugging my apartment and following me . . . maybe.
Probably.

Definitely.

'And besides,' she went on. 'You know we told Grandma –
everyone in the family actually – that you . . . died. How
would we explain to her – and her friends – what Nikki
Howard was doing, joining us for our family vacation?
Obviously, you couldn't be Em around her . . .'

Of course. My obituary. The memorial service. The
story about my gory death by plasma screen TV on CNN.

'Right,' I said. My bones did that frozen thing again,
the way they had outside the Stark Megastore, the scene
of the accident that had caused all this. Only this time I
wasn't outside, with so many windows filled with posters of

Nikki Howard smiling blandly down at me. So there was no rational explanation for why I suddenly felt like I was freezing cold. 'Grandma thinks I'm dead.'

How stupid of me to have thought I was going to her condo for the holidays with the rest of my family. How stupid of me to have brought that tote bag, sitting over by the door, filled with wrapped gifts for all of them, to take down to Florida to put under Grandma's tree.

Everyone thought I was dead.

I was Nikki Howard now.

Em Watts was dead.

'It's OK,' I said with a careless laugh – or a laugh that I hoped sounded careless. It actually sounded more brittle, I think, than careless. Suddenly I was blinking back tears – where had those come from? – but I hoped Mom and Frida couldn't see them. 'How dumb. I totally forgot about Stark. And the contract. And everything. Jeez. I'm so stupid.'

'Honey.' Mom put down the paper and got up off the couch to wrap an arm around me, even though I took a step back, away from her. 'Are you all right? We probably should have discussed this, but I just assumed you'd be working anyway, so—'

'I'm fine,' I said, still moving away from her. I didn't want her to see my tears, that I wasn't fine. Also, I was afraid that her touch would cause me to crumble. 'Actually, it's much better this way, because Lulu is having this huge party, and I was worried about how I was going to break the news to her that I wasn't going to be able to be there, and now I won't have to. So, phew!'

Mom didn't look convinced that I was all right.

'You know what?' she said. 'This is silly. We'll just stay here in town for the holidays this year. I'll give Gran a call. I'm sure we can work something out—?'

Frida didn't seem to hear what Mom had just said. She was too excited about something else. 'Lulu's having a party?' she asked. 'A holiday party? Am I invited?'

Yeah. Forget everything I said about Frida being so much more mature now.

'No,' I said. I started reaching for the outdoor things I'd only just put down, like Cosy's coat and leash and my gloves and stuff. 'You know what? I forgot I promised Lulu that I'd pick up some stuff for her party, and here it is getting close to five and the party store is going to close since it's Sunday, so I better go—'

'Em,' Mom said, reaching for me again, looking as if her heart was breaking on my behalf.

But I was too quick for her. I sidestepped her and was halfway out the door and down the hall before either of them seemed to realize what was happening.

'I'll call you guys later,' I tossed back over my shoulder as I heard Mom say my name again.

But I was hurrying towards the elevator, hoping I'd get there before the tears started, and before either of them caught up with me . . .

And I made it, but only just. I actually managed to get past the doorman and into the driveway in front of our building, under the protective canopy, before I burst.

And then my face melted. Or at least that's what it felt like. The tears in my eyes overflowed, coursing hotly down my cheeks. I couldn't see anything in front of or around me, because it all kind of disappeared into a hot mess of little dots and smears, like the Impressionistic paintings in the nineteenth-century wing in the Metropolitan, as the tears took over everything. I'm pretty sure there was snot involved too.

And even as I was doing it – crying, I mean – I knew it was ridiculous. I never actually *liked* going to Grandma's that much, except for the beach and her pool. Her condo was way too small for the four of us plus her, and I always had to sleep on a fold-out cot that was too short for me, and she gave us frozen bagels for breakfast instead of the real kind you could get here in New York, still warm from the oven, crusty on the outside, and warm and gooey in the middle.

But somehow, being told I *couldn't* go, because I was dead . . .

Well, it just made me wish I'd stayed down at the bottom of the ocean last night. It had been so *nice* down there, so quite and calm and, OK, cold, but still. No one had been *demanding* things of me, like Climb This Cliff, Find My Missing Mom, Wear This Diamond Bra, or Don't Go To Florida With Us, You're Dead, Remember?

Although I guess in a way I was at the bottom of that ocean again. I was just as cold anyway, and just as alone –

except for Cosy – and soon I'd have to go out into that sleet, and then I'd be just as wet, since I didn't bring an umbrella.

Suddenly I decided I couldn't take it. I just couldn't take it! I knew I must have looked like an idiot, but I didn't care. There was no one around. Only a fool would have been out in weather like this anyway. I decided just to stand there. At least until a cab went by and I could try to hail it.

Because no way was I walking home in this crappy weather.

Then I felt a hand on my shoulder. Thinking it was Eddie the doorman, asking if I wanted him to flag down a cab – which, good luck finding one in this weather – I turned my head, sniffling. I still couldn't exactly see because of my face melting, but I could sort of vaguely make out a masculine shape beside me.

'What?' I asked, sniffling.

'Nikki?' a familiar voice asked. As familiar to me, almost, as my own. Or as familiar as my own voice used to be, before my larynx was crushed beneath three hundred pounds of plasma television.

It wasn't Eddie. It was someone else who lived in my parents' building. I'd just forgotten that little fact during the pity party I'd been throwing for myself.

And for a second I nearly choked on my own tears.

Because it was Christopher.

Eight

Great. There's nothing a girl wants more than for the guy she's been crushing on since like the sixth grade or whatever to find her standing outside his building on a miserable wintry Sunday afternoon, sobbing her guts out.

There was absolutely no way I could think of to get out of this one either, other than the obvious – suicide. I contemplated simply running away from him and throwing myself under the first cab I saw speeding down Bleecker Street. But I wasn't sure I'd be able to see clearly enough, what with the sleet and my sunglasses and tears and all. I figured I might just end up throwing myself under a parked car.

Besides, I had Cosabella with me. And I wouldn't want anything bad to happen to her.

I reached up and hastily swiped at my face with my gloved hands, hoping the suede would absorb some of the moisture spilling out of my eyes so I could at least see him properly.

This turned out to be a huge mistake, however. Because it revealed that Christopher was standing there in *his* leather jacket (when had he gotten one of those?), looking down at me (unlike my dad, Christopher was not shorter than Nikki Howard) with an adorable mixture of confusion mingled with concern on his face. He was obviously just coming home from somewhere, and in typical male fashion had remembered to wear neither a scarf *nor* a hat, so the sleet had caused his short blond hair to stick to his head, and the cold had turned the tips of his ears and his cheeks bright red.

This only made him look cuter, however, if such a thing is possible. I mean, even his lips had turned red, which I know was a weird thing to notice about a guy – much less to think looked cute.

But then, I'd had my brain taken out of my body and put into someone else's. I was about as weird as you can get.

'Hey, how's it going?' Christopher asked. He'd barely said three words to me since I'd slapped a set of glow-in-the-dark dinosaur stickers down in front of him in the school's computer lab, hoping he'd get the message that I was really his best friend trapped in a supermodel's body (he didn't). But he seemed to take the fact that I'd just shown up in front of his apartment building, weeping behind my Gucci sunglasses, in his stride. 'Cold out today, huh?'

'Um,' I said, 'yeah.' I tried not to look at his lips. I looked at the canopy stretching over the apartment building's driveway instead. They'd painted it an ugly looking grey. The paint was flaking off in parts of it.

'Were you shopping or something around here?' Christopher asked me. I don't suppose he could figure out any other reason why I'd be in his neighborhood. It would never occur to him that I might be stalking him, or standing here thinking about how much I wanted to kiss him. He wasn't the kind of guy who would think that girls fantasized about that kind of thing. At least, not about him.

That was one of the reasons why I loved him. When I wasn't thinking about how much I'd like to strangle him for being so dense as to not realize I was me, Em Watts. Just inside somebody else.

'Yeah,' I said, staring at a particularly large flake of paint peeling off above his head. 'Yeah, I was. But . . . it's sleeting so badly. And there . . . were no cabs.' Did that sound reasonable? Would he believe it?

Apparently so.

'And you didn't think to bring an umbrella when you went out,' Christopher said with a little smile. 'Just like me.'

I couldn't help lowering my gaze to his hands. They were gloveless and empty and huge. And would have looked so much better if they were somewhere on my person. I knew exactly where too.

God, what was wrong with me? I used to think it was just Nikki's body that was wanton. Now I was starting to wonder if my brain was catching up with it.

'You want to borrow one?' Christopher asked. 'I mean, I do actually own one.'

I dragged my gaze from his fingers to his face. 'One what?' What was *wrong* with me? I couldn't even follow a simple conversation any more. Either Stark Enterprises had attached a few wires wrong when they'd put my brain into Nikki's head, or I had it really, *really* bad for this guy.

'Uh,' Christopher said, looking down at my feet, 'I think there's something wrong with your dog.'

I glanced down at Cosabella. She was trembling all over from the cold because she'd been standing with her paws in an icy puddle, and I'd been too busy crying – and lusting after my secret crush – to notice.

'Oh!' I bent down to scoop her into my arms. 'Cosy! You're freezing!'

'Why don't you come on up,' Christopher said, 'and I'll get you an umbrella and you can let your dog defrost for a minute before you both head out again?'

I was looking down at Cosabella when he said this, holding her close to me in the hope that my body heat would eventually warm her enough so that she'd stop shaking.

So I was pretty sure he didn't see the blush that flooded my cheeks. At least, I hoped not. It was a happy blush, since this stroke of luck – his inviting me upstairs to his apartment, where I hadn't been since before the accident – was totally unexpected, considering the sucky twenty-four hours I'd had up till then.

'I guess,' I murmured into the puff of fur growing out of the top of Cosabella's head. 'Thanks.'

It wouldn't be cool of course, if I let on how I felt about his invitation – I wanted to shriek with joy and dance around like a maniac. I had to act calm as we walked past Eddie the doorman. I prayed as Christopher and I passed that Eddie wouldn't say anything like, 'Forget something?' Because how would I explain to Christopher what I'd been doing in his building a few minutes ago?

On the other hand, maybe it would be a good opener. I could be like, 'Well, the truth is, Christopher, I was here seeing my mom and sister. Yeah, they live in this building. Because they're Em Watts's mom and sister. Get it? GET IT?'

But Eddie was preoccupied with a tenant who had called down to complain about something, so Christopher and I just breezed by and managed to get in the elevator without incident.

It was a slightly awkward, silent ride up, but Christopher broke the tension by looking over at me as I was clutching Nikki Howard's dog and saying, 'So. You don't really go everywhere in a limo, do you?'

I smiled some more into Cosy's fur. I still hadn't taken off my sunglasses – I didn't want him to see the full extent of what had been going on under there. It was possible I'd escape all this without him ever knowing I'd been standing down there bawling my eyes out, not exactly the impression I wanted to make on him.

I just said, 'Uh, no.'

I was obviously not at my witty best when I was around Christopher. Which made no sense, because I used to be able to talk non-stop around him. This was a problem that I was going to have to do something about one day.

But right then, seeing as how I was just barely hanging on emotionally, I figured monosyllabic answers were OK.

Now was really not the time to dive into the whole *Guess what? I'm not really Nikki Howard* thing. Not when I was on the verge of bursting out into hysterical sobs – or laughter – at any moment.

'Yeah,' Christopher said, nodding. 'I figured the rumours were bull.'

I smiled enigmatically – as enigmatically as I could. I mean, let's face it: I was in the elevator – with Christopher! I was going to Christopher's apartment on a Sunday afternoon! It was just like old times! It was hard to be enigmatic when I was kind of bursting with happiness.

The elevator doors slid open on Christopher's floor – which, thankfully, was seven stories up from my parents' floor, so I was unlikely to run into either my mother or Frida – and he said, 'It's to the right,' and held the door open for me. Christopher had never held doors open for me back when I'd been in my old body. Not that I would have expected him to. It was just . . . well, it kind of caused my happiness to dry up and make me realize . . .

This wasn't old times. It wasn't old times at all.

'It's right here,' Christopher said, pulling out his keys.

Christopher threw open the door and I went inside, nearly tearing up again at the familiar sight of piled-up newspapers everywhere (the Commander read every newspaper he could get his hands on in the morning, so he'd know exactly what was going on in the world. I always thought it would be easier to use the Internet, but he read that too) and the faint scent of leather (most of the Maloneys' furniture was upholstered in soft leather handed down from some ancient estate long since entailed away from the family, and was much too large for a tiny faculty apartment).

'Here,' Christopher said. 'Let me take your coat.'

Trying to hide my shy smile (I know! I felt shy! Around Christopher, of all people!), I pulled off my gloves and began untwining my scarf, then shrugged off my leather jacket – but not before kneeling down to help Cosabella off with hers first.

The one outdoor item I didn't take off, when I was done disrobing both of us and had handed everything to Christopher to stack on the antique bench in the front entranceway, was my sunglasses. My excitement wasn't the only thing I was trying to hide.

'Have a seat,' Christopher said when I followed him into the living room. He shoved a stack of the *Times*, the *Wall Street Journal* and the *Washington Post* out of the way, just letting them crash to the floor in order to make room for me on the cracked brown leather couch. 'Do you want some coffee or tea or hot chocolate or something?'

Refreshments. He was offering me refreshments. Like I was a real guest.

Which in a way I was, I guess. I always should have been . . . Em Watts, girl. Not Em Watts, sexless friend from seven floors down.

For some reason, however, that had never seemed to occur to Christopher. Not until I started wearing much tighter shirts. In someone else's body.

92

'Uh, some tea would be great,' I said, putting Cosy down. She was better now that we were inside, where it was warm. She'd stopped shaking and was looking around for a place to curl up and take a nap. 'Could I just use your bathroom for a second?'

Christopher said, 'Sure,' and showed me where it was, and I followed him, pretending I didn't know where I was going, even though of course I'd been in his bathroom a thousand times before.

Once safely inside, I shut the door and whipped off my sunglasses and squinted at my reflection in the shaving-cream-flecked mirror above the sink (Christopher and his dad had a housekeeper, but she only visited every other week. Or at least she used to. Judging by the mess, it was hard to tell if she still came at all any more).

Actually, I didn't look that bad. You could barely even tell I'd been crying. I wiped off a little mascara where it had smudged. Just a wave of the lipbalm from my Miu Miu tote (which I kept there to prevent chapping, because you can't imagine how the make-up artists get on your case when you present yourself to them with chapped lips that they then have to exfoliate), and I was good to go. I gave myself a smile for luck, and noticed how the bathroom smelled like Barbasol, Christopher's shaving gel of choice. I stood there and inhaled it for a while, because it smelt like him.

Yeah. I was that far gone. I couldn't even be mad at him for treating Nikki better than he had ever treated me. Because I realized he just didn't know any better.

He hadn't understood what he'd had in me until I was gone.

Except that I wasn't gone. That was what he hadn't figured out yet. Though how I was going to let him know that – in a way he was going to be able to comprehend – was what *I* hadn't figured out yet.

But checking for tear stains wasn't the only reason I'd gone into the bathroom, of course. I reached into my tote, pulled out my pocket bug detector and turned it on. It seemed almost too much to hope that Stark hadn't hit the Maloneys' place as well my parents'. But since I hadn't yet been able to establish any kind of meaningful contact with Christopher, there was always a chance they hadn't bothered to slip any surveillance equipment in there.

Except . . . that they had. At least if the antennae was working properly. The signal was strong and steady. Even after I smacked it a few times.

Jeez! Thanks, Stark. Thanks a lot.

Sighing, I put away the detector, washed my hands and came out. Well, at least I'd dodged a bullet in the form of any embarrassing questions about why I might have been weeping. Christopher couldn't have noticed my little crying jag outside.

'So why,' Christopher asked, after I'd settled on to the couch and he'd come out of the kitchen with a steaming mug of mint tea for me in one hand and a cup of coffee for himself in the other, 'were you crying down there, anyway?'

Nine

I stared at him.

Great. I wasn't going to tell him. I wasn't going to tell him a thing.

'I wasn't crying,' I said, taking the mug from him. Oh, excellent response, Em! Score one for you.

'Yeah you were,' he said. He sat down on the other end of the couch, after first kicking off the *Los Angeles Times* and the *Seattle Intelligencer*. Cosabella, who had made herself at home on the cushion between us, watched the individual sections of the paper fall to the parquet floor with her ears perked in curiosity. 'I mean, I guess you could try to say that your eyes were just watering with the cold. But it looked pretty obvious to me that you were crying.'

I stared at him speechlessly. What was there for me to say, after all? I was busted. I took a tiny sip of the hot tea and hoped to find inspiration in its mint flavour. Except . . . no. Nothing.

'You don't have to tell me if you don't want to, of course,' Christopher went on. 'But I don't see what you've got to lose. I don't know anybody you know, so it's not like I'm going to tell anyone.'

I looked around the apartment, half afraid a paparazzo or even someone from Stark was going to pop out from behind a piece of furniture and snap my photo.

Christopher had barely spoken three sentences to me since I'd come out of my coma and started attending Tribeca Alternative again. Why would they put transmitters in *his* home? Even Stark could see he was more interested in McKayla Donofrio than he was in me. What was their problem?

'My dad's at his office right now,' Christopher said, seeming to read my thoughts – although not entirely correctly. 'Last day before finals. All his students are panicked.'

'Oh,' I said. I wished he'd read my *other* thoughts. The ones where I wanted him to put down that coffee mug and kiss me. And realize that I was his old friend Em and not Nikki Howard. Although that might put a damper on the whole kissing scenario, since Christopher had never expressed the slightest interest in making out with me when I'd been alive. In my old body, I mean.

'It's just,' I said slowly. Why *not* tell him? Why not tell him I was his old friend Em, that I wasn't dead after all? I couldn't tell him verbally, because somewhere in this apartment was a listening device. But I could write the truth down, couldn't I? Then destroy the evidence when I was through?

Yeah, why not? Christopher wouldn't tell anyone.

Except his dad, of course. Who was such a conspiracy theorist that, when he found out his apartment was bugged – as he would, since I'd have to tell Christopher that's why I was writing instead of just telling him my secret – he'd surely insist on going to every news organization in the country with the story. The Commander hated Stark almost as much as I did. There was no way Christopher would ever get him to keep quiet about what they'd done to me . . . or the fact that they'd bugged his apartment.

And then Mom and Dad would be ruined, if not have to serve actual jail time, for breaking the contract they'd signed. Those millions of dollars they'd have to pay back for my surgery, legal fees and fines? Even Nikki Howard didn't have that much in her bank account . . . not that I'd have access to that money any more, after the Commander went to CNN.

No. Just no. I couldn't tell Christopher the truth. Not now.

And the way things were going? Maybe not ever.

'It's just –' I said again, stalling for time. What could I say? What? How about . . . well, some semblance of the truth, I guess? Just not the *whole* truth. '– I got some bad news today.'

'Really?' Christopher looked concerned. This was how he used to look when I'd tell him about a bad grade, or a fight with my sister, or my character losing a life on *Journeyquest*.

That's when I realized . . . What was I saying? I couldn't tell him about what had just happened with my mom . . . that I was upset that I couldn't go to Florida for winter break with my family. Because they weren't supposed to be my family any more.

But I had to say something now that I'd blurted out the

thing about getting some bad news. Only what? That I'm a Stark Angel? Oh God, no . . . Christopher wouldn't have the slightest bit of sympathy. Anything but that. But what else?

'My mom's missing,' I heard myself say.

Oh. Great. OK, yeah, so I didn't mean to blurt out *that*. But it was too late to stuff the words back in my mouth now.

Christopher stared at me, his blue eyes wide.

'Your *mom* is missing?' he echoed.

Only when the words were out of his mouth did it occur to me that possibly this was the part I shouldn't have mentioned after all. Maybe leading with being a Stark Angel would have been better.

'We're not close,' I said lamely. 'She's, uh –' Wow. How do I get myself out of this one? – 'been missing a while, and I only just found out because we don't talk on a regular basis –'

Then I realized maybe this wasn't the most tactful thing to say either. Christopher and his own mother weren't close, due to his having chosen, when his parents were divorcing, to live with his father and not his mother. But this, he'd once confided to me, wasn't because of any particular dislike of his mother or a surfeit of affection for his dad, but because his younger sister had chosen to live with their mother, and Christopher had felt it only fair that one child side with their father, who'd also sued for full custody. Which is how he'd ended up living in my building.

'How long has she been missing?' he asked. He was absently petting Cosabella, who'd fallen asleep with her muzzle on his knee.

'A couple of months,' I replied, a little surprised by the intensity of his interest. But then I guess it would be alarming to hear that someone's mom was missing. If you were anyone except my agent Rebecca, that is. 'Maybe . . . three.'

Christopher got a faraway look in his blue eyes. 'Right around the time of the accident,' he murmured as he stared off in the direction of the television. 'It makes sense.'

My eyebrows went up. 'Excuse me?' I asked.

His gaze snapped back towards me. 'Nothing,' he said. But it was clear it wasn't nothing.

'What have you done to try to find her?' he asked. 'Has anyone filled out a missing person's report?'

'Um,' I said, 'yeah. I guess.'

'You guess?' Christopher looked confused. I couldn't blame him. I was confused too. What was going on, exactly? I was really starting to wonder if maybe grief over my death had sent Christopher around the bend. Chopping off all his hair the way he had – it used to be to his shoulders – wasn't the only change I'd seen in him since I 'died'. He'd gotten too intense, spent too much time alone in the computer lab in school, not talking to anyone. Including me, despite my efforts to draw him out.

'Well, my brother's the one who's looking into it, really,' I said. 'All I've done is call my cellphone service provider. To see if she called and maybe I missed it –'

Christopher shook his head. 'It could take months before they get back to you with that information.'

I looked at him and shrugged. 'I know. But what else can I do?' I hated feeling this helpless. Especially in front of Christopher. Back in my old body, I'd always made a point to do everything for myself in front of him, like if I showed the slightest female weakness, he might think less of me somehow. If there was a bug on the floor? I squashed it. If something was too high for me to reach on a shelf? I got a chair and climbed it. If the lid to the peanut butter jar was on too tight? I'd have gone all the way to my own apartment and asked my dad to open it before I'd have asked Christopher.

But now . . . now I was wondering if this had been the wisest strategy. I mean, did you really get guys by acting like you didn't need them? That had not been how I'd gotten Brandon to kiss me last night. I'd asked him for help getting back to New York, and next thing I knew, we'd started making out, and he'd asked me to be his girlfriend.

If I wanted to make out with Christopher, wouldn't it have behoved me to have acted like I needed him? Just a little bit?

And OK, I hate girls like that – the Whitney Robertsons of the world. But hey. Didn't she have the hottest boyfriend in school (if you considered Polo-wearing, thick-necked jocks hot)?

'McKayla Donofrio's father is with the Office of the Attorney General,' Christopher offered, obviously trying to be helpful. 'Maybe he could do something for your mom.'

McKayla Donofrio? How did Christopher know what her dad did for a living? Although knowing what a snob McKayla was, she'd probably bragged about it in class one day when I hadn't been there. She bragged all the time about being a National Merit Scholar and head of Tribeca Alternative's Business Club. She even bragged about being lactose intolerant. Having a father in the Office of the Attorney General would be only slightly less prestigious to a girl like McKayla.

On the other hand, maybe Christopher and McKayla were dating. Hadn't I caught her staring at him more and more often as the semester had gone on, especially since he'd cut his hair and started wearing more black (what was up with that, anyway)? And hadn't I seen his gaze stray more than once in her direction? But then, I'd just thought he was staring blankly at whatever was in front of him out of abject boredom.

There couldn't be anything going on between the two of them. There could *not*.

And yet . . .

Suddenly, I felt like crying all over again. The thought of Christopher with McKayla on top of everything else was more than I could handle.

And that's exactly what I needed, someone from the Office of the Attorney General of the state of New York poking around in Nikki Howard's business. Please.

'Hey.' Christopher reached out and laid a gentle

hand on my shoulder. I was so startled – I'd been busy picturing the two of them at one of McKayla's Business Club meetings, his fair head and her dark one bent over some kind of PowerPoint presentation together, I'd almost forgotten he was there – that I jumped. 'Are you all right?'

'I – I'm fine,' I said. My eyes were filled with tears again. I reached up hastily to wipe them away. 'Just . . . allergies. Sorry. I should probably go . . .'

I got up, wanting to leave before I had even less control over my tear ducts. I was turning into a total basket case. Also, *allergies*? In winter? Right. Brilliant, Em.

'You're really upset about this,' Christopher said, gazing up at me. He hadn't fallen for the allergy excuse. 'Aren't you?'

'Well,' I said, sniffling. Did I feel a twinge of guilt over the fact that he was mistaking my tears for concern over Nikki Howard's missing mom, when they were, in fact, tears for him? Yeah. But so what? It was kind of hard to feel bad about it when he was gazing at me so worriedly with those bright blue eyes of his. 'I mean, yeah. She's my mother.'

Oooh, nice one, Em. Laying it on kind of thick, aren't you?

'Look.' Christopher seemed to come to some kind of decision in his head. 'Before you go . . . just let me try something.'

He got up – jostling Cosabella, who sighed and curled up into a ball – and crossed the living room, heading down the hall. I realized he was heading towards his bedroom. What was going on?

'Uh. Christopher?' I called after him when a few minutes passed, and he didn't reappear. Clearly he wasn't just getting me an umbrella.

'In here,' he called back. 'It's OK. Come on in.'

I followed the sound of his voice, wondering what on earth he was up to, since getting me an umbrella shouldn't have taken that long.

I found myself freezing like a statue in his bedroom doorway, however.

'All of this would be a lot easier,' Christopher was muttering from the chair in front of his desktop, 'if we could crack their firewall –'

But I was barely listening. That's because sitting there on top of Christopher's messy bookshelf, which was sagging in the middle because there were so many hardbacks piled on to it, was a framed photo of . . .

Me.

Not McKayla Donofrio. Not Nikki Howard. *Me*. Emerson Watts.

It was the photo they'd used at my memorial service. It wasn't very flattering, in my opinion. It was a school photo, the one I'd told Mom not to even bother buying, because in the proof one of my teeth was doing this weird snaggle thing (I always thought I'd have time to get that fixed one day. No such luck). She'd gone ahead and bought it anyway, because . . . well, because of what happened.

And now a copy of it was sitting in Christopher's

bedroom, on such prominent display that you couldn't go anywhere, really, without feeling like it was looking at you.

'Hey, Felix.' Christopher, ignoring me, was speaking into his computer.

A squeaky voice came on over the computer, and I saw Christopher's fourteen-year-old cousin Felix, the one who was under house arrest in Brooklyn for some kind of computer-hacking crime, on Christopher's monitor.

'Didn't you just leave here?' Felix wanted to know. 'What'd you do, forget something?'

'I've got my friend Nikki here,' Christopher said. 'Her mother is missing. Can you run her Soc and see if anything comes up?'

'A girl?' Felix's voice rose an octave. 'You got a girl in your room?'

'Yeah, I got a girl in my room,' Christopher said in a calm voice. He didn't blush or anything, the way he might have in the old days. This, to me, was only clearer proof there was something going on between him and McKayla.

But then . . . what was with the picture of me?

To tell the truth, I couldn't believe the way he was . . . well, taking charge. That just wasn't Christopher. Christopher was Doritos and the Discovery Channel, not ordering people around and Skyping his cousin to consult about 'running' a missing woman's Social Security number.

This change in him was kind of freaking me out. In

a good way. Except for the photo of the old me, and the McKayla part.

'Can you help her?' Christopher asked his cousin.

'Of course I can help her,' Felix said. He sounded like a kid. Which wasn't that unusual, since I could see from the monitor that that's what he was . . . skinny neck, tufted black hair, pimples and all. 'Let me see her.'

'You don't need to see her,' Christopher said.

'I want to see her,' Felix said. 'I have to sit cooped up in here all day by myself. If you've got a girl in your room, I want to see one.'

'You can't—' Christopher began.

I took a quick step so that I was viewable in the lens of the camera on Christopher's monitor. 'Hi, Felix,' I said, just to shut him up.

Felix let out an expletive and abruptly disappeared from view. 'Chris,' he whispered from somewhere off camera. 'That's Nikki Howard. You didn't tell me the girl in your room was Nikki *Howard*.'

'Well,' Christopher said, sounding faintly amused, 'the girl in my room is Nikki Howard.'

'How,' Felix wanted to know from wherever he was hiding, 'did you get *Nikki Howard* to come into your room?'

Christopher looked over at me. He was smiling a little. 'She basically followed me here,' he joked. I couldn't help smiling a little back at him. If he was doing all this to make me stop crying, it was working. Wow. I should have tried a few tears on Christopher years ago. I probably could have gotten him to change the channel all those times he'd insisted on watching those boring episodes of *Top Gear*. 'Do you think you can help her, Felix, or not?'

'Of course I can help her.' Felix said again, reappearing on the computer monitor. He'd combed his stick-uppy black hair and put on a different shirt. 'Hey, there, Nikki,' he said, in a much deeper tone of voice. 'How you doing?'

'Uh,' I said, laughing a little, in spite of my unease about the situation, 'I'm fine.'

'Great. That's great,' Felix said. 'So, just give me your mom's Social Security number, and we can get down to business.'

I glanced at Christopher. 'The police already checked this stuff out, I think—'

'The police!' Felix's scorn was explosive. 'You think they have the resources I do, even though they did take away my Wi-Fi connection and now I have to piggyback off my neighbour's? Trust me, unless she's dead or living off the grid, I'll find her. Just cough up the digits, babe.' Christopher gave him a warning wag of his finger, and Felix apologized. 'Sorry, I mean, Miss Howard.'

'I don't actually have that number on me,' I explained. Then, seeing Felix's look of dejection, I added quickly, 'But I guess I can get it—'

'Great!' Felix perked right up. 'As soon as you do, text me! Or maybe you could come over, actually. My mom makes really good chilli—'

Christopher reached out and switched the monitor off. Felix disappeared in a flash.

'He's kind of a freak,' Christopher explained. 'But he

really does know what he's doing, believe it or not. That's why the judge gave him six months instead of just a slap on the wrist. My dad sends me over there every Sunday to try to be a good influence on Felix, but I think it's the other way around. Anyway, you can just give the number to me when you have it. And I'll make sure he gets it.'

'Uh, thanks,' I said, glancing up at my picture, which was leering toothily down at us. I glanced hastily away from it. 'This is really nice of you.'

Christopher shrugged. 'You can make it up to me, actually. I mean, if you want to.'

I could? All sorts of ideas how I could make it up to him went through my head. The tongue trick, even though I still didn't know what it was, sprang foremost to mind, which was disturbing. I had to go sink down on Christopher's tightly made bed (the Commander believed a tidy bed was a sign of a tidy mind) before my knees gave out from under me.

'Oh?' I managed to squeak out when I could finally speak.

'Yeah,' Christopher said. 'So. Just how loyal are you to your boss anyway?'

This was such an unexpected question, I blurted, '*Who?*' without thinking.

'Your boss,' Christopher said again. 'Robert Stark. How much do you like him?'

Taken completely aback, I stammered, 'W-Why?'

'You work for a company that reported three

hundred billion dollars in sales last year, most of the profit of which went to line your boss's pocket. I'm just wondering,' Christopher said calmly, 'how you feel about him.'

Instead of answering, I stood up. Then I walked over to Christopher's bedroom window. To his surprise, I leaned over and yanked it open, letting in a blast of cold air, as well as the steady patter of the sleet and loud traffic sounds from Bleecker Street below. The acoustic interference, I hoped, would make it hard for anyone listening to our conversation to hear what we were saying.

'What are you doing?' he asked me curiously. He had to raise his voice a little to be heard over the traffic.

I waved my hand around my head. 'Did it ever occur to you,' I asked, 'that they could be listening?'

Christopher stared at me. 'Who could?'

'Stark,' I whispered. My heart gave a little thump as I said it. Not so much because of the thought of Stark listening to us, but because Christopher was looking at me . . . really looking at me, like he was actually seeing me for the first time.

Only, of course, he wasn't.

Christopher laughed. '*Stark?* Here? Are you serious?'

I was *dead* serious. But of course, I couldn't tell him that. Especially not now.

'Christopher, you shouldn't underestimate them,' I said instead. 'They . . . they know things.'

He laughed some more. 'You're paranoid.'

'Maybe,' I said, going back to my perch on his bed.

'Maybe you should try being a little paranoid too.' Then I sighed and said, 'Richard Stark wants me to parade around on national television in a ten million dollar bra made out of diamonds. How do you *think* I feel about him?'

Christopher smiled. When he smiled, something strange happened to my insides. It was like they turned to liquid.

'That's what I was hoping you'd say.'

And then he told me what he planned to do. And what he needed from me.

And my world, which had already been upside down, flipped over one more time.

'Felix and I have been trying to find a wormhole to get us into Stark's corporate mainframe for ages,' he said. 'But we haven't been able to. Their firewall is that good. So instead of a back door, I think we're going to have to try going in through the front door.' Christopher had stopped smiling and regarded me seriously. 'Do you think you could get us a username and password for someone who works at Stark Enterprises? Someone high up would be best, but at this point we'll take anyone . . .'

I just stared at him.

This was what he wanted from me? A lousy username and password?

It so figured. Why was I even surprised? I mean, the guy had a picture of a dead girl on his bookshelf. Not a small one, either, but an eight by ten glossy, with eyes that followed you everywhere you went.

Great. Now I was starting to get jealous of *myself.*

'Christopher,' I said, shaking my head. 'What you're

talking about . . . it's crazy. I mean . . . what are you guys going to do once you get into their system?'

He looked surprised.

'Take it down,' he said in a *What else?* tone of voice.

Take it down. Like it should be so obvious. Also like it would be that easy. Like he was Robin Hood, and Stark Enterprises was a coach full of gold he was going to rob.

'Isn't that a little . . . childish?' I pushed some of my hair behind my ears as I tried to figure out how to phrase what I was going to say next without offending him. 'I mean, OK, yeah, so their system goes down for a few hours. You'll make some Stark cellphone owners mad, whatever. Maybe you'll get on Google News. But . . . what's the point? Just to show you can? Your computer is bigger than their computer? Big deal.'

'No, no,' Christopher interrupted, shaking his head. 'You don't understand. I mean, the point is to take it down. *To take Stark Enterprises down.* Forever.'

Ten

It would have been obvious to anyone looking at me as I staggered into school on Monday morning just before the late bell rang, a cup of tea clutched in one hand, and my Marc Jacobs tote full of overdue assignments and my Mac Air in the other, that I hadn't had a good weekend. I know I looked particularly heinous. I'd tossed and turned all night, unable to sleep not just because Lulu Collins was hogging my Frette sheets and duvet, but because the guy I'm hopelessly in love with? Yeah, well, *he's* in love too.

Only not with McKayla Donofrio, it turns out. He's in love with a dead girl.

Oh, and did I mention that he plans to obliterate the company I work for? Yeah.

Not, of course, that I myself was all that enamoured of Stark Enterprises. But I didn't want to destroy it, necessarily. After all, I actually liked a few people who worked there.

Not that Christopher had been kind enough to share with me yesterday the details of what he and his cousin Felix intended to do once they'd gotten the information they need. Why would he tell me? I was just some bubble-headed model.

He hadn't put it that way, of course. But it was clear he

didn't think I'd 'understand' and that I was 'better off not knowing'.

Of course, part of that was my own fault for pretending not to understand the simplest things about computers when I'd first 'met' him.

But there hadn't been any pretence in my reaction to his statement that he was going to take down Stark Enterprises. I couldn't help myself. I'd been honestly horrified. I'd blurted out the first thing that sprang into my mind, and that was, 'But . . . *why*?'

Christopher had just smiled in an enigmatic way and said, 'I have my reasons.'

I hadn't missed the way his gaze had flicked, just for an instant, towards my photo.

Great. Just great! It was perfectly obvious now what was going on. My death, like the deaths of so many tragic heroines before me, had caused another one . . . in this case the death of Christopher, only on the inside. His heart had died, and where fun, joyful Christopher used to be – the Christopher I had loved, the Christopher with whom I'd played so many rounds of *Journeyquest*, the Christopher whom I'd longed to notice me as not just a gal pal, but as a girl – stood an evil supervillain.

Why had I been so surprised? It happened all the time in comic books. Christopher was now going to use his powers for evil instead of good in order to avenge my death. What other explanation could there be?

Just to be sure, I'd asked, 'Well, is one of the reasons what happened to your friend who died at that Stark

Megastore? Because I'm pretty sure that was the fault of the protester who shot that paintball at the plasma screen she was standing under.'

Christopher had looked at me without expression and said, 'And who was responsible for making sure that plasma screen was secured well enough to the ceiling that an assault from a paintball attack wouldn't cause it to come crashing down?'

'Well, Stark,' I'd said. 'But—'

'Stark has to be held accountable for what it did.'

Oh my God! I couldn't believe how upsetting this was.

But also, in a way, how kind of hot it was. I mean, what girl wouldn't want a guy to go on a wild computer-hacking rampage against a majorly environmentally irresponsible corporation, just for her? Especially one that was basically holding her in corporate slavery to it, and which had just the day before almost made her get eaten by sharks.

The only problem was, he wasn't doing it for me. Well, I mean, he was, but he didn't know it. Because he thought Em Watts was dead.

And now more than ever, I couldn't tell him I wasn't. Because it was obvious he'd completely lost it. Who knew what he'd do if he knew the truth? In seconds he might spill it all over the blogosphere, in order to get his 'revenge' on Stark.

And where would that leave me? And my parents? In bankruptcy court, that's where. Oh, sure, Stark would go down.

But so would the Watts family.

It was bad enough Christopher had been doing all this crazy virus programming and Stark probably knew it, given that they were bugging his place, and there I was, sitting in his apartment. I just couldn't believe any of it was happening. Christopher, my sweet, funny best friend Christopher, had turned into this dark, cynical crusader for global justice? Since *when*?

'Do you really think,' I'd said, trying to figure out how I was going to handle this, 'that this is what your friend – Em, I think you said her name was – would want? I mean, what if you get caught? You could get house arrest, like your cousin. Or worse, actual jail time, if you're tried as an adult.'

'I don't care,' Christopher had said, shaking his head. 'It'd be worth it.'

A chill had gone up my spine. It was obvious now that Christopher's transformation was a hundred per cent complete. All that was missing was his black cape and a jagged facial scar.

'You'd risk possible incarceration,' I'd asked in astonishment, 'for a dead girl?'

His next words had rocked my world to its core:

'She was worth it,' he'd said simply.

If I could have picked up a knife and jammed it in Em Watts's heart right then, I would have, I hated her so much at that moment. Never mind that Em Watts was me. I couldn't look at her picture a second longer. I'd had to get out. I'd had to get out of Christopher's lair slash bedroom.

Especially because of the whole still-wanting-to-kiss-him thing.

And him so very definitely *not* wanting to kiss me. Because he was in love with a dead girl.

I don't know what I did or said after that. Somehow I'd found myself in his front hallway, jamming my arms back into my coat, and suiting Cosy back up into hers. It shames me to say I think there might have been some more of those unshed tears in my eyes . . .

But I don't think he noticed. This time.

And of course now I had to decide . . . did I give him what he wanted and risk the jobs of all the people I worked with on a pretty much daily basis (if what he and Felix had planned were to succeed, which, let's face it . . . what were the chances? I loved Christopher, and I don't think there's anything he couldn't do if he set his mind to it. But bring down a bazillion dollar corporation like Stark with a computer virus, or whatever he was planning? Let's get ever so slightly real)?

Or did I blow him off and try to find Steven's mom some other way?

Plus the whole thing about getting him to like me as I was now, in Nikki Howard's body. Because when I was standing there in the hallway, trying not to let him see how freaked I was, he was definitely giving off a Let's-get-the-pretty-girl-out-of-here-now-since-she's-not-coughing-up-the-info-we-need vibe.

Oh, he'd been polite enough. He'd given me that umbrella he'd promised and everything.

But he hadn't exactly begged me to stick around or anything.

Was it any wonder I'd been up all night? And had done zero studying for finals?

As soon as I got to Tribeca Alternative, I wandered into the ground floor ladies' room, hoping to snatch a minute in the mirror to do some kind of repair work to my face prior to encountering Christopher in first period Public Speaking. I had no idea what I was going to say to him, but I knew I'd feel more confident if I had some lipgloss on. The merits of lipgloss had long been praised by my sister, but ignored by me, until professional make-up artists had started slathering it on me every day, and I saw the results in the mirror and the pages of the magazines Nikki's face routinely graces. It could really boost a girl's self-esteem, and anyone who thought otherwise had never tried Nars Triple X.

It was funny that as I was thinking this my sister came barrelling out of the ladies' room and crashed right into me.

'Em – I mean, Nikki!' she cried, as hot tea sloshed out of the cardboard cup I was holding, and all over the floor beside us. 'Oops! Oh no, I'm so sorry!'

Her friends – Frida rarely travelled without a pack of fellow junior varsity cheerleaders around her – all stared at me owlishly. Even though I'd been going to Tribeca Alternative (in my current incarnation) for almost two months now, the student body still hadn't gotten used to seeing me around the halls, and I was the recipient of a lot of gawking and even the occasional catcall, though I was probably among the more conservative dressers there. Belly, cleavage, and thong baring ensembles weren't tolerated by the administration, but that didn't rule out the occasional 'accidental' flash of tanned flesh from Whitney Robertson and her ilk. I, however, kept what I had going on strictly under wraps. Of course, it would be no secret after New Year, thanks to the Stark Angel fashion show.

'Hey,' I said to Frida, 'thanks.' I was being sarcastic about the tea, which had burned my hand. I wiped it on my Temperley top, which was fortunately dark blue and wouldn't show the resulting stain.

'I'm so glad I bumped into you. We really need to talk,' Frida said, grabbing my arm and dragging me into the bathroom she'd just vacated. 'You guys go on without me,' she called to her friends. 'I gotta chat with Nik for a sec.'

Nik. Nice one. Her friends would be so impressed.

Fortunately the ladies' room was empty, as Frida ascertained after a quick stall check.

'How could you run off like that yesterday?' she demanded, dropping my arm as well as the polite tone she'd adopted in the hallway in front of her friends. 'Mom and I were so worried about you. And then you wouldn't return any of our calls.'

I just blinked at her. This was too much for me to handle so early in the morning on basically zero sleep and no caffeine. Not that I ever got to have much caffeine anyway, since I found out it's forbidden on Nikki's acid reflux diet (which she'd fortunately kept taped to the side of the refrigerator). One cup a day was all she could handle, I'd discovered, or it was reflux city.

'I was having a really bad day,' I said. This wasn't a very good explanation, I knew. But it was all I had.

'And you left that big bag of presents for us!' Frida went on. 'Just left it, without saying anything!'

'Those were for you guys to open when we all got to Grandma's,' I said. I didn't want to think about the fun present-fests we used to have down in Florida, the free-for-all of gift wrap and dreidels and chocolate Santas. I'd never experience any of that again, I knew.

'I *know*,' Frida said. 'That was *so* nice of you . . .'

I knew she'd already shaken the distinctively wrapped, robin's-egg-blue box I'd gotten her, and figured out by now it contained exactly what she's always wanted . . . something all her friends here at Tribeca Alternative had, but that our parents could never afford to get her . . . a pair of diamond stud earrings.

'Look,' I said uncomfortably. I didn't like thinking about how she was going to be opening that box down in Florida without me being there to see her expression when she did. 'I have to go. The bell's going to ring and I haven't even been to my locker yet.'

'No,' Frida said, reaching to grab my wrist again. But this time not the one holding the tea. 'Nikki, Mom and Dad and I talked. That's why we kept calling you. Mom didn't think you'd be so upset about not going to Grandma's. She thought you'd be going somewhere fabulous like Paris or whatever and wouldn't care—'

'I really have to get going,' I said. I didn't want to hear this. She was going to say they'd decided to have some kind of lame Christmas-Hanukkah party here in the city for me before they leave, with a gift exchange and hot cider and a viewing of *A Christmas Story* or something.

But it wasn't going to be the same without Grandma and the beach and her stupid frozen bagels. Which I couldn't eat anyway, in this dumb body.

'– but now that we know you're going to be around, we're going to change the whole thing,' Frida went on. 'We're skipping Florida this year. We're going to stay here in the city, and Gran's agreed to fly up! So you can come over. We can say you're my friend from school—'

'Free,' I said. I did not want to hear this.

'Come on, Nik. I know it won't be the same, but it'll be fun. Gran's even excited about coming to the city in winter, and you know how hard it is to get her to come here when it's cold—'

'Free!'

Frida jumped, but whether because of the bell or the fact that I'd shouted at her, I didn't know. In any case, I'd gotten her attention.

'We're going to be late to class. We'll discuss it later, OK?'

'OK,' Frida grumbled, looking hurt. 'But, jeez, I thought you'd be happy. I mean, I agreed to give up going to cheerleading camp so I could stick around here in the city and be with you.'

Suddenly I didn't want my tea any more, caffeine fix or not. I dumped the entire thing into a nearby trash can and made my way out of the ladies' room.

'That doesn't make me happy, Frida,' I hissed at her from between gritted teeth as she trotted along behind me. 'I want you to do what *you* want, not what you think I want.'

'But I *am* doing what I want,' Frida said. 'I really want to come to your party.'

I staggered to a halt and whirled round to face her, even as the last of the latecomers were running past us, trying to get to class before tardy slips were given out.

'Wait a minute.' I stared down at her. 'Did you weasel out of going to Florida just so you could come to Lulu's party?' It would totally be like her to have done this. Frida was so obsessed with glitz and glamour, she'd gnaw her own arm off in exchange for a chance to brush up with the right celebrity.

Frida's blush revealed the truth before she could say a word. 'No, not exactly,' she said.

I threw my hands into the air in exasperation and turned around again to head back to class. I was done.

'What?' Frida trailed after me. 'I thought you'd be happy! I mean, you looked so sad yesterday! Now you'll have Mom and me to hang out with—'

'You're incredible,' I said. 'You know, Frida, yesterday I went out of my way, slogging through terrible weather, not to mention risking getting Mom mad at me, to stick up for

120

you, all because you were so adamant about going to that cheer camp. And as soon as you got a better invitation, you totally dropped it. What happened to your being such an integral part of the team? What happened to you being the base?'

Frida hurried along beside me, her mouth opening and closing like a goldfish. She was trying, I knew, to think of an excuse for her behaviour. But there was nothing she could say, because there was no excuse.

'I know you think you're doing me this big favour,' I said. 'But you're not actually doing it for me, are you? Because you're the one who's really getting something out of it. Well, I've got news for you, Free. There are some things that are more important than parties. Such as being there for your teammates. Did you ever think of how they're going to feel when they find out you've ditched them so you can party with Nikki Howard and Lulu Collins?'

I'd reached the classroom where my Public Speaking class was held, and turned at the doorway to glare down at her. Frida's eyes were filled with angry tears.

'I *thought* I was being there for my sister,' she said.

'Yeah,' I said. 'Well, funny how you only remember you have a sister when you want something, like someone to side with you against your mother or an invitation to a kick-ass loft party. Which you're not invited to, by the way.'

I stormed past her just as Mr Greer called, 'Ms Howard?

Are you joining us today? Or are you going to stand out in the hallway, chatting?'

'Sorry,' I muttered. I sailed into the classroom and slid into my seat . . .

. . . which just happened to be in front of Christopher.

This was so not shaping up to be my kind of day.

Eleven

Christopher was actually awake, for once, and greeted me with a smile.

'How's it going?' he asked.

'Oh,' I began, telling myself, *Don't you dare smile back, Em Watts, no matter how much you might want to because of how much you love him and what that smile does to you! He's evil! And even if he's not, he doesn't like you! Well, he does, but not the real you. The dead you.*

And that's just wrong. And so is what he and his cousin want to do.

Right?

But before I had a chance to say anything more to Christopher, Whitney Robertson, who was sitting one desk over, leaned forward and whispered, 'Oh my God, is that top Temperley? It's so nice.'

'How was your weekend?' Whitney's henchwoman, Lindsey Jacobs, seated in the row beside hers, was also leaning forward eagerly. 'I saw online that you were in St John with Brandon Stark.' There were photos of our trip online? Great. If there were any of Brandon and me making out, I was going to murder someone. 'That must have been incredible! I would give anything to get out of here for a couple of days, the weather's been so miserable. And with Brandon Stark! He's so hot.

How could you even stand to come back? I'd have killed myself.'

She had no idea.

'Ladies.' Mr Greer sounded snide. 'So sorry to interrupt. But some of you might recall that it's the last week of the semester, and we're finishing up our final three-minute oral presentations, which will count as three quarters of your grade, before winter break.'

I couldn't help groaning inwardly. I was completely unprepared for this. It was going to be my turn to give my presentation sometime soon, and I hadn't had a second to work on it. When I'd got home from Christopher's last night, I'd been astonished to find Lulu home instead of out partying with her friends, and in the kitchen making, of all things, coq au vin.

Since I'd never seen her cook anything more complicated than microwave popcorn, I'd been sure she was suffering some kind of stroke and had almost called for an ambulance.

But it hadn't been a breakdown. Lulu had been cooking for Nikki's brother Steven, whom she'd sent out in search of 'a really crunchy French baguette' to go with the meal she was preparing.

'I want your brother to think I can cook,' Lulu had informed me when I'd asked her what the heck was going on. 'No, wait, maybe I don't. Wait, which do you think he'd think is cuter, a girl who lied and tried to cook just for him, or a girl who really knows how to cook?'

I'd given her a weary look and said, 'Lulu. I'll tell you

what's not cute. You, right now. This is pathetic. If you want Steven to like you, why don't you try being yourself? That's what you've always told me, remember? To just be myself?' Not that it'd ever worked. Well, it had, of course. Just not with Christopher.

I could have worked on my homework after dinner, I suppose, but somehow I'd ended up on the couch between Steven and Lulu, while he told her (after she'd prompted him) about his job as radio man on the sub on which he served.

And then when I'd tried to sneak off to work, Lulu had followed me, clearly aching for a little girl talk, asking over and over again, 'But . . . do you really think he likes me?' and 'Do you think he'd mind if tomorrow I bought him a new shirt?'

'Lulu,' I'd said to her, 'you just met him. Why do you like him so much already?'

Lulu sighed and snuggled down into the pillows beside me. 'Because he's just so . . . amazing.'

So far, the most amazing thing I'd seen about Nikki's brother Steven was that he'd volunteered to wash all the really big pots Lulu had used making the coq au vin, the ones that wouldn't fit into the dishwasher and that Lulu had been going to leave for Katerina to wash when she got to the loft in the morning.

But I had to admit . . . for a guy, that *was* pretty amazing.

Still, if I'd used our girl chat time to do my homework instead of listening to how amazing Steven Howard was,

I'd probably have felt a lot less like throwing up than I did the next morning, when I saw Mr Greer flipping through his roster.

'So, if we could get straight to business,' Mr Greer said. 'I'd like to call on . . .'

Not me, I prayed. *Not me, not me, not me, and I swear I'll stay home and study till midnight every night this week.*

'. . . Christopher Maloney.'

Christopher got up and went to the front of the room. I noticed with some chagrin that I wasn't the only girl in class whose head turned as he walked by. Christopher's look in the past few weeks had gone from preppy Polo shirts, which used to cause him to blend right in with the Jason Kleins of the school – Whitney's boyfriend and reigning king of the Walking Dead – to wearing his newly acquired black leather jacket indoors. McKayla Donofrio (I swear I was going to rip that tortoiseshell hairband right off her head, and not even care how much hair I took with it) stared as he went past her, and both Whitney and Lindsey's eyebrows shot up as well . . . and not, as in the past, because they were making fun of him, but because his form-fitting jeans didn't leave much to the imagination.

'And –' Mr Greer said from his desk when Christopher reached the front of the room and indicated he was ready to begin. Mr Greer timed all our speeches with an oven timer. At Tribeca Alternative, considered one of Manhattan's finest prep schools, things were nothing if not high-tech – 'Go!'

'Stark Enterprises,' Christopher began, 'is now the

world's largest corporation, surpassing even the oil companies and pulling in almost three hundred billion dollars a year.'

Wait. *What?* Christopher's three-minute final oral presentation was on *Stark Enterprises?*

I felt myself begin to sink down in my seat.

From the sound of it, he wasn't about to say anything good either. Not that I had anything good to say about Stark. But it was just slightly embarrassing that I, the Face of Stark, was sitting here in the classroom while a fellow student went on a rant about my employer. I could feel everyone's gazes nervously sliding towards me.

'Stark Enterprises,' Christopher went on, 'declares a profit of over seven billion dollars a year, and yet, with more than one million employees – this country's largest business – the average employee makes only fifteen thousand dollars a year before taxes for full-time work, hardly enough to sustain the average household in America. But Stark employees only receive medical benefits after two years of work, and then at such high premiums that they often have to supplement them with government subsidized health-care programmes. Essentially, many full-time Stark employees, who aren't allowed to unionize, find themselves depending on Medicaid to pay for their health care. Meanwhile, Robert Stark, Stark CEO and chairman, routinely appears on the Forbes List of wealthiest people in the world, generally in the top ten, with a personal worth of somewhere around forty billion.'

Hearing this, several people began muttering . . . and

not just Lindsey and Whitney, who whispered that Brandon Stark was worth a lot more than they thought. I knew what was coming next (if I told them Brandon wasn't my boyfriend): they were going to want to know if I could get them his cell number.

'During the past twenty years,' Christopher went on, 'it's been illustrated again and again that while on the surface Stark Megastores seem to provide convenience and low prices to the consumer – and Stark Enterprises receives tax incentives for building their stores in many towns – that convenience comes with a cost . . . and that cost to the communities in which these megastores appear may prove irreparable, since they wipe out locally owned businesses that didn't get tax breaks and don't sell cheap, knock-off products made exclusively in China, so they can't compete with Stark's rock-bottom prices. These megastores turn whole communities into ghost towns as locally owned businesses are forced to close. And who suffers because of this? We do, the taxpayers, when states and cities then have to finance downtown revitalization programmes, which usually fail, since it's easier for everyone to shop at Stark, where the parking is more convenient.'

I looked around to see how people were reacting to all this. Normally, this early in the morning, most of the class would have been asleep – including Mr Greer, who had a bad habit of dozing through his students' oral presentations.

But weirdly, everyone was wide awake, and paying total

attention to Christopher. This, of course, only fed into his rant.

'Stark keeps costs down by outsourcing every step of the way, paying nothing to the American worker,' he continued. 'And Stark Quark, this computer Stark is launching after the New Year, is no exception. Not a single person involved in the manufacture of it was employed in this country. And to guarantee every kid in every American household will be clamouring for one this Christmas, Stark has arranged for the new Quarks to come with the only available copies of *Realms*, the new version of the *Journeyquest* RPG, and have been doing an aggressive ad campaign for the PCs for weeks now –'

I sank even lower in my chair. No one here could have missed the commercial, which had gone viral on YouTube, showing Nikki Howard plinking around on a Quark keyboard resting on her bare stomach while floating on a raft in a Stark-brand bikini in a laptop-shaped pool. The Quarks are waterproof (well, splashproof. You couldn't actually drop them in water, as I discovered when I accidentally did just that), and come in a variety of colours. The ad shows Nikki in a different coloured bikini to match each of the colours the computers come in, while a boppy rock tune plays in the background. There's no mention, of course, of how technically useful the laptops are . . . just that they're pretty.

Kind of like Nikki Howard, I realized when I thought of it.

'If we want to keep America from going the way of

ancient Rome,' Christopher continued, seemingly unaware of the uncomfortable atmosphere as I overheard Lindsey humming the Quark jingle, 'which in the fifth century found itself in a similar situation, with a collapsing economy and a society dependent on imported goods, we have to become producers again, and stop consuming so much. Otherwise, people like Robert Stark are going to continue getting insanely rich off our laziness, our refusal even to go buy our music at a music store, books at a bookstore, food at a grocery store, and clothes at a clothing store, because it's more convenient to buy all these things in one place. Some of us are so lazy, we'd rather waste fossil fuels driving a few miles to get all of them in one store, made overseas at a discount price – even if the quality is sub-standard – than buy products in a few local stores, which were made in the good old USA. Let's take a moment to think about what this is doing to the communities we live in, not to mention to the American spirit – murdering them. Because that, not progress, is the true legacy of Stark: murder.'

There was a moment of silence as what Christopher had said sunk in, during which he simply looked out at us with his ocean-blue eyes. Not just out at *us* in general, I realized after a few seconds, but out at me . . . yes, me, directly at *me*, like I was there in the room as some kind of representative of Stark.

Which might technically be correct. But, hello, I was the *last* person who needed convincing of Stark's evilness. Look what they had done to me.

I mean, sure, they had saved my life.

But they had also forced me completely to give it up too, in most of the ways that matter. I couldn't even spend the holidays with my family. Give me a break.

And OK, I completely agreed with every point Christopher brought up about Stark in his speech. But what did he expect *me* to do about it? Quit because my boss was the devil? Yeah, well, I *couldn't* quit.

Not that I could mention this in front of everyone.

I had no choice but to sit up straighter in my seat, fold my arms, and stare right back at him. Even though of course doing so caused me to have to look at those lips again . . . those lips that yesterday I'd so foolishly thought might be close to finally brushing mine. I still wanted them to. Desperately.

I was smiling bitterly to myself about this when the oven timer on Mr Greer's desk went off, and I jumped, as did a few other people in the room. Everyone except Christopher, who just kept staring at me, cool as an iced mocha latte.

Then someone – McKayla Donofrio. Of course. That suck up. Was there nothing she'd stoop to in order to get Christopher's attention? – started to clap. A few seconds later, more than half the class was applauding. Like they really meant it too, not sarcastically like they sometimes did when someone did something stupid like drop their tray in the cafeteria.

And Mr Greer was going, 'Excellent work, Christopher. Really excellent work. Strong, persuasive argument. I think you went a little under three minutes, but I won't take off any points for that, because it was such an improvement over your last piece of work. You can take your seat now.'

Christopher went back towards his seat. I didn't miss the swift glances both Whitney and Lindsey, who were among the people applauding, gave him as he passed them. I couldn't believe how quickly Christopher went from being a social pariah to almost revered by them. It was as if they could sense how dead he was inside . . . just like they were.

And yet a part of me refused to believe Christopher really *was* one of them, a member of the Walking Dead. I knew he couldn't really be dead inside. Not the Christopher I loved. He was, after all, only doing what he was doing for revenge . . . revenge for what happened to me. That thirst for revenge had made him blind to everything else, like the fact that I wasn't really dead . . . that I was sitting right in front of him – turned in my seat to face him, as a matter of fact, and saying, 'Nice speech.'

Well, what else was I going to say? Everyone was watching to see how I was going to react. I had to play the game.

Christopher nodded. 'Thanks. Do you have that information we talked about yesterday?'

'Part of it,' I said, and fished from the depths of my tote bag the Social Security number I'd cadged from Steven that morning. I slid it across his desk towards him. 'I'll try to get the rest of it soon.'

I wasn't entirely sure this was true – or how I was going to get it for him if I did decide that's what I was going to do. But I wasn't ready to say I wouldn't help him when there was still a chance he might find Mrs Howard.

And when there was a chance that, by helping him, maybe . . . just maybe . . . he might stop hating me.

He took the slip of paper and put it in his jacket pocket, just as Mr Greer was calling the name of his next victim – fortunately not me.

'Everything I said up there,' Christopher said, 'is true, you know.'

His words burned. And he knew it.

'Yeah,' I said, 'I'm aware of that.'

'And yet you're still loyal to Robert Stark.' He was smiling a little. I didn't get what the smile was about. It was like he knew something – something about me.

But how could he, when the most fundamental thing of all continued to escape him completely?

'I don't have what you want,' I said.

'But you're going to get it for me,' Christopher said. He was so confident. He had never been this confident when we were friends. About anything. It was sexy . . . but also a little frightening. 'Right?'

'Um,' I said, just as Nikki's cellphone, deep in my tote, began to chime 'Barracuda', letting me know I had a text message, 'I'll let you know.'

McKayla Donofrio, who'd been about to begin her three-minute oral presentation on whatever incredibly boring topic she'd chosen, no doubt about the dairy industry and its unfairness to the lactose intolerant, glared in my direction.

'OK,' she said, 'what's with Fergie? That's not cool, whoever didn't turn off their cell.' She said *whoever*, but from the direction of her gaze, she clearly meant me. 'You could extend some common courtesy, you know.'

'Sorry,' I said, digging through my tote. 'Sorry, sorry.' I found and turned off my cell.

But not before I saw the text from Rebecca.

Rehearsal going on for Stark Angel show right now, she'd written. **Where are you????**

Twelve

Three months ago if you'd asked me what I thought I'd be doing during finals week, hanging out in my underwear at a fashion show with a bunch of the world's top supermodels would not have been high up on my list.

In fact, it wouldn't have been anywhere on my list.

And by hanging out in my underwear at a fashion show, I mean, *About to go out onstage wearing nothing but*.

Except that they didn't call it underwear. They called it *lingerie*.

And it wasn't a stage: it was a *runway*.

Yeah. I was about to publicly humiliate myself wearing fewer clothes than I had ever worn in public in my life, including in the locker room at school, where I'd always made sure to have on *something* that covered me from armpits to mid thigh at all times, even if it was only a towel. Forget about showering with my fellow students in Tribeca Alternative's prison-style showers – one nozzle for four to six girls at a time – in the locker room. It was impossible to work up a sweat during what passed for physical education class at TAHS, so there was no need to shower, anyway.

Well, impossible for me, considering that, in the past, whenever a volleyball or whatever came near me, I'd always make sure I stepped calmly away to avoid it.

See? No sweat. No need for a shower. Problem solved.

Only now it appeared as if karma was sending me a great big power serve for all my slacking off in PE. I not only got to parade around in my underwear at the real deal on New Year's Eve (an event where I'd be humiliating myself in front of a live audience of four hundred photographers, journalists, cameramen, fashionistas, designers, stylists, art directors and your everyday run-of-the-mill celebrities such as Sting and John Mayer, and various other celebutantes who'd have gathered at the Stark Enterprises Sound Studio in midtown for the occasion), but I'll have to endure several dress rehearsals, where I'd be half-naked in front of assorted sound and camera people, light and technical crew, stylists, and don't let me forget my fellow models.

One of whom – I think her name was Kelley – was peering at me right now as we sat amid the craziness backstage, wardrobe assistants running around trying to get us all sorted out and fitted with our wings and various assigned bras and panties and thongs so they'd know if they'd ordered the right amount for the Big Night.

'Are you worried, Nikki?' Kelley leaned over to ask me in a thick southern accent. 'Cos you look worried.'

'Uh –' I was totally shocked that she was speaking to me. No one had spoken to me all day, except for the stylists, one of whom warned me about my chi. In his opinion, it could have used some realigning – 'maybe a little.'

I smiled queasily at her. I really did think I was going to heave the chocolate-covered strawberries I'd just scarfed from the catering table. Why couldn't I follow the advice on the list of forbidden foods on the refrigerator back in the loft? Chocolate was definitely on it.

'You'll be fine!' Kelley said. She had huge brown eyes, made to look even larger by the liquid liner around them. 'If the lights get to be too much and you can't see, just feel for the stage with your feet. If all you touch is air, don't put your foot down. That means you're at the end of the runway. You don't want to step off into thin air. You know what happens then.' She made a splatting noise.

This didn't reassure me. If anything, I felt more like throwing up than ever. I was going to be so blinded by the studio lights, I was going to walk off the end of the runway? No one had mentioned this to me before. I was already completely unsteady on the six-inch platform Louboutins they'd handed me. My sassy catwalk strut? It wasn't all that sassy, it turned out.

But I said, 'Great, thanks,' anyway, to be nice.

'Gosh, Nikki,' Kelley said, looking a little surprised. 'You're the one who told me that about the lights when I was just starting out. Remember?'

I blinked. I'd screwed up. As usual.

'Of course,' I said, with what I hoped was a fierce laugh. Nikki was nothing if not fierce. Right?

Kelley didn't fall for my alleged fierceness. Well, why should she have?

'You really *did* bang your head and get amnesia, like everyone is saying.' Kelley looked at me pityingly.

'What does it feel like?' another girl – this one as fair as Kelley was dark – wanted to know, as we waited for someone to come over and tell us the director was finally ready for us.

I was surprised – surprised Kelley and the other girl were even talking to me. We'd been in the studio for hours rehearsing . . . or waiting around, really . . . but none of them had said a word to me, even though I'd figured, you know, being in the same business, some of the girls *had* to have known Nikki, and maybe even been friendly with her.

But either these girls were just too shy (doubtful, given their outgoing personalities) to say hello, or Nikki had done something to irritate them – which, knowing Nikki, was the most likely explanation.

'What does what feel like?' I asked, starting to freak. Not that this girl was speaking to me. But that she *knew*. Only how could this gorgeous girl, sitting there so coolly in a water bra and thong, have found out about my surgery?

Or maybe she didn't know. Maybe she was a plant, sent by Stark, to try to screw me up. See if I'd talk.

Yeah. That's how paranoid I've gotten. It's amazing what happens when you start thinking you're being spied on all the time, the tricks your mind starts playing on you . . .

'*The diamond bra*,' the blonde girl said. 'You're wearing ten million bucks on your chest, Nik. What does that feel like?'

I looked down. Oh, yeah. I was completely cracking up, that was obvious.

'Oh,' I said, 'it's really uncomfortable. Diamonds, being

the hardest substance on earth, aren't the best material with which to make a bra. Well, technically, that's aggregated diamond nanorods. But you know what I mean.'

Oh, wow. I sounded like the biggest nerd. And nothing like Nikki Howard . . .

The blonde girl – whose name, I seemed to recall from the stylist, was Veronica – just stared at me. But thankfully, Kelley seemed to get a kick out of my reply – as did a couple of the other models nearby – and giggled.

'Diamond nanawhatevers,' she echoed. 'What have *you* been doing since I last saw you? Taking science classes at night school?'

'Well,' I replied, 'not night school, exactly, but high school—'

It was at that moment my non-Stark-brand cellphone chimed. I checked it to find a text from Frida.

I'm sorry, Frida had written. **Plz dont b mad! I luv u! U should c me, I cant stop crying! Plz call back!**

Honestly. I would give anything to have the biggest crisis in my life be that my big sister said I couldn't go to her holiday loft party. I mean, suppose Mom could see me now, in a ten million dollar diamond bra and sheer black lace-trimmed panties. Oh, and did I mention the angel wings?

And PS, I was so not calling back. I was having my own personal drama right then. I did not need to get sucked into my little sister's, which could wait until my own was finished. Which would be never, at the rate things were going.

'That's an awesome phone,' Kelley said admiringly. 'And what's the name of that ringtone?'

I looked at her in surprise.

'You can download it for free off the Internet,' I said, knowing how lame I must have sounded to those twenty-something models. Just wait until they found out my ringtone is called Dragon Battle Cry and from an online RPG called *Journeyquest*.

Except . . . they didn't seem to care. In fact, Kelley gasped and handed me her Stark-brand phone.

'Ooh, me,' she said. 'Do me? I want.'

'Me too!' the other models squealed. All but Veronica, who looked around at her friends like they'd lost their minds. *Have some dignity*, her look seemed to imply.

'Ladies!' Alessandro, the show's stage director, clapped his hands to get our attention. 'It's time! Exactly like we rehearsed last time, all right?'

Except, of course, when we'd rehearsed we'd been in our regular clothes, because the lingerie hadn't arrived yet. Not to mention our wings.

Also, it was hard to hear him, thanks to the pulsing beat that had started out on the runway.

'Oh, and the musicians are here now,' Alessandro said unnecessarily. 'So let's see if we can walk in time with the music.'

All the girls who'd gathered round me, wanting me to download the geekiest ringtone possible on to their phones, had run off to get into their places for the show, and Shauna, my agent Rebecca's assistant, had hurried over to whisper, 'OK, Nikki? Don't freak out, but they've made a last-minute change. When you come out wearing the diamond bra, Gabriel Luna is going to play his new song, "Nikki". I said don't freak out.'

'What?' I couldn't hear her because of all the noise onstage.

But I was pretty sure she'd just said that the hottest new sensation on the Stark record label, who just happened to have written a song about me, was going to be singing it when I came out onstage wearing nothing but wings, a bra, and a pair of panties. A *diamond* bra and panties.

A song about *me*.

This was really not what I needed to hear just then. I had been successfully avoiding Gabriel Luna for weeks now.

It wasn't that I didn't like him. I actually did. But like with Brandon, not in *that* way. I liked someone else *that* way.

So I didn't really need to be hanging out with some other guy – especially one who was writing love songs about me – when my heart belonged to another.

Who, OK, it turns out now was in love with another girl – a dead girl – and might happen to be a supervillain. But no relationship is perfect.

'Rebecca said not to tell you about Gabriel before,' Shauna said with an apologetic smile, 'so you wouldn't get nervous.'

I just stared at her. I wasn't nervous. Not exactly.

The truth was, I wasn't nervous at all.

I was pretty sure I was having a nervous *breakdown*.

'Try not to think about it,' Shauna said, spinning me around to face a line of tall, impossibly thin girls all getting ready to go onstage. 'Take deep breaths. Just concentrate on your breathing!'

My breathing? What was she talking about? Gabriel Luna, on whom my little sister Frida and all her friends were crushing in the biggest way – that accent! Those eyes! That dark hair! – was going to be singing a song about me while I was prancing around in front of him in my underwear, and I was supposed to concentrate on my *breathing*? I was hyperventilating. I needed to *stop* breathing so much, actually.

Like I didn't have enough problems with Christopher and Steven and Nikki's missing mom and all. Now I had to deal with this?

And sure, most girls, such as my sister, would die to hear all those *I love you*'s coming from a guy like Gabriel.

I love you is always great when it's coming from the right guy . . . not to mention when it's not just lines from a pop song manufactured to propel the singer to the top of the charts. It wasn't like Gabriel's *I love you*'s meant anything. He barely knew me. We'd had a few, mostly chance, encounters. We'd never even been out on a date. We'd never even kissed. Well, for any significant amount of time. He didn't love me. He couldn't.

And even if he did, it didn't matter, because of Christopher.

In front of me, the girls were taking off, one by one,

like graceful butterflies, swooping out from backstage on to the runway and into the blindingly bright lights, which the tech crew was still adjusting in the rafters of the vast, dark studio that seated hundreds. Those seats were empty now, but on the Big Night . . .

OK, try not to think about that now. I was attempting to control my breathing, and not think about what was going to happen when I stepped out there . . .

And then suddenly the girl in front of me – I didn't realize it was Veronica right away, because her massive wings had hidden her from my view until just then – turned to say, 'You know, Nikki, you have some nerve.'

I looked at her blankly. 'I'm sorry?'

'Yeah, you better be sorry,' she said. 'After what you did, I can't believe you have the guts even to look me in the face.'

What *I* did to her? I'd done nothing all day but memorize my blocking and eat chocolate strawberries and feel like I was going to throw up. I'd barely said a word to anyone . . .

Oh, wait. She must mean what Nikki did to her.

'I'm sorry,' I said. This time I meant it as an apology and not *Excuse me*. 'I really don't remember what you're talking about—'

'Oh, right,' Veronica said. The music was so loud, I could barely hear her.

But I could read the hatred in her eyes clearly enough.

'You might have all the other girls eating out of your hand, with your weird ringtones and your oh-I'm-so-nervous routine,' she said. 'But I know the truth. I know this whole amnesia thing is a scam. And I know you're still in touch with Justin.'

I blinked at her. '*What?* Justin who?' She better not have meant Justin Bay, Lulu's ex . . . and Nikki's too, incidentally. Or maybe not incidentally, since it turned out Nikki had been seeing him behind Lulu's back.

And now, apparently, behind Veronica's back too.

Veronica glared at me. 'Don't play dumb with me. I know you still email him,' she spat. 'And I'm just warning you. You better watch your back.'

Wait . . . what? That made no sense at all.

'I don't email anyone named Justin,' I insisted. I couldn't believe this was happening. Although that made it like most of the things in my life these days. I wished I was wearing a little more clothing. I might have felt less exposed. However, at least I knew if she tried to stab me or something, my diamond bra would stop any sort of blade. And probably most bullets. 'I can assure you—'

'I know it's you,' Veronica snapped back. The music was thumping, and the girl in front of her had just taken off for her turn down the runway. 'You stay away from him. Do you hear me?'

'I've never –'

It didn't matter though. She was gone, sashaying out on to the stage in front of me, the ends of her wings drooping on to the highly polished metallic floor.

Great. So I had yet another enemy.

What was wrong with Nikki, anyway? What was she

doing, going after her friends' boyfriends, when she could have had any single guy she wanted (except Christopher Maloney)? Were single guys not enough of a challenge for her? She had to go after guys who were taken?

It was tough being one of the most beautiful women in the world, I guess. When almost every guy you met fell all over himself trying to be with you, you naturally found yourself only drawn to the ones who didn't.

But why did that nutcase think Nikki was still emailing her boyfriend?

'Nikki,' Shauna hissed at me, 'go!'

I realized the music had changed. It wasn't the pounding techno-pop it had been a minute before, when all the other girls had been heading out on to the stage. It had turned into a more mellow, haunting melody.

A second later, I heard a deep male voice singing from the stage: 'Nikki, oh, Nikki . . . the thing of it is, girl . . . in spite of it all . . . I really do think . . . I love you.'

If I hadn't been hyperventilating before, I was definitely about to now. Oh, great. Gabriel Luna, a guy I'd met maybe four or five times in my life, *loves me*? Yeah. I don't think so.

Well . . . it was just a song. Just a song that, as soon as it hit the airwaves when the show went live on New Year's Eve, everyone was going to be humming, instead of the Stark Quark song. Or at least, I supposed that's what Gabriel Luna and the Stark record label were hoping.

'Nikki,' Shauna said again, '*go!*'

I went. I wandered out on to the runway in a daze. I

was trying to remember my sassy catwalk strut, but it was really hard when all I could think was, *Gabriel Luna loves me. Really?* No. No, he couldn't. Every time I saw him I was doing something boneheaded, like getting carried around by Brandon Stark, or being in a hospital recovering from a transplanted brain. He didn't love me. This was all just a publicity stunt. A Stark-engineered publicity stunt. After all, that's why he was in this country and not back in his native England in the first place, right? To further his career.

But as I moved out more centrally on to the stage, and I saw him there with his guitar, wearing a faded blue shirt beneath a brown suede jacket over jeans, I could sort of see why Frida and her friends were so gaga over him. I mean, he looked really cute. And he was looking right at me, not smiling, not frowning, just *looking*, super-intently, as he sang, 'It's not the way that you walk, girl . . . the way that you smile or the way that you look . . . it's just the way you move me . . . the way that you move me . . . that makes me say, Nikki, oh, Nikki . . . the thing of it is, girl . . . in spite of it all . . . I really do think . . . I love you.'

All I could think was what I thought every time I saw him, which was, *Oh my God. Frida's right. He* is *kinda hot.*

But at the same time I realized he wasn't *my* kind of hot. If that makes any sense.

I was trying to keep my gaze on where I was going – down the runway – but the truth was, I could hardly see two feet in front of me, the lights were so bright, plus they were reflecting up off the diamonds in my bra – and that was a lot of reflection, let me tell you. There were diamond rainbows dancing everywhere before my eyes. I couldn't see a thing as I looked out towards the lights – nothing except rainbows. I tried to remember what Kelley had told me about feeling with my feet for the edge of the catwalk so I didn't sassy-strut my way right off it.

But it was hard to do that without inching along like I was walking the plank on the Pirates of the Caribbean ride at Disney World.

Alessandro seemed to realize I was in trouble and shouted from somewhere out in the vast emptiness of the studio, 'Yes, Nikki! You're doing fine! Now . . . turn!'

I turned on his command, trusting he wouldn't lead me astray. And he hadn't. Suddenly I was facing away from the lights, and I could see again. What I saw was Gabriel at the opposite end of the catwalk. He was grinning at me a little now. Only through some trick of the lights, for a moment his dark hair looked gold, and his blue eyes seemed to belong to someone else.

'The thing of it is, girl . . . in spite of it all . . . I really do think . . . I love you.'

God! What I wouldn't give to hear those words coming out of Christopher's mouth. About me. Not me the way I was, but me the way I am now.

And OK, maybe his song *was* only a publicity gimmick.

But I knew that somehow, coming from Christopher, I'd have believed those words. I'd have believed them in a second. Why, oh why was it Gabriel and not Christopher saying he loved me?

And then suddenly, right as Gabriel was hitting his third chorus of *I love you*'s, my foot landed on something that was not catwalk *or* air. I didn't know what it was, but it was soft . . . and it was slippery.

And it caused my feet to go flying right out from under me.

Only since I wasn't really an angel, and my wings didn't actually work, I didn't just float lightly off into the air.

I came crashing down, hard.

Thirteen

'Just keep your gaze straight ahead, don't look into the light.'

That's what Dr Higgins told me as I sat on the examination table in front of her. She was flashing a beam from a penlight into my eyes. I guess she wanted to see if Nikki's brain had come loose or something after my huge and embarrassing tumble on the catwalk at the Stark Angel dress rehearsal.

'Honestly,' I told her, doing as she asked and looking straight ahead. 'I'm fine.'

'Shh,' she said. 'Don't talk.'

I'd been assuring everyone that I was fine – except for my wounded dignity (and backside) – but everyone had just shushed me. I guess they all thought no one could take that hard a tumble and not be hurt. Alessandro was the one who'd insisted I be checked out by a medical professional.

And of course, when the Stark security limo stopped, and I found myself in the Stark Institute for Neurology and Neurosurgery, I wasn't surprised. I was right back where I'd started. Well, sort of.

'Are you experiencing any double vision?' she wanted to know. Dr Higgins was all business. Apparently she, and not Dr Holcombe, who'd been part of the team who'd performed my brain transplant, was the one on call tonight. 'Headache? Nausea?'

'No,' I said. 'No, and no. I told you. I just slipped. On this.' I held up the object I'd slipped on, which I'd found a few seconds after I'd sat up. A bunch of feathers, wadded together and tossed on to the runway. They'd clearly been ripped from a set of Stark Angel wings.

It wasn't hard to guess who they'd belonged to either. The last angel to walk out on to the stage before me, and one who had a particular grudge against me: Veronica.

The first face I'd seen hovering above mine after I'd landed was Gabriel's, his blue eyes filled with concern. Gabriel Luna's blue eyes, I'd noted. Not the eyes I'd been fantasizing about seeing: Christopher Maloney's.

'Nikki? Are you all right?' Gabriel had wanted to know, putting an arm round me – as best he could with the tangle of wings behind me.

'I'm fine, I'm fine,' I'd assured him. 'I just slipped on something – there was something on the runway . . .'

And I'd looked to make sure I was right, and there it was. Thank God. It wasn't just me, and my utter inability to be fierce in six-inch heels.

I'd made out like it must have been an accident. Alessandro's face had darkened when he saw what Gabriel was holding up – because he'd seized the clump of feathers from me and turned to face the director with indignation. That's when Alessandro began to swear in a steady stream, primarily at the costume mistresses, for not gluing the feathers down hard enough.

150

I hadn't corrected him. I don't know why. I knew Veronica had done it, and on purpose – *You better watch your back:* more like right in front of you – but I'd had other, more important things to worry about.

Like the fact that I'd known I was going to end up here, at the Institute.

And not just because they were worried about my head either. Or at least how attached it was to the inside of my skull.

I knew they'd use this opportunity to give me a little lecture about . . . well, my behaviour lately.

And sure enough . . .

'There was an incident in St John a couple of days ago,' Dr Higgins said, looking down at a thick white manila file she was holding. 'You fell there as well.'

God! I knew they were watching me. I just knew it. When were they ever going to leave me alone?

Oh, that's right. As long as I'm the Face of Stark, making them millions? Never.

'I slipped,' I corrected her. 'I didn't fall.' Of course, technically I'd sort of jumped. But she didn't need to know that. 'They were making me hold on to this cliff, and it was really slippery, and I couldn't hang on any more.'

'I see,' Dr Higgins said, still looking down at the file. 'You went to visit your family recently too. And that boy, Christopher Maloney.'

It was a statement, not a question. I could only stare at her. What could I say in response, anyway? I knew the deal: I got to live in exchange for their watching – and listening in on – my every move. What was there to say about it, really?

'You know we'd like you to limit visitations with people from your past,' Dr Higgins went on. 'It will only cause people to wonder how you know them, and you wouldn't want unnecessary attention drawn to them, would you?'

'No,' I said, 'but . . .' Suddenly I felt like punching something. Or someone. I'd changed out of the diamond bra and panties and wings and back into my normal clothes, so I didn't look like quite as big a freak sitting there in her office as I might have.

But I was still, I realized, a plenty big freak. Which I could handle, actually, because I'd always been a big freak.

It was the fact that there were people *spying* on me all the time – and not just the paparazzi – that was kind of hard to bear without breaking something.

'I know it's hard,' Dr Higgins said sympathetically, as if she could read my thoughts. But she couldn't . . . because if she could she'd have looked more scared. Besides, surely my thoughts were still my own. Stark didn't own them. Yet. 'Of course you miss them. And we don't expect you never to see them. That's why we let you go to school with your sister. But you really need to cut back on the personal visits. You won't assimilate into your new life as easily if you keep trying to cling to your old life. Do you know what I mean?'

I thought of Christopher. Wasn't that exactly what he was doing, clinging to his old love, Em (even if he'd never once acknowledged, while I was actually around, that he liked me), instead of embracing the here and now?

'Maybe,' I admitted, more so she'd shut up and let me leave than because I thought it was really true, 'I'm just having a rough transition period.'

'Acknowledging that,' Dr Higgins said with a smile, 'is half the battle towards overcoming it. Now –' She looked down and turned a page in my file – 'about Nikki Howard's brother.'

All my internal alarm sensors went off. Stark knew! Stark knew about Steven!

Then again . . . of course they did. Why wouldn't they? They knew everything.

Dr Higgins looked up from the file and smiled at me again. 'I know you feel bad about his mother, and want to help. But really, all you had to do was ask. Because of course we at Stark would be happy to do anything we can to help resolve this unfortunate and really quite sad situation.'

I blinked. 'Wait . . . really?'

'Yes, of course. It's odd that Steven Howard came to you and not us first, but considering the circumstances—'

I shook my head. 'What circumstances?'

'Well, his mother's . . . condition. I'm sure he was a bit embarrassed.'

'Condition?' I stared at her. What was she talking about? 'What condition?'

Dr Higgins closed my file and crossed the room to sit at her desk, where her computer was. Because Dr Higgins had been out of the office, she had to turn the computer on and let it boot. While it did this, she said, 'I'm not surprised he didn't mention it, but Mrs Howard is not a well woman. If she should contact you, or Steven, it's important, whatever outrageous things she tells you, that you remember that. She has a long history of mental illness and, I'm sorry to say, drug and alcohol abuse.'

I stared at her in shock. Dr Higgins looked up from the computer screen, saw my startled expression, and nodded.

'It's actually not that unusual that she's disappeared like this. She's done it before, many times –'

I listened with growing disbelief to Dr Higgins as she continued.

'– of course, if you do hear from her, you should contact us at once, and we'll take care of it. Mrs Howard needs immediate medical care.'

What was going on here? What was Dr Higgins doing? This was not the person Steven Howard had described to me – not that he'd gone into much detail at all about his mom. Still, this didn't jibe with what he'd said about his mom not being the type to leave her business unattended.

Who was telling the truth? Dr Higgins? Or Steven?

'Um,' I said. Dr Higgins was typing something into the keyboard in front of her. 'OK.'

'I'm glad we had this little talk.' Dr Higgins straightened, came over to me, and patted me on the back, then helped me down from the exam table. 'Sometimes it's nice when it's just us girls, isn't it?'

'Yeah,' I said. You mean, when we don't have lawyers

from Stark Corporate around, telling me what I can and can't say? 'It sure is.'

'Goodnight,' Dr Higgins said, and shook my hand at the door to her office. 'If you experience any headaches, double vision, nausea, or any other symptoms at all, don't hesitate to call.'

I assured her I'd call, then, as Dr Higgins returned to her computer, no doubt to input every detail of our conversation into my file, I allowed myself to be escorted by Stark security through the dark and silent – at this time of night – hallways to the hospital's front entrance, where the Stark limo was waiting to take me back to the loft.

Only, when I got there, I found that the press was waiting. Hordes of them. They must have been tipped off by someone that this was where I'd been sent, because otherwise how could there have been so many of them? The flashbulbs started going off, instantly blinding me the second I set one foot out of the door. It was a good thing those security guys were there, giving me their strong arms to support me. Otherwise I'd have suffered another embarrassing tumble as they led me down the hospital steps, to the limo waiting below.

'Nikki!' a paparazzo cried. 'Are you all right?' White flashes burst all around me. I could barely see the cement steps underneath my feet.

'What happened, Nikki? Care to comment?' another wanted to know.

'Nothing,' I said, trying to give a casual laugh. 'I was just a klutz, that's all. I'm fine. See? Nothing broken. Except my pride.'

'Nikki, was this fall related to what happened to you a few months ago, when you suffered from a hypoglycaemic incident at a Stark grand opening and had to be hospitalized?' someone else asked. Flash. Flash. Flash.

'No, nothing like that,' I said. 'I just trip –'

But I didn't get the full sentence out of my mouth. That's because my vision had finally cleared enough for me to see that, waiting next to the limo, was a guy. A dark-haired, blue-eyed guy, wearing jeans and a brown suede jacket. He was holding an enormous bouquet of red roses. And grinning. At me.

'Hello there,' Gabriel Luna said with a smile.

'Why, hello,' I said. I glanced around, pretty sure I knew the answer, but wanting to make sure I wasn't about to make a fool out of myself again. 'Have I got the wrong car?'

'No,' Gabriel said, 'this is your car. So. How are you?'

'I'm fine,' I replied, still not quite believing what I was seeing. Gabriel Luna was waiting with a big bouquet of roses next to my car. In front of the paparazzi, who were snapping tons of photos of us both now. What exactly was going on? Was this because he loved me or something?

'Oh, these are for you.' Gabriel seemed to remember the roses suddenly, which he passed to me. Tons more flashes went off. 'A bit sappy, I know,' he whispered, so the paps couldn't hear him. 'But my manager thought it would be a good idea.'

I took the beautiful bouquet. 'Your . . . manager?' I

whispered. I didn't understand anything that was going on.

'And your agent,' Gabriel said, still smiling away as everyone took our photo. He was opening the limo door and helping me inside. 'They go to the same gym. Anyway, what with the song and the show and us both working for Stark and all, they just thought, well, it wouldn't be such a bad idea for us to be seen out and about together. I know it's a bit stagy, but it can't hurt to have the fans think we're an item now, can it?'

'Oh,' I said, finally catching on. 'You mean your song . . .'

Gabriel grinned. 'Right. The song.'

We were in the car now, and my security guys had slammed the door behind us and were shooing the paparazzi away, even as they clamoured for just one more shot, and called things like, 'Nikki! Are you and Gabriel Luna going out? Where are you off to? How long have the two of you been seeing one another?'

It was much quieter in the car, with the door shut. Gabriel looked at me with his dark eyebrows raised enquiringly, and said, 'I hope you don't mind. Your agent said it was all right.'

'Oh,' I said. What could I say? That I was going to kill Rebecca later? 'No. It's fine.'

'Good,' Gabriel said. 'And of course, I don't want to keep you. I'm sure you must be exhausted. And if you want to get back to your place, that's fine. But if you wanted to get a bite to eat –'

Suddenly I realized I was starving. It had been a long time since those chocolate-covered strawberries. And I had so many things to do – finals to study for, an oral presentation to prepare, a sister to make up with, Nikki Howard's mother to find, and her brother to ask something really horrible. Not to mention Christopher waiting for an answer about whether or not I was going to help him bring down Stark Enterprises.

'Sure,' I said, without a second more hesitation. 'Why not?'

Which was how I found myself, an hour and a half later, at Dos Gatos, the underground club where you needed to be a celebrity even to know it existed, since it looked like an ordinary diner on the outside.

But when you said your name, a guy with a walkie-talkie would let you through a door marked Employees Only, into what was really an elevator. And suddenly, you were in one of the hottest clubs in town. There I sat, sharing a cosy booth in the corner with Gabriel Luna, beneath the flickering candlelight from dozens of Mexican lanterns hanging overhead, while he explained the genesis of the song 'Nikki'.

'The Nikki in the song isn't necessarily you,' he was saying. We'd finished a platter of bite-sized carne asada tacos, sprinkled all over with bright green bits of cilantro, and a pitcher of Key lime margarita (virgin, of course. I doubted Gabriel would have allowed it to be served any other way, with the reputation the tabloids had given me).

'Really,' I said. 'So it's about some other girl named Nikki you happen to know?'

He grinned. 'OK. Well, maybe she's you. But she's more the *idea* of you –'

In the candlelight, a wave of his dark hair cast his eyes into shadow, so his expression was hard to read. 'I'm saying there's the public Nikki, the one that everyone thinks they know. And then there's the Nikki underneath, the one that you won't seem to allow anyone to know.'

I looked at him. Gabriel was smarter than I'd given him credit for. 'You really think that? You think I push people away?'

'You're the one who's been impossible to reach these past few weeks,' he said, with a gentle laugh. 'If I didn't know better, I'd think you were seeing someone.'

I bit my lip. The truth, of course, was that I *was* seeing someone. Well, at school. He just didn't know it.

Except that now . . . well, now, that person had made it clear he was in love with someone else.

And OK, that someone else was me . . . but me as I used to be.

'Wait a minute,' Gabriel was saying now, reaching out to push back some of my long blonde hair, which had partially fallen across my face. 'There *is* someone else, isn't there?'

Oh God. Why did his eyes have to be so blue? Like someone else's eyes, actually. Only bluer, because they contrasted so nicely with his dark hair and long curly eyelashes.

'There . . . was,' I murmured, looking everywhere but at Gabriel's face, and cursing Nikki for having such an insufferable physical weakness where guys were concerned. Because when his fingers brushed the skin on my cheek, I felt myself melting. Just a little, the way I had when Brandon had touched me that night in St John. Why couldn't Christopher touch me like that? *Why?* 'But not any more. He likes . . . another girl. Not really, but . . . well, he might as well.'

Gabriel raised one ink-black eyebrow. His hand had slipped from my cheek around to the back of my neck. Uh-oh. 'Sounds complicated.'

'You have no idea,' I said.

And that's when it happened. Gabriel began to knead the back of my neck with his fingers.

I don't know what came over me after that. Or rather, I do: it was all Nikki Howard's fault. Nikki's body's fault, I mean. Because the next thing I knew, it had happened again. That thing Nikki's body was always doing, when it went all melty at a guy's touch.

And the worst part was, Gabriel *knew*. I mean, he could tell. I knew he could tell because, suddenly, he scooted closer to me on the cushioned bench, and his other hand reached up to cup my face.

And then even though I didn't want to – even though there weren't any paparazzi around to take a photo of us together – I let him tilt my face up towards his, and didn't move away when he pressed his mouth down against mine. I know! I let him kiss me. In fact, I kissed him back, kissed him with all the pent-up emotion I'd been feeling for days now.

The worst part of it was, the emotion I felt? It wasn't for Gabriel. That much I knew. It was pent-up passion for someone else. Someone with eyes just as blue as Gabriel's.

But someone who would never, ever in a million years cup my face in his hands and lean down and kiss me, much less write a song about me. Or notice that there was a public Nikki, and then a different Nikki underneath.

Gabriel didn't kiss me like someone whose manager's idea it had been to bring me roses. He'd slipped both his arms around me now, and was kissing me like he meant it, and had been waiting around for exactly this to happen, like everything leading up to it had only been appetizers, and finally, *finally* we'd gotten to the main course.

Which was why it was a bit disheartening when I realized what I felt about him was exactly zero. And when I started to become aware that the soft chatter from other diners all around us had gotten a bit quieter suddenly, as if everyone had stopped eating to stare at something.

Which, I realized as I broke the kiss and drew away from Gabriel a little, was *us*.

'Uh,' I said to him, ducking my head so that my hair covered my burning face. I started digging through my tote for my lipgloss. 'Whoa.'

'Sorry,' Gabriel said. He reached for his water glass. The conversation level of the diners around us picked up again, and not a moment too soon. 'I probably shouldn't have done that.' His voice wasn't completely steady.

'No,' I said. I held my compact up over my face so I could check my reflection and reapply my gloss without going outside the lines . . . but also in the hopes that he wouldn't be able to see how hard I was blushing. 'It's all right. Really.'

'And you're quite certain there's someone else?'

'Yes,' I said gently. 'I'm sorry, but there is.'

'Shame,' he said, grinning, as he set down his now-empty water glass. 'I think we'd have gotten along famously. Even though you're impossible.'

'I'm impossible?' I clicked the compact shut. I wasn't blushing any more. 'I'm not the guy who stuck the name of a girl he barely knows in a song about how much he loves her. I'm trying to overlook the fact you chose a girl who just happens to be the face of the corporation that owns your label, by the way.'

'You don't honestly believe I wrote a song about you to get press, do you?' Gabriel asked, looking hurt.

The truth was, I didn't know what to believe any more. Everything I'd ever believed these past few months had turned out not to be true. Parents who were supposed to be there to protect you actually couldn't always do that, corporations who were allegedly evil occasionally saved your life, and brainiacs, like me, turned out not to know anything at all.

What *could* I believe any more?

'It's kind of hard not to notice that you've decided to let

Stark introduce your song about me to the world by having you sing it at a fashion show for underwear,' I pointed out. 'Or am I wrong?'

Gabriel appeared startled for a minute. Then, out of nowhere, he started to laugh.

'Touché,' he said. 'But my agent is making me do that last part. I was against doing the Stark Angel show from the start.'

'Well,' I said. I was trying hard not to smile. Because it wasn't funny. Except it sort of was. 'I wasn't exactly thrilled about doing the Stark Angel show either.'

'I guess maybe we have more in common than either of us thought,' Gabriel said.

'Right,' I said, rolling my eyes. Though it was hard to keep on being a sarcastic, tough model when he was being so nice. 'We're both corporate slaves.'

'But that doesn't mean,' Gabriel said, 'what I said in the song isn't true. There is something about you, Nikki, that I haven't been able to get out of my head since we met. But until tonight, you never seemed to want to let me in.'

I smiled at him miserably. 'Believe me, Gabriel,' I said, 'this is one head you're better off staying out of.'

Fourteen

Hanging out with a hot British singing sensation way past midnight on a school night probably wasn't the best way to prepare for finals.

In fact, it was pretty much the best way to guarantee you weren't going to perform your best the next day.

Another good way to assure you were going to bomb was to come staggering into your loft and find your big brother waiting up for you.

Except, of course, he's not really your big brother.

'Where's Lulu?' I asked. Steven was sitting alone on one of the white couches, watching TV. Almost all the lights were out in the loft, and I nearly tripped over Cosabella as she darted over to greet me when I stepped out of the elevator.

'She went to bed,' Steven said, switching off the sound of the show he was watching. I was almost not even surprised to see what it was. *Shark Week*. Yeah. Nothing surprised me any more. 'Which is where you should have been hours ago, isn't it? Don't you have school in the morning?'

The idea of Lulu going to bed before me was so laughable I almost choked. I knew she only did it to impress Steven with how responsible she was. As if.

'Uh, yeah,' I said. I collapsed at one end of the couch on which he was sitting and began tugging at the high-heeled boots I was wearing. They'd been killing my feet all day – except during the brief interlude when I'd been wearing the Louboutins, during which my feet ached in a different way. I almost longed for the Stark-brand imitation Uggs. 'I better head to bed. Sorry I was out all day. Rehearsal ran late. Did you get dinner?'

'Lulu took care of me,' Steven said with a nod. 'She made sure I got the entire tour of downtown Manhattan, including Chinatown, Ellis Island and the Statue of Liberty.'

'Wow,' I said. Cosabella hopped up on to the couch beside me and I absently stroked her ears. 'That's a lot. No wonder she went to bed. Aren't you tired too?'

'I am,' Steven said, 'but I wanted to wait up for you. We need to talk.'

I was instantly seized with alarm. I knew I hadn't exactly been spending the hours since I'd last seen him doing what I'd said I'd do – hiring a private investigator. In fact, I'd been doing very little in the way of looking for his mom . . . unless you counted giving Christopher Mrs Howard's Social Security number.

Then there'd been that piece of information Dr Higgins had told me. Which was not exactly the kind of thing you wanted to share with a guy. At least not at one in the morning.

'What?' Steven said before I could say a word. 'What are you not telling me?'

I blinked at him, wondering how he knew.

'Um,' I said, 'I did hear something –'

165

How do you tell someone you've heard their mom is crazy?

I guess you just blurt it out. Which I did. Because I couldn't exactly hide it, could I?

'Do you think it's possible maybe, what with you away, and her relationship with me not being the best, Mom might have just . . . snapped? I hear she wasn't the most mentally stable person in the world to begin with,' I said, all in a rush. 'People at Stark say—'

'People at Stark say?' Steven stared at me like I was the one with a screw loose. Which couldn't possibly be true, because I just had all my screws examined, and they'd been ruled completely tight. 'What do the people at Stark know? They've never even met her!'

'Don't be mad,' I said. I was starting to feel worse than ever. And I didn't mean my sore feet. 'I'm really sorry. But maybe, because you're her son, you don't want to see that—'

'See what?' Steven demanded. 'That Mom worked her whole life to feed and put two kids through school single-handedly because Dad ran out on us when I was seven and you were two? That none of us ever heard from him again, but Mom still managed to get you everything you ever wanted for Christmas, even though we could barely afford it? That when you wanted ballet lessons because your best friend had them, Mom took on an extra job, working even more hours, just so you could have those too? And now you don't want to bother looking for her because someone at Stark told you she was off her rocker?'

Whoa. I'd screwed up. Big time. Why had I believed Dr Higgins's version of things, instead of Steven's? Why had I fallen for the lies of a doctor who worked for a corporation I knew to be evil?

I knew why, actually. Because it had been easier than doing the right thing – the responsible thing – which was actually helping Nikki's brother. Especially when I'd been so wrapped up in Christopher's drama since yesterday. I couldn't believe how stupid and selfish I'd been, worrying about nothing but *me*, when Nikki's family had been in so much real trouble and pain. What did I have to be concerned about, really? Whether or not Christopher liked me? Whether or not people saw me in a bra made out of diamonds? Here a woman was missing – a woman who'd sacrificed so much for her kids.

I bowed my head, so Steven couldn't see the guilt on my face, and said to Cosabella, who'd crawled into my lap, 'I'm sorry.'

There were a couple seconds of uncomfortable silence before Steven asked, his voice cracking, 'Who *are* you?'

I lifted my head and just stared at him.

'W-what?'

'I mean it.' I wasn't the only one who'd been staring. Steven couldn't seem to take his disconcertingly blue eyes off me. 'I honestly don't have the slightest idea who you are. Because you're not my sister. You look like her. And your voice sounds like hers. But the words coming out of your mouth aren't anything like the things she'd say.'

A small croaking sound came out of my mouth. I managed to formulate it into, 'I h-have amnesia—'

'Enough with the amnesia thing,' Steven snapped. 'You aren't Nikki. She'd never apologize to me for anything. You have to be some kind of twin they found somewhere and put in her place for some reason. I'll admit they did a good job. A really good job, since you look exactly like her, even down to that –' He grabbed my hand, the hand I was resting on Cosabella's furry head, and pointed to a tiny crescent-moon-shaped scar on the back of it. 'What'd they do, carve you up to make you look identical? That must have smarted.' He threw my hand down again. 'Hope you're getting paid a lot.'

I didn't know how to handle this. No one at Stark had prepared me for this, or told me what to do in the event it occurred. I was starting to feel panicky. What was I supposed to say? No one had ever not fallen for the amnesia line. I'd talked to hundreds of Nikki's friends and co-workers and, while they'd all agreed the 'new' Nikki was a little strange, none of them had ever accused me of not being Nikki at all . . .

I just shook my head, look at him and said, 'I don't know what you're talking ab—'

'You know *exactly* what I'm talking about,' Steven said. 'Just tell me. What happened to Nikki? What, did she get fired for getting too full of herself or something? It wouldn't be the first time. Where is she, anyway?'

I reached up with a shaking hand to push some of Nikki's hair from my face. I glanced around the room . . .

then at the ceiling, at the tiny holes next to the halogen lights. Then I pressed a finger to my lips and pointed upward. Steven followed my gaze, then looked back down at me as if I was insane. A second later, I reached for the remote, and hit the volume button. The sounds of *Shark Week* filled the apartment. Then I got up and walked over to the music system and switched on the last track that had been playing. Lulu's voice filled the loft, crooning that she was a cat, and how much she needed to get scratched.

Then I went to the loft's floor to ceiling windows, and threw them all open, letting in blasts of cold air and the sound of the traffic from Centre Street below.

'What are you doing?' Steven demanded, looking at me as if I was demented.

But instead of answering him, I sat down again, and looked urgently up into his face.

'I can't tell you what happened to your sister,' I said, not raising my voice to be heard above the cacophony of the television, the music, and the traffic sounds. 'I'll get in really big trouble if I tell you. Well, *I* won't, but my family will.'

Steven looked down at me as if I was nuts.

'So you admit you're not her.' His voice was hard.

I nodded my head. 'I do,' I said. 'I mean, I am, partly . . . on the outside.'

'What do you mean, on the outside?' Steven glared. 'That makes no sense.'

'I know.' I was staring down at Cosabella, who had gone completely limp across the couch between us, as if she was in a coma, she was so relaxed, in spite of all the noise. God, I'd have given anything to have been a dog just then. 'I can't explain it. But you have to believe me. Nikki – the Nikki you knew – is gone.'

'Gone?' Steven asked. 'What do you mean, gone? Gone as in . . .' He looked disbelieving.

'Yes,' I said. 'She had an aneurysm. It was like a ticking time bomb in her head. She had a rare congenital brain defect—'

'No, she didn't,' Steven said. Now he didn't just look disbelieving. He looked like he was going to burst out laughing. 'Who told you that? Did *she* tell you that?'

'Um, no,' I said. I was pretty sure laughter wasn't the correct response when someone told you that your sister had died of an aneurysm to the brain. 'I never met her, exactly—'

'So what's this BS about her having some kind of genetic brain defect?' Steven wanted to know. 'Nikki was healthy as a horse. My whole family is. None of us has any genetic defects, believe me, and especially not Nikki. She hit her head falling off the back of the bleachers in school when she was in the ninth grade, and they did a CAT scan *and* an MRI, and there was no sign whatsoever of any brain defect. Who told you there was?'

I swallowed. Then I said softly, 'Stark.'

'Stark.' He snorted. 'The same people who told you my mother's a fruitcake.'

I opened my mouth, then closed it again. 'Um . . . yeah.'

170

'And you believe them?'

I couldn't really tell him I had pretty good reason to believe them. That, if it wasn't for Stark, I wouldn't be there talking to him.

I chewed my bottom lip before I replied. 'I have no reason not to,' I said finally. It seemed like the most diplomatic answer.

'Let me ask you something,' Steven said, leaning forward. 'When did all this happen? You stepping into Nikki's shoes, so to speak, and her having this so-called aneurysm?'

'It wasn't so-called,' I protested. 'People were there. They saw it. It was during the grand opening of a Stark Megastore. It was on CNN. It really—'

'Fine,' he said with an impatient wave of his hand. 'When?'

'About three months ago,' I said.

He seemed to do some mental arithmetic. 'Around the same time,' he murmured.

'Around the same time as what?' Then it clicked. 'As when your mom disappeared?' I looked at him curiously. 'But . . . what would the two things have to do with one another?'

'I don't know,' he said. 'But it's a little bit more than a coincidence, don't you think? And now, with Stark feeding you this story about my mom being mentally unhinged—'

'You're saying you think *Stark* had something to with your mom's disappearance?' My mouth had gone dry.

Why *wouldn't* Stark have had something to do with his

171

mom's disappearance though? Stark spied on me all day and night. Stark knows everything, sees everything. *Stark's legacy is murder.*

'Isn't it obvious?' Steven asked. 'Look at you. You're so paranoid about Stark, you can't even talk about it without turning on every piece of electrical equipment in the apartment. Do you honestly think this place is bugged?'

Instead of answering, I leaned over to reach for my purse, then pulled out my bug detector and turned it on. The audible alert clicked faster and faster the closer I waved the antennae towards the ceiling and the holes above our heads.

'And don't say it's a piece of junk,' I said, referring to the transmitter, 'because I paid nearly five hundred dollars for it.'

Steven blinked. 'Oh,' he said, 'it's a piece of junk, all right.'

'It isn't,' I insisted. 'I know they've got something in here, recording what we say. They knew you were here. They know all sorts of things they couldn't know otherwise.'

'I'm a communications electronics technician,' Steven said patiently. 'With the United States Navy. And I'm telling you, what you're holding is a piece of junk . . . which isn't to say it doesn't work.'

I felt a cold chill up my spine. 'Really?'

'Really,' he said. He took the detector from me and stood up, holding the antenna towards the ceiling himself. The clicking grew in intensity and volume.

'How long have those been there?' he asked, nodding towards the holes.

'I don't know,' I whispered. 'I just noticed them one day.'

'Not good,' he said. He took the transmitter from me and switched it off, then threw it down on to the couch. 'What are we going to do about it?'

'What do you mean, what are *we* going to do about it?' I asked.

'Two women are missing,' Steven said, 'and Stark obviously knows why.'

'Only one woman is missing,' I said through my too-dry lips. 'I told you, Nikki is—'

'Gone, right, you said that. Only she's not really, is she?' He looked down at me expectantly from where he stood.

'No,' I said. 'Legally, she's alive. Because legally, she's me.'

Steven stared down at me. He waited a beat. Then he said, 'You're kidding me. Right?'

'I'm not,' I said. My heart was thumping hard within my chest. I had to tell him. I had to tell him the truth. He deserved to know. It was *his sister*, after all. I had to make him understand. 'This is your sister Nikki's body. But her brain is—'

Before I knew what was happening, he'd reached down and seized me by both shoulders, hauling me to my feet, and startling Cosabella, who yelped. He didn't seem to notice though.

'What the hell are you talking about?' he demanded, giving me a shake. 'How can *this* be my sister's body?'

Suddenly I was having trouble seeing him, thanks to all the salt water coming out of my eyes.

'I can't tell you,' I cried. 'They already may have made your mother vanish. Do you really think I want to get on their bad side? You don't understand. You don't understand what they're like, how powerful they are, how much money they have –'

Steven's grip on me was pretty hard. I had a feeling he could leave marks on my arms, which wouldn't look too good on the Stark Angel taping, if they didn't fade by New Year's . . .

'This is crazy,' Steven said, giving me another little shake to emphasize each syllable. Cosabella, watching from the couch, let out a nervous bark. '*You're* crazy, do you hear me? Every word that comes out of your mouth is nuts.'

'I'm not nuts,' I insisted. 'It's called a brain transplant. My brain in your sister's body—'

That seemed to stagger him. But he didn't let go. '*Stark? Stark* did this? If Stark did all this – if they're really doing this – then why doesn't anyone know? Why haven't you told anyone?'

'I told you,' I said to him, through gritted teeth. 'We *can't* tell anyone. Anyone, do you hear me? Stark says they'll put my parents in jail if I tell anyone! And they'll do it too. Whatever ideas you might have about going to the press or whatever, get them out of your head right now. It won't work. Stark owns the press. I'll help you find your mom if I can.'

'How?' he asked, his fingers loosening on me. 'How are you going to do that?'

How *was* I going to do that? I couldn't mention Christopher and his crazy scheme with Felix. Firstly, it was so nuts, there was no chance of it succeeding. And secondly, I didn't want Christopher more involved in this than he already was. I loved Christopher, in spite of the fact that he didn't love me – or at least, the fact that he only loved some dead girl I used to be, not the me I was now. I couldn't drag him into all this, not if what Steven suspected was true, and his mom had disappeared because of what had happened to me, and to Nikki. It was too dangerous.

And yet . . .

And yet if Christopher and Felix really could do what Christopher said they could . . .

'I know some people who say they can find her,' I heard myself saying.

Miraculously, Steven dropped his hands.

'Who?' he asked.

It was at this point the door to my bedroom eased open and Lulu stuck her tousled head out.

'What's going on out here?' she wanted to know, blinking sleepily. 'What's all this noise? Why are you yelling? Why's Cosabella so upset?'

Steven backed away from me.

'Nothing,' he said to her, reaching for the remote. He

switched the TV off. 'Just a family squabble. Go back to bed.'

Lulu didn't listen to him. Instead, she came padding barefoot out into the living room. Rather than wearing her usual negligee, she had on a pair of oversized pink flannel pyjamas with enormous cherries on them. They belonged to Nikki and Lulu had had to roll the legs up at the bottom.

'No, seriously, you guys,' she said. 'What's up? Hey, are you listening to my CD?'

'Yeah,' I told her, reaching up to push my long hair out of my eyes. 'Everything's OK, really. Go back to bed.'

'No.' Lulu tottered over and plopped down on to the couch next to Cosabella. 'It sounded like you guys were fighting. I don't want you guys to fight. I mean, I never had a brother or sister so I always kinda wished for one so I could have fights. But still. What was the fight about?'

I looked over at Steven. He was scowling at the white carpet. Since it didn't seem like he was going to say anything, I shrugged, and just said, 'He found out about the spirit transfer.'

Lulu looked up at Steven, then reached for his hand, which looked huge in comparison to hers.

'Oh, poor baby!' She squeezed his hand. 'You miss the old Nikki, don't you?'

He looked down at her incredulously. 'The old Nikki? What are you . . . ? You *know* about it?'

'Sure,' she said, tugging affectionately on his pinkie for him to come sit next to her on the couch. He resisted, of course. 'We all do. Well, me and Brandon. We even went and kidnapped Nikki from the hospital after it first happened. She didn't like it. But we thought she'd been a victim of Al-Qaeda! Or the Scientologists. Only it turned out it wasn't either of them. The old Nikki was just gone. And this new one was here to take her place. We've decided we like her better than the old one though. At least I do. I don't know about Brandon. Why?' Lulu looked from one to the other of us. 'Is that a problem?'

Steven just shook his head. 'I need an aspirin,' was all he said.

But he let Lulu pull him down on to the couch beside her, where he sat with his head sunk into his hands. He looked like a man defeated. I didn't really blame him.

'Do you need a neck massage?' Lulu was asking him. Even though he didn't reply, she was already reaching over to rub his neck. 'I give totally good neck massages. They just about turn Nikki to Jell-O. Our housekeeper Katerina taught me how. And she was trained at some of the best spas in Gstaad. It's all about getting the tension out right *here . . .*'

'What did you say about finding Mom?' Steven asked me.

'I know a guy,' I whispered. I was desperate to make the situation right. Although I wasn't sure how it could ever be right again. His sister was dead, even though he didn't seem to want to believe it.

And of course somehow I felt like it was all my fault, even though I knew it wasn't.

'What guy?' he asked.

'A guy who's really good with computers,' I said, softly. Softly enough, I hoped, for none of the bugs in the loft to pick up. 'He says he can find your mom.'

I didn't want to say that this guy was the fourteen-year-old cousin of someone I'd been crushing on since like the seventh grade. Steven looked suicidal enough. He stared at me while Lulu kneaded his neck. Weirdly Lulu's neck massage didn't seem to have the same effect on him that neck massages had on me.

'How?' Steven asked. 'How can he find her when the police can't?'

'I don't know,' I whispered, 'he just says he can. Look, I don't see what we have to lose.' Except everything, including my life, when Steven found out 'this guy' was an adolescent.

'When can we go?' Steven asked without further hesitation.

I felt my heart lurch. I hadn't expected him to agree so quickly. What was I doing to Christopher? To Felix?

On the other hand, if their plan worked, maybe there'd be no Stark to come after us later . . .

Yeah. And maybe Nikki Howard was going to be the next president of the United States.

'Um. In the morning, I guess,' I said.

'Great.' Steven nodded. 'Let's do it.'

Lulu looked pleased. 'Fantastic!' she said, applying her elbow to his trapezius muscles. 'And you know what? You're feeling less tense to me already!'

'Thanks.' Steven gave her a brief smile, then got up and started heading towards her room. 'I'm really beat. I'll . . . I'll see you both in the morning.'

When he got to the door to Lulu's room, he paused, however, and turned to look back at me.

'What should I call you?' he asked.

My voice sounded almost unnaturally soft in the large loft, after our shouting match. The traffic sounds from the windows were loud, even though it was so late at night. We lived, after all, in the city that never slept. On the speakers, Lulu was making noises like a cat. Whatever Stark was picking up of this conversation, it was bound to be confusing them.

'Nikki,' I said to Steven. 'It's my name now.'

He stared at me for what felt like ages. I couldn't have begun to read his expression if I'd tried.

Then he turned abruptly and disappeared through the door, closing it quietly behind him. I glanced at Lulu.

'Well,' she said, with a big smile on her freshly scrubbed face, 'I think that went OK. Don't you?'

I collapsed on to the couch beside her with a frustrated moan. It was going to be, I knew, another sleepless night.

Fifteen

'This is so exciting,' Lulu kept saying.

'It's really not,' I assured her. I couldn't figure out why she'd insisted on coming along. Well, actually, I was starting to get a good idea. I just couldn't believe it. I was pretty sure it had to do with the six feet of manliness striding along the hallway beside us, doing his best not to let steam shoot out of his ears at the realization that he was, of all places, in a Manhattan high school.

Worse, a Manhattan high school at seven forty in the morning. With one of the nation's leading teen supermodels, who was smuggling in her miniature poodle in a Louis Vuitton tote, as her best friend, the celebutante daughter of one of the nation's most celebrated film directors, struggled to keep up alongside her, despite the fact that she was wearing a pair of five inch heels. It wasn't like anybody was staring at us or anything, as we tottered down the hall beside one another. Much.

What I couldn't believe was that she was being so obvious about it. Lulu, and her obsession with Nikki Howard's brother, I mean. I was glad she'd at least dressed somewhat normally, in vintage Jordache jeans and a leather bomber jacket over an Alexander McQueen shirt (I had to wrestle the Chloé shirt and Citizens of Humanity jeans I wanted to wear away from her. Which was ridiculous because I'm about a foot taller than she is, so I don't know how she thinks she can get away with wearing Nikki's stuff).

But still. Up this early, for a guy? I guess I shouldn't talk. When the dinosaur-sticker thing had failed, in the first few weeks I'd come back to school after my surgery, I'd done some pretty stupid stuff myself, I guess, in the hopes a certain boy would admire me . . . I'd given myself a thirty minute blowdry every morning that Christopher had never even noticed, worn a surprisingly painful (Stark-brand, of course) push-up bra that, ditto, he'd never even glanced below my chin to admire.

I guess I know what it's like to be in Lulu's designer shoes.

But excited to be at TAHS? Believe me, there was nothing exciting about being at Tribeca Alternative High School, as Steven had already pointed out. It was actually the opposite of exciting, if you asked me.

But then, Lulu had never been in a real American high school before. She was looking at all the students as we passed them by (and as they ogled us in disbelief, whispering, 'Isn't that . . . ?'), going, 'Oh my God, she's so cute!' or, 'Isn't he sweet!' like she was talking about puppies and not actual real-live fifteen and sixteen-year-olds. It was as if she didn't realize these people were just a year or two younger than her.

The truth was, because they hadn't been as gifted genetically as she was, they did look almost as if they'd descended from another species.

But that was no excuse for Lulu's behaviour.

Especially when she saw Frida hanging out with a group of junior varsity cheerleaders by one of their lockers and cried, 'Oh my God, look, Nikki! There's Frida! Hi, Frida!'

Frida freaked when she saw us . . . particularly Lulu. Her friends' jaws all dropped as well. They'd dined with me upon occasion in the TAHS cafeteria, where haute cuisine extended as far as hamburger and no further. So Nikki Howard was no longer quite the big deal she once might have been.

Frida had bragged to them that she knew Lulu. I was pretty sure none of them ever believed her.

But here was Lulu Collins – who had graced the red carpets of so many movie premieres, the covers of so many magazines and the arms of so many skeevy rock-and-roller boyfriends she really should have thought twice about dating (but who was I to criticize, seeing as Nikki Howard dated some of Lulu's boyfriends as well, behind her back?) – in person, strolling down the hall towards them and greeting Frida. They stared at her in total awe.

'Oh my God, Lulu,' Frida cried, looking as if she was about to wet herself, 'I . . . I can't believe you're here. And, Nikki! This is amazing! I was just talking about the two of you. You know, about your party?'

'Oh, you have to come,' Lulu said. 'You should all come. It's tomorrow night. It's to die for, really. Everybody will be there. Marc, Lauren, Paris. They love it. It's the best.'

I could see the girls doing quick mental calculations

in their heads – Marc *Jacobs*, Lauren *Conrad*, Paris *Hilton*. I said, under my breath, to Lulu, 'Lulu, they can't come. They're in high school.'

'Well,' Lulu said, looking blank. 'So are you.'

'But I'm not fourteen and living with my parents.'

'Could someone,' Steven asked, 'explain what we're doing here? I thought we were trying to find my mother.'

'We are,' I assured him. 'Come on.'

I looked at Frida and her friends dispassionately. 'You guys can't come to our party. You're under age. Come on, Lulu.' I grabbed Lulu's arm and began steering her away. Too late however, since I heard an all-too-familiar voice call Nikki's name, and a second later Whitney Robertson was upon us, her alter ego Lindsey and boyfriend Jason Klein not far behind, oozing Axe body spray.

'Nikki, hi.' Whitney was eyeing Steven hungrily, not even bothering to hide her interest in him for Jason's sake. Their relationship had always been full-on dysfunctional anyway, if you ask me. Which wasn't that unusual, considering I'd long suspected Jason of being a cyborg. 'I didn't know it was bring-a-hunk-to-school day.'

Steven looked appalled. I didn't blame him. Whitney was like tooth decay: you didn't have to know her more than five seconds before you started to realize she needed to be removed.

Accordingly, I ignored her and kept going, heading towards the computer lab, even though I could hear Whitney crying, 'Nikki? Nikki!' in the distance. Lulu followed me, making sure Steven stayed close beside her by keeping a hand clamped on the front of his jacket. Steven didn't appear to notice.

'What are we doing here?' he asked again. 'How can –'

But I'd already reached the doors to the lab, through which Christopher was just leaving in order to get to Public Speaking before the bell rang. As always when I saw him, my heart skipped a beat. Today he was wearing a black Ramones T-shirt under his leather jacket. His hair was still a little damp at the ends from his morning shower, and his jeans were as form-fitting as ever.

To say he looked surprised to see me would be an understatement . . . and then I was followed by Lulu, whom he surely recognized (he was as upset with her father for butchering the direction of the *Journeyquest* movie as I was) and a moody, six-foot male blond version of me. Christopher's jaw sank nearly to the floor.

'Uh, hey,' he said.

'I need to talk to you,' I said. It was difficult to get the words out when my heart was hammering so hard in my chest. But I managed.

'Now?' Christopher's gaze drifted past me towards the clock hanging in the hallway. 'Class is about to start.'

'Yeah,' I said. I reached out and took his arm. I knew he didn't feel the electric pulse that leaped from my skin to the leather of his jacket. But I sure did. 'We aren't going to class today. We have to go to your cousin's house.'

Christopher shifted his backpack from one shoulder to another, looking from me to Lulu to Steven then back again. His expression was impassive.

'Look, Nikki,' he said, 'if this is about your mom, I thought we—'

'I have that thing you asked me for,' I said. 'The password? So let's just go, OK?'

His blue-eyed gaze swept over me searchingly. I expected him to ask about finals. The old Christopher would have. The old Christopher would have said, 'But this is the first semester of our junior year. Colleges will be looking at our grades this semester. If we screw up, it will be held against us. McKayla Donofrio is already a National Merit Scholar. We can't mess this up.'

But this wasn't the old Christopher. This was supervillain Christopher.

He looked me right in the eye and said, 'Let's go.'

And then we were heading for the nearest exit, even as Frida, who it turned out had been trotting behind us the whole time, was crying, 'Wait! Where are you going? You guys? The bell is going to ring. You can't just leave.'

'Grab a cab,' I said to Christopher, 'and tell it to wait. I'll just be a second.' I peeled off from the group and swung around to grab Frida by the shoulder.

Then I pinned her to the nearest locker with one hand.

To say that she looked surprised by this turn of events would have been the understatement of the century. But this was too important to play the kindly big sister. I couldn't let her mess this up for me. I had Steven to think of.

'Go to class,' I told her. 'Forget that you saw me here today.'

'Where are you guys going?' she wanted to know. 'You can't cut class this week. It's finals. You'll flunk!'

'I mean it, Frida,' I said. 'Tell your friends the same thing. None of you saw us.'

'What's going on?' Frida was starting to look scared now.

And you know what? She had a lot to be scared of.

'Where are you taking Christopher?' she asked.

But I'd already turned and was jetting down the hall and towards the doors through which Lulu, Christopher, and Steven had just bailed.

'I'm gonna tell,' I heard Frida calling after me. 'I mean it, Em! I mean, Nikki! Wait!'

Her voice was cut off by the heavy metal doors to the school slamming shut behind me as I hurried down the side steps, in the bitter cold and drizzle, to the waiting cab.

Sixteen

Lulu was shouting, 'Hurry!' to me – as if the taxi she had just climbed into might take off without me.

'I'm coming, I'm coming,' I told her. Christopher was waiting on the corner with his hand on the open taxi door. His face had settled back into impassivity again, as if he was used to being pulled out of school every day by supermodels and their entourages.

'Where, *exactly*,' Steven wanted to know as I slid into the back seat where he was sitting next to Lulu, 'are we going?'

'This guy's cousin is a computer genius,' I said, pointing at Christopher, who was seated up front next to the driver. I was pretty sure Christopher couldn't hear what we were saying through the thick bulletproof barrier separating the front and back seats. The driver had the Bollywood music turned up pretty loud. 'He says he can find your mom.'

Steven looked confused. 'He's with the NYPD? What was he doing in your high school? Is he a narc?'

'Um,' I said, beginning to see some inadequacies with my plan, 'no.'

'Did you see that girl's top?' Lulu wanted to know. She was apparently talking about Whitney. 'It was so . . . trying too hard.'

'But he's with the government,' Steven said. 'Tell me he's got some kind of connections with a governmental agency.'

'Not exactly,' I said to Steven.

'I mean,' Lulu went on. 'It was practically see-through. And not in a good way. You didn't like that top she was wearing, Steven, did you? That girl back there?'

'Are you telling me,' Steven asked, ignoring Lulu and Cosabella, whom I'd let out of my tote and who was prancing on his lap, peering excitedly at the traffic all around us, 'that he's really just a *high-school student*?'

'You know what?' Christopher had turned around in the front seat and was looking back at us through the plastic barrier. It was clear he *could* hear us after all, despite the tinny music urging us to *Soniya dil se mila de* and *Just Chill*. 'Don't worry about it. If she's alive, Felix'll find your mom. Just sit back and relax, all of you. It's taken care of.'

Which was exactly what a supervillain *would* say. Especially as he was taking you to your execution.

But wouldn't a truly threatening supervillain have been waving a weapon of some kind at us?

Yeah, no, not so much. Also, we were all heading into this of our own volition. Well, more or less. I guess I didn't have a choice, really. It was help Steven find his mother, or let him go public with what he knew. I could just see it now . . . Steven on the national news, making appeals for help finding his mom, and then casually mentioning, 'And by the way . . . the girl currently occupying Nikki Howard's body isn't really my sister. I don't know who she is, but somebody please do an exorcism to get her the hell out, OK? Thanks.'

That'd go over real well with Stark, I bet.

Lulu was on her cellphone next to me. 'No,' she was saying, to someone on the other end of the line, 'you have to make sure the caterer knows to deliver everything through the service elevator in the back. Last time they made a few deliveries from the front and they scratched the brass in the elevator and the building management got really mad. Understand? Good.' She hung up.

'Is this party all you ever think about?' Steven asked. He sounded really irritated.

Lulu looked past me and over at him. Her expression was stunned.

'No,' she replied, 'of course not!'

'It's just a party,' Steven said. 'I throw parties all the time. You get a keg and you pour out a couple of bags of pretzels. You put on some music and you invite your friends. It's not that big a deal.'

Lulu threw me an incredulous look. Since I wasn't exactly the world's greatest expert on parties, I was unable to contribute to the conversation. I've been to some parties with Lulu, it's true, and they seemed a bit more complex than *getting a keg* and *pouring out a couple of bags of pretzels*. The last one we went to involved a fire-eater. But I figured I'd let her handle the situation.

'This isn't just an ordinary party,' she explained carefully. 'Sushi chefs from Nobu are going to be making hand rolls on the spot. There's going to be every type of call liquor you can imagine, with bartenders who are also expert astrologists. I'm having a chocolate fountain installed on that little outside deck. And DJ Drama is going to be spinning.'

Steven just shook his head. 'Why? Why are you doing all that? Who are you trying to impress?'

'Impress?' Lulu said the word as if it was foreign. 'I'm not trying to impress anyone –' Which wasn't exactly true. Lulu'd been spending a lot of time lately trying to impress Steven. Still, not in a bad way, the way Whitney Robertson and the rest of the Walking Dead try to impress . . . well, me. Everything Lulu does, she does from a motivation of a hundred per cent goodness. No one who knew her well could ever say otherwise. Steven, I'm sure, was just upset with the way things were going, and nervous about his mom.

I hurried to intervene. 'Lulu likes to entertain,' I said. 'She's compensating for a less than satisfactory childhood. She'd really like it if you could be there.'

Steven hesitated . . . then, seeing my expression, which was beseeching – I was sending him a telepathic message which read, *Come on, dude. She has a huge crush on you. Don't diss her. Just say you'll come to her party. I don't care if she's not your type. Just say you'll come. Come on, throw the girl a bone* he shrugged and sank more deeply back into the seat as Cosabella's panting made a steamy spot on the window beside him. 'Sure. Of course. I appreciate the invitation. It sounds great.'

Lulu wriggled all over with excitement. 'It is going to

190

be great!' she enthused. 'We're having some of the trapeze artists from Cirque du Soleil, you know? They're installing trapezes from the ceiling, because our ceilings are so high. It's going to be freaky! People should be able to see them through our windows from all over Manhattan!'

Lulu went on about the party almost the entire way to Felix's house, which we finally pulled up in front of about ten minutes later. It was a nondescript attached home in a pleasant-looking middle-class neighbourhood. We stepped out into the cold, miserable rain, which disturbed Cosabella so much – she looked up at me with a perplexed expression like, *Why, Mom? Why would you do this to me?* – that I had to lift her and stick her back in the tote, where she snuggled happily down again.

Then, ducking his head against the steady mist of rain, Christopher led the way down the walk and up the stoop to the front door, where he lifted the American-eagle shaped door knocker and let it drop.

'Why do I have a bad feeling about this?' Steven asked me as we waited for the door to be answered.

'It'll be fine,' I said. Though I didn't actually believe this. Especially, I suspected, when Steven saw who we'd come to visit.

I wasn't wrong. A minute later, the door opened and a plump middle-aged woman wearing jeans and a Stark-brand sweater with a sparkly American flag on it cried, 'Christopher! What are you doing here on a school day?'

Christopher smiled and said, 'Oh, they let us out on winter break already in the city, Aunt Jackie.'

Aunt Jackie beamed and said, 'And you came to see Felix? And brought your friends? How sweet of you. Aren't you a nice boy?'

If only she knew.

'Well, don't stand out there in the cold,' Aunt Jackie cried. 'Come in! Come in . . .'

Felix's mother shepherded us inside, where it was warm. And decorated in everything you could buy at a Stark Megastore. I'm not kidding. I recognized a Stark-brand shelving unit, a Stark entertainment set, even a Stark-brand television. Felix's family had the complete Stark living room, down to the matching green Naugahyde Stark-brand love seats Christopher's aunt and uncle evidently sat in to watch the Stark Shopping Network at night. I could even smell Nikki perfume emanating from Aunt Jackie, a fairly noxious combination when added to the fact she had something baking in the oven in the kitchen. Nikki's perfume didn't go well with food. Or anything, really.

'You're just in time,' Felix's mom was saying, confirming my suspicions, as she bustled around. 'I'm about to take a batch of my world-famous brownies out of the oven—'

'Gee, that's great, Aunt Jackie,' Christopher said. 'Maybe later. Right now we have to talk to Felix. Is he downstairs?'

'Of course,' Aunt Jackie said with a laugh. 'Where else would he be?' She kept looking nervously at Lulu and me. At first I couldn't figure out why, then I remembered: we were Nikki Howard and Lulu Collins. She'd probably seen us before on *Entertainment Tonight* . . . not to mention my face on the tag of just about everything she'd ever bought. Maybe she couldn't place *how* she knew us, but she knew we looked familiar.

On top of which, it couldn't be every day girls came over to visit her little Felix. Or, more like, ever.

'We'll just go say hi to Felix,' Christopher said, nodding his head for us to follow him as he made his way across the orange shag carpeting towards a nearby door. 'We'll only be a minute. We won't stay long.'

'I'll tell you what,' Aunt Jackie said. 'I'll bring the brownies down to all of you. Would you like some milk with them? Or, I know! Hot cocoa! It's so cold out . . .'

Felix's mom apparently hadn't noticed one of us was in his twenties.

'That's OK, Aunt Jackie,' Christopher said. 'We'll be fine.' He yanked open the door and I saw it led to a long, narrow staircase into the basement. Christopher started down the stairs and, apprehensively glancing over my shoulder at Steven and Lulu, I followed him.

This, I knew, was it.

It wasn't as scary as heading into the Batcave exactly. Unless posters from the movie *Scarface* were scary. Which were what greeted us as we descended into Felix's parents' basement. They were everywhere. They covered almost every bit of wall surface in the basement, giant blown-up posters of Al Pacino, who starred in the movie, in all sorts of different costumes and poses.

Someone, I was beginning to suspect, had a bit of a gangster complex.

It wasn't really very hard to figure out who. I mean, I was guessing it wasn't Christopher's Aunt Jackie.

The basement apparently served as a laundry room as well as an exercise room. There was a set of weights – which looked as if they hadn't been touched in ages – as well as a treadmill from which bits of laundry were hanging to dry. At least down here, though, you couldn't smell the sickening scent of 'Nikki'. The air smelt crisply of washing detergent.

A corner of the basement had been converted to a media centre. Well, of sorts. Computer monitors that appeared as if they'd been scrounged from other people's garbage cans hung suspended from the ceiling by what looked like bungee cords. Some of them also sat on milk cartons or perilously leaned on entertainment consoles (Stark-brand, of course).

Sitting in the middle of this construction was a thin, hunched figure. The figure wore baggy jeans, a green velour shirt and multiple gold chains. He was playing an online game involving a stick shift.

'Die,' he was saying to one of the many computer monitors in front of him. 'Die, die, die, die, die!'

Behind me, I sensed rather than saw Steven freeze. Lulu crashed into him.

'Oh,' she said, *'excuse* me!' Steven didn't react. He was too stunned.

I didn't blame him.

The figure in front of the computer monitors turned its head. I recognized Felix from the other day. He smiled. I half expected to see that some of his teeth were capped in gold. But they weren't. Just braces.

'Christopher!' he exclaimed. 'My man! And you've brought visitors . . .' His voice trailed off as he saw just who his visitors were . . .

I thought there was a strong possibility Felix's eyes might bulge so far out of his head that they'd disconnect from his retinas entirely . . . especially when he saw Lulu. At the last minute, however, he pulled it together.

Then he said, 'Ladies! Hello. Welcome to the Men's Den. Good to have you here. How thoroughly excellent of you to come. Did the matriarch offer you brownies?'

'You have *got* to be kidding me.' Steven's voice, behind me, was wooden.

'Just give it a chance,' I said to him quietly.

'I will not give it a chance.' Steven sounded like he was being strangled. 'That is a *child*.'

'*Au contraire, mon frère*.' Felix, evidently overhearing him, pulled up a trouser leg to reveal an evil-looking black plastic device attached to one – surprisingly hairy – ankle. 'Does *this* look childlike? I assure you, it's anything but. This is a state-of-the-art in-house arrest-tracker system. Tamper-resistant. Communicates wirelessly to the docking station upstairs in the kitchen. It's connected to a transformer and the phone line. It will notify the police the minute I step outdoors. Hardly something your average fourteen-year-old boy would wear now, is it? But then,' Felix added, with a pointed glance in my direction, 'I'm extremely mature for my age, as I'm sure you ladies can tell.'

Steven tensed up and looked like he was about to slug the kid. But Lulu laid a gentle hand on his arm, murmuring soothingly, 'Oh, Steven, come on. Listen to Nikki. Just give it a chance.'

Christopher, meanwhile, was leaning up against a support post, a small smile playing across his lips.

'Everyone,' he said. 'My cousin, Felix. Felix. Everyone.'

'This,' I said, pointing, 'is Steven—'

Christopher held up a hand. 'I think it's probably better if it we keep it anonymous,' he said. 'I mean, as anonymous as we can, considering there are celebrity superstars among us.'

'Don't think just because you're famous, Ms Howard and Ms Collins,' Felix let us know, 'that I'm going to treat you any differently than I would if you were any other attractive lady. I actually know some celebrities – some of my best friends are celebrities, though I can't mention names, of course, because I'm too chill – and I know how upset they get when people make a big deal out of their fame. So you don't have to worry. I'm cool about the celebrity thing.'

Lulu and I exchanged glances. Then I said the only thing we possibly could say, under the circumstances, which was, 'Um . . . great. Thanks.'

The truth was, people said this kind of thing to me a lot. Everybody wanted me to know they weren't the kind of person who was impressed by celebrities, and that they were going to treat me like a 'normal person'.

Except that just by telling me that, they weren't treating me like a normal person.

Christopher – who had to know his cousin was a bit of a tool, but was mostly keeping his gaze averted, as if he wanted to avoid the whole situation and escape off into his own little world – asked, 'Nikki, do you have that information we asked you for?'

'Oh.' I was startled. Christopher was the one who'd always treated me like a non-celebrity. To the point where he almost treated me like a non-human at times. 'Yeah . . .'

I still wasn't sure how I felt about ratting out Stark to Christopher and Felix. On the one hand, I honestly didn't think their plan was going to work. I mean, we were talking about Stark, which according to Christopher was the largest corporation in the entire world. Were two teenagers really going to be able to take it down with their little hack?

Yeah, so not.

On the other hand, they were so going to get caught. One of them was already wearing an ankle bracelet and, from the looks of things, living in a basement, playing video games and eating brownies served by his mother all day . . . on the surface the most ideal of existences for a kid, but in reality actually kind of horrible, with his obviously made up relationships with 'celebrities' and delusions of grandeur. Was that really the sort of future that I wanted for Christopher?

No, of course not.

But if that was true, would I have gone to school this morning, pulled him out of class during finals week, and dragged him all the way out to Brooklyn to his cousin's house?

I wasn't sure. But I had to do something. Because my days of doing nothing but running around with a bug detector in my pocket were over.

'It's Doctor Louise Higgins,' I heard myself saying. 'That's the username.'

Seventeen

Felix didn't waste any time. He turned around and headed straight for his computer chair in the centre of all his mismatched monitors.

'And her password,' I said, remembering the way Dr Higgins's fingers had flown over her keyboard, 'is Miss Kitty, one word, all lower case.'

'Sweet,' Felix said, typing.

'What,' Steven said, taking a few steps forward, so he could see what was coming up on the computer screens flicking before us, 'does any of this have to do with my missing mother?'

'It's just,' I said, 'what I had to do in order to get them to look for her.'

'And we're men of our word,' Felix said. 'Behold.' He reached for a bunch of papers that had been spitting out of one of his many printers while we'd been standing there, then waved them in the air. 'The last known whereabouts of Dolores Howard, also known as Dee Dee, also known as your mom.'

Steven snatched the pages from Felix's hand as Christopher came over to watch Felix, who, completely uninterested in any of us any more, turned back to his keyboards.

'Does it work?' Christopher asked his cousin. 'Are we in?'

'Oh yeah,' Felix said, sounding pleased. 'We're in.'

'Wait a minute.' Steven was looking down at the papers in his hands, shuffling through one after another, peering at each one. 'This doesn't say where she is. This just says her Social Security number hasn't been used to register for any new jobs or credit cards or places to live since she disappeared.'

'That's right, buddy.' Felix's fingers flew over the keyboards in front of him while the various monitors flickered with information that, to me, just looked like jumbles of numbers and incomprehensible data.

'But –' I felt my blood run cold on Steven's behalf – 'Christopher, you said Felix could find her.'

'Unless she's dead.' Christopher didn't even bother looking over at me. He pointed at one of the computer monitors and said to Felix, 'Look. Look at that.'

'I know,' Felix said.

Lulu crossed the room, her high heels clacking on the cement floor, and came to stand very close to Steven. Then she reached for his hand, the one that wasn't holding the pages of information about his mother. She didn't say anything. She just reached for his hand, then squeezed it.

He didn't seem to notice.

'So you think his mother is dead?' I demanded. I didn't mean to sound harsh, but I was angry. Not so much at Felix, because for all his brains he was just a kid who thought he was a gangster, and didn't know better. But Christopher. I knew he knew better – he should have been showing more concern for Steven.

But all his attention was completely glued to those stupid slapped-together computer screens. I hadn't any doubt he was eager to get started on his diabolical scheme to bring down Stark Enterprises and avenge the wrongful death of Em Watts . . . a girl he had never even bothered to kiss while she was legally alive.

But he could at least have looked over at us. He could at least have said he was sorry. A man's mother was dead!

'What?' Christopher must have felt the intensity of my gaze, since he finally glanced over. 'What are you talking about?'

Felix looked over at us too.

'Dead?' he echoed. 'I didn't say she was dead. Did I say she was dead? No. No unidentified bodies fitting Dee Dee Howard's age, description or dental records have turned up anywhere in the past few weeks in any of the databases I tapped . . . which was all of them, by the way.' Felix shrugged as he turned back towards one of his keyboards and started typing again with lightning speed. 'It's possible, of course, that someone corked her and then threw her in a lake somewhere. Floaters don't usually pop up to the surface until spring, when the temperatures rise and the gases in the bodies start the decomposing process—'

'Hey, man,' Christopher said, prodding his cousin in the shoulder. 'That's not cool.'

Felix shook his head. 'Sorry. We know that's not what happened.'

I stared at him, not sure if I could start feeling relieved. 'We do?'

'We do,' Felix said. 'Take a look at page four.'

Steven quickly flipped through the pages he was holding, until he found the fourth page. 'These are my mom's bank records,' he said, sounding a little incredulous. 'How did you . . . ?'

But Felix cut him off before Steven could finish his question. 'Check out the withdrawal she made shortly before her last few cellphone calls.'

'Her cellphone records are here? How . . . ?' Steven's voice trailed off. Then, his eyes widening while he was reading the page in front of him, he looked up at Felix and asked, in a shocked voice, 'Nine thousand dollars? She withdrew nine thousand dollars from her savings account before she disappeared? And no one bothered to mention this to me before?'

Felix had already turned back to his keyboard however.

'When there's no sign of foul play,' Christopher said, his gaze as riveted to the computer monitors as his cousin's, 'there isn't exactly a reason for the cops to do a thorough forensic accounting investigation, if they even have the manpower for it, which they don't, usually.'

'And it's pretty common behaviour,' Felix added, 'for someone heading underground to make large cash withdrawals. You want to go off the grid you can't be flashing your Visa around, or using the ATM. They'll find you in a red-hot second. Whoever your mom's running from, she doesn't want to be traced. She's paying cash for everything.'

Steven glanced back down at the pages he was holding. 'She owns a dog-grooming kennel, for God's sake. She's never been in trouble with the police – or even the IRS, for that matter – in her life. Who would she be running from?'

'Stark,' Christopher said. He said the word as bleakly as someone else would say the word *death*.

'Stark?' Steven flung him an incredulous look. 'But why?'

'Give us twenty-four hours –' Christopher nodded at the mishmash of computer screens in front of him – 'And we'll find out.'

'And we'll bring 'em down!' Felix let out a whoop, not unlike the kind a kid his age would release upon plummeting over the particularly steep summit of a roller coaster.

Only this wasn't a roller coaster. I doubted Felix had ever been on an actual roller coaster in his life. He just didn't seem like a roller-coaster kind of kid.

Felix raised his left hand for Christopher to high five. Christopher, however, ignored him. Felix lowered his hand sheepishly.

'So this is what this is all about,' Steven said. He didn't sound pleased. In fact, he sounded disgusted. 'You two are going to hack into their computer system and "bring down" Stark Enterprises?' He looked at me. 'You knew about this?'

'That's what they wanted,' I said. Why was he trying to make me feel bad about my decision? I was helping him. Wasn't that what *he* wanted? 'In exchange for the information about your mom. A Stark administrative employee username and password.'

'Great,' Steven said. He looked down at the papers in his hand. 'And we still don't have the slightest idea where my mom is.' He looked over at Christopher and Felix. 'How can they be so sure she's even alive? Someone could have held a gun to her head and made her withdraw that nine grand, then dumped her body at the bottom of the lake, like the kid said.'

'No.' My voice was soft. 'You said she took her dogs with her. If someone took her by force, they would have left the dogs. Christopher's right. She's on the run. She has to be.'

I glanced over at Christopher and Felix, who were not paying even the slightest bit of attention to us any more, they were so caught up in their world of destruction and – in Christopher's case, at least – revenge. We didn't exist to them any more. Maybe we never had, except for what they could get out of us.

'Let's just go now,' I said. 'Come on.'

We started towards the staircase, only to see a Stark-brand imitation Ugg appear on it. A second later, Aunt Jackie's voice was calling as she came down the stairs, 'Yoo-hoo! I've got those brownies for you! Fresh from the oven! And look who I found outside. Your little friend. She said you all ran off so fast, you left her behind.'

Following right behind Aunt Jackie, holding a tray full of mugs containing steaming hot chocolate, was my little sister Frida.

Eighteen

'Don't be mad,' Frida said.

I was sitting in the make-up chair at the Stark sound studio. Hopefully this dress rehearsal would go a little better than yesterday's fitting and run through.

Of course, dragging my little sister along with me hadn't exactly been part of the plan.

'I'm just so worried about you,' she said.

Jerri, the make-up artist was attaching the last of a set of individual faux-fur eyelashes over mine. I was trying not to move for fear of being stabbed in the eye with a pair of tweezers.

'I didn't know who that guy was,' Frida was saying, referring to Steven. 'I thought he might have been kidnapping you or something.'

'This really,' I said, 'isn't a good time to talk about it.'

'But when *can* we talk about it?' Frida asked. 'You wouldn't talk about it in the cab back to Manhattan. Why can't we talk about it here?'

Because, I wanted to tell her, this is Stark Central. And while the room wasn't bugged (I'd checked), everyone – meaning Jerri – was listening.

Just like the cab driver on the way back into Manhattan had been listening.

Besides, the less Frida knew, the safer she'd be. Of

course, she didn't know this. And if she had, she wouldn't have agreed.

She was slumped on the chair behind mine, clutching the Dolce & Gabbana backpack I'd snagged for her at the runway show I'd done for them. She looked totally miserable. She'd been looking like that all afternoon. Although I didn't know what she had to be so bummed about. She'd got to miss out on a day of school – even better, a day of finals.

And then, while I'd been yelling at her about that down in Felix's basement, Nikki's cellphone had gone off. It had been Rebecca, telling me I was late for rehearsal – again.

I'd tried to drop Frida off back at school, but she wouldn't get out of the cab. No, she was sticking to me like glue.

Only glue would be more pleasant.

'Of course I grabbed a taxi and told the driver to follow yours after you just stormed out of school like that,' she was prattling on. 'He thought I was kidding. But I told him it was a matter of life or death. If that lady who was making the brownies hadn't kept me in the kitchen talking my ear off about the fact that Nikki Howard was downstairs in her basement visiting her kid, I would have been down there a lot sooner to rescue you.'

'Frida,' I said with a nervous glance at Jerri, 'I wasn't—'

'Well,' she said sullenly. 'It's not my fault you didn't need rescuing. Or so you say.'

'You *skipped*,' I said to her reflection in the wide make-up mirror in front of me, hoping to change the subject, 'your finals.'

'What about you?' Frida demanded. 'You skipped too. You ran off to Brooklyn with a total stranger. I'll admit he was cute, but—'

'He's not a total stranger,' I said. 'He's Nikki's – I mean, *my* – brother.'

Frida stared at me with her mouth hanging open for a full minute before she burst out, 'Your brother? But what were you doing in a Brooklyn basement with Christopher, Lulu Collins and Nikki Howard's *brother*?' She said all this just as Gabriel Luna came strolling into the dressing room.

Perfect timing. Of course.

'Sorry,' he said. 'Am I interrupting anything?'

'Oh, hi, Gabriel' Jerri said, the smile on her face huge. You could tell she was enjoying every moment of this, even though she had no idea what was going on, or who Frida was to Nikki Howard. She was just enjoying the fight. 'Are you here for a touch-up? Have a seat.'

'No thanks,' Gabriel said, looking with loathing at all her brushes and powder puffs. 'It's only a dress rehearsal.'

'Gabriel Luna,' Frida breathed. Her cheeks immediately burst into flame. 'Um, hi!'

Gabriel studied her. It was obvious he recognized her. They'd met at the Institute back when he'd visited me – or, rather, Nikki – after the accident. Just who he thought she was in relation to me – we'd never exactly discussed it – remained sketchy.

'How are you doing?' Frida asked Gabriel before he could say hi back. Her sisterly concern for my well-being was momentarily lost as she greeted her crush. Her room back home was papered in Gabriel Luna posters the way Felix's basement was with Al Pacino. She Google-searched him relentlessly on her Mac back home. 'It's been ages.'

'I'm fine,' Gabriel said. He turned his attention on me in my make-up chair. 'Brooklyn? Really?'

'It's a long story,' I said, shooting Frida a look. She didn't notice, however, having eyes only for Gabriel Luna and the fact that he was standing in the same room and breathing the same oxygen as she was.

Not that I blamed her. It probably *was* kind of hard for her to concentrate on anything else, given the fact that Gabriel had on the performance clothes Stark had ordered him to wear, a pair of pretty tight tuxedo suit trousers, the vest that matches the tuxedo suit, and a white button-down shirt open to midway down his chest, with the sleeves rolled up. This could be a very distracting look . . .

But only on someone as attractive as Gabriel, as was proved a second later when Robert Stark strolled into the dressing room wearing a very similar get-up. Maybe that was because Robert Stark's shirt was buttoned up to his throat, and his bow tie was actually tied. Or possibly because he was followed by his son, also wearing a tux . . . but at the same time, a look of extreme agitation, as if the dressing room before the Stark Angel fashion show dress rehearsal with his father was the last place in the world Brandon Stark really wanted to be.

Especially when he saw me. We hadn't communicated with one another since the awkward private plane ride home the other morning after that kiss we'd shared at the hotel back in St John.

When Brandon noticed me there in the dressing room, his scowl grew even more menacing.

Nice to know I have that effect on boys. I mean, Christopher doesn't even know I exist, and Brandon Stark practically throws up when he sees me. Having my brain transplanted into a supermodel's body was doing wonders for my love life all right.

'Nikki!' Robert Stark cried. He threw out his arms wide to greet me. I was so startled I didn't know what to do. It was the first time Robert Stark had ever openly acknowledged me. 'So good to see you! Don't you look beautiful?'

It took me a second, but I soon saw why he was being so effusive. A string of photographers were following the two Stark men. Flashes went off as the CEO of Stark embraced the Face of Stark. Our photos would appear in countless newspapers tomorrow morning.

'Uh,' I said, 'thanks.'

'And Gabriel Luna.' After letting go of me, Robert Stark turned and held out his hand to Gabriel, who shook it. The photographers got this shot too. Robert made sure to turn to the camera, smiling toothily. 'So glad to have you on board here at the Stark label. Hope you play well tonight. Just a rehearsal, I know, but we've got the Stark stock investors in the audience for your run-through before their big holiday dinner tonight. They couldn't be more excited about seeing it.'

'Thank you, sir,' Gabriel said. He looked completely baffled by the whole thing. The head of the corporation that owned his label greeting him personally? This had obviously never happened before in the entirety of his career. 'I hope they enjoy it.'

'Just wanted to personally extend my thanks,' Robert Stark was saying. 'I wanted my two biggest stars to know how important they are to me. So we wanted to make sure you got these.'

He snapped his fingers and Brandon, standing behind him with his scowl deepening again, went, *'What?'* in an annoyed voice.

'The bag, Bran,' Robert Stark said, his smile never wavering. 'The *bag*.'

Brandon rolled his eyes, then held up a large red velvet bag he'd apparently been lugging around . . . and none too happily either. Robert Stark reached inside the bag and withdrew a foot-long box containing a Stark Quark – colour: red – which he handed to Gabriel.

'Happy holidays,' Robert said. 'First one off the boat. I hope you enjoy it.'

Gabriel looked down at the computer. His face was impassive. 'Thank you, sir,' he said again. It was hard to tell what he was thinking. But *Why the hell is this guy giving me this?* would have been high on my list of guesses.

'And here's one for you,' Robert Stark said, reaching down into the bag and fishing out a pink Quark for me. Because, you know, pink equals girls.

'Oh, gosh,' I said, gazing down at the computer I'd

pretended to be so fond of in the Stark Quark ad (only that one had just been an empty shell, not the real thing). My Mac Air was a thousand times more user-friendly and in the long run less likely to break down.

But it also cost five times more, retail. And didn't come with *Realms*, the new *Journeyquest* game, on it.

'I always wanted one of these,' I lied. 'How did you know?'

Behind his father, Brandon kept his gaze averted from mine. I couldn't tell if he knew I was lying or not.

'Santa knows all,' Brandon's dad said with a chuckle, and some of the reporters laughed.

Brandon muttered something about handing out free laptops to celebrities as opposed to the poor. I raised my eyebrows just as his father asked, in the same hearty voice, 'What was that, Bran?'

'Nothing, sir,' Brandon mumbled. I caught his eye and, for a moment, as our gazes met, something seemed to pass between us. I don't know what exactly. I was so surprised at what Brandon had said, I hardly knew what to think, to be honest.

And then it was gone, and Brandon was glaring stonily ahead again.

'And who's this?' Robert Stark asked, when he finally noticed Frida.

'Oh,' Frida said, looking mortified. 'I'm no one. Just a friend of . . . Nikki's.'

An FON! Frida had just called herself an FON!

'Well, tonight, young lady,' Robert Stark said, reaching

down into the red velvet bag, 'any friend of Nikki Howard's is a friend of mine.' And he pulled out a bright orange Quark and handed it to her.

Even though a moment before Frida had been acting as if she was suicidal, and she'd never in her life expressed the least interest in owning a Quark, she let out an excited scream and began jumping up and down.

'Oh, these are the ones that aren't on sale until Christmas! Thank you, thank you, sir!' she yelled, throwing the arm that wasn't wrapped around her gift around his neck, and planting a kiss on his cheek. 'Oh, *thank you!*'

The reporters got *lots* of photos of this. Excited young teenage girl embracing one of the richest men in the world? It would be all over Fox Business News in about five minutes.

And not just because it was a cute shot either. It was sickening really, watching the way Stark operated . . . giving away something for free, something that the individual didn't even know she wanted, and thus incorporating in her a feeling of goodwill towards both him and the company . . . and ensuring that Frida would go fully Quark from now on, with products she'd only be able to buy at a Stark Megastore.

That's why the man was a genius. And a billionaire.

'Well,' Robert Stark said. 'Happy holidays to you all. Have a great performance. I have to be off. Can't keep the investors waiting.'

He gave a big wave, and turned to leave, Brandon following, tight-faced, behind him with the bag.

I wondered what would happen if I cleared my throat and said, 'Excuse me, Mr Stark? What about the Stark Institute for Neurology and Neurosurgery, and what you people do there? I mean, the whole brain-transplant thing. Do you have any comment on that?'

The truth was, probably nothing would happen. Robert Stark would just blink at me with those blank eyes of his and say he didn't know what I was talking about. And later, I'd get sent back to the Institute and get another lecture by Dr Higgins. Or maybe they'd send Dr Holcombe this time, or, if they really wanted to scare me, some of Stark's lawyers to threaten my family.

I wasn't supposed to talk about what had happened to me, of course.

But no one had ever said I couldn't talk about . . .

'Excuse me,' I said, 'Mr Stark?'

Robert Stark turned in the doorway and looked back, still smiling pleasantly from his interlude with my sister.

'Yes, Nikki?' he asked.

'I was just wondering,' I said. My heart was in my throat, but I didn't care. I knew I had to keep going. I couldn't stop thinking about Steven's face down in that basement, and knew I had to do something.

And this was my opportunity. Maybe my only opportunity.

'Do you know where my mother is?'

There were a few seconds of silence after I asked this, as my words sunk in. Then everyone began buzzing among themselves. Her mother? Did she just say *her mother*?

'Pardon me?' Robert Stark said, his dark eyebrows raised.

'My mother,' I said. I was aware that the reporters were scribbling my words down frantically, some of them holding mini-recorders in my direction. I tried to enunciate more clearly. 'She's missing. I was wondering if you might have any idea where she is?'

'How would *I* know where your mother is, sweetheart?' Robert Stark was grinning as if I'd said something hilarious.

'Well,' I said, 'because she disappeared right after my *accident*.' I put special stress on the word 'accident'. A stress only he and I – and Frida, of course, who was staring at me in astonishment – would understand. 'And no one has seen or heard from her since. I was hoping maybe you might be able to shed some light on where she could have gone.'

'No,' Robert Stark said, shaking his head. His smile had disappeared. 'Sorry, kid. I can't help you there. Can't help you there at all.'

He couldn't seem to get out of there fast enough after that. Brandon followed him, looking back at me curiously.

After Robert Stark was gone, the level of tension in the room went down a millionfold. At least to me. Which was weird, because the reporters, instead of following him, stuck around. They shoved microphones and cameras in my face and asked, 'Nikki Howard, is it true your mother is missing? Would you care to elaborate?'

It was weird but . . . it turned out I *did* care to elaborate . . . at least as much as I could without giving away the whole brain-transplant angle of the story, which really didn't have anything to do with Nikki's mother anyway – at least so far as I could prove. Soon I had the reporters' names and affiliate stations and had given them exclusive interviews (Gabriel had handed me his tuxedo jacket to wear over my bra before doing so, which I considered decent of him), and had promised to have Steven email over a photo of his mom for the reporters to air on their shows.

It turned out Nikki Howard having a missing mom was big news.

Really big news.

This was something I should have thought of before. I mean, being a supermodel wasn't all just about strutting around in ten-million-dollar bras. People were interested in you. And if your mom went missing – especially around the holidays – that was front-page stuff.

Or at least, it could be, if I worked it right. I was thinking this was something I needed to get my publicist on . . .

'Why didn't you tell *me* about your missing mom, *Nikki*?' Frida asked in a tight little voice after the last of the reporters had left the dressing room with their big scoop. 'I thought we were close enough that you could tell me *anything*.'

What was she even talking about? Of course I couldn't tell Frida anything. She was too young. And it was too dangerous.

The truth was, I'd forgotten Frida was even there. Which was probably why she was glaring at me now, her eyes filled with tears.

'Don't feel bad,' Gabriel said lightly to Frida. 'I had dinner with her last night, and she didn't say a word to me about it either.'

'Last night?' Frida gasped. 'You guys had dinner together last night?' She couldn't have sounded more wounded if one of her Google searches had turned up images of Gabriel and me actually making out.

Great. Just great.

'Yeah,' I said quickly. 'We had dinner. Because we're in this show together, so we grabbed something after rehearsal. As *friends*.'

It was too late though. There were even more hot tears in her eyes. 'I saw the photos of you two by the limo on PerezHilton.com,' she said. Oh no. 'But I didn't think . . . I mean, you *like* him?' she demanded. 'He's your boyfriend now? What about Christopher?'

'Of course he's not my boyfriend,' I said. How could this be happening? 'Frida, stop—'

'What's going on?' Gabriel asked, looking bewildered. 'Who's Christopher?'

'No one,' I said. 'Gabriel, would you mind leaving us alone for a moment?'

'Of course,' Gabriel said, backing from the room, a wary eye on Frida, who looked like she might go supernova any minute. 'I'll just see you onstage, all right, Nikki?'

'That'd be good,' I said to him. As soon as he was gone, I whirled towards Frida, who was glaring at me like I'd just written You Suck on her wall on Facebook, and said, 'Frida, get over it. He's way too old for you. And there's nothing going on between us anyway. We just work together.'

The truth was, I was kind of glad she was distracted from asking me what I'd been doing in Brooklyn, anyway. Better that she be mad at me for going out with Gabriel Luna – however innocently – than be wanting to know more about what I'd been doing all morning with Christopher.

Except that it turns out that wasn't why she was mad. Or not entirely.

'Who *are* you?' she demanded.

I blinked down at her. 'What do you mean, who am I? You know who I am . . .'

'No I don't,' Frida shot back. 'You're doing all this stuff to find someone else's mom, and meanwhile you don't even care about your *real* family any more.'

'Frida,' I said in a tight voice, 'you know that isn't true.'

'Yes it is,' Frida said. 'We changed all our plans for you. I'm not going to cheerleading camp because of you. And you don't even care. You're spending all your time worrying about Nikki's family. Because you're turning into Nikki!'

I felt something inside me go cold. 'You know that isn't true,' I said, through lips as numb as if they had been smeared with plumper.

'You're the worst sister,' Frida snapped. 'You don't even care about me any more! Just your new family!'

I had to admit that hurt. Everything I'd done, I'd done to protect her. Well, OK, maybe not the part where I'd accidentally made out with Gabriel Luna. I'd only done that because I'd been so hurt and lonely about Christopher.

But the fact that I had gone through with this whole model thing so Mom and Dad wouldn't be in violation of the contracts they'd signed? I'd done that for Frida. How would she enjoy living in bankruptcy, with no Wi-Fi or Juicy Couture?

And she had the nerve to say I was a bad sister?

'Go get my bag,' I said in a cold voice. 'Take money out of it, get a cab and go home.'

'Gladly,' Frida said, just as coldly. 'I can't believe we decided to stay here for Christmas for you. I wish we were going to Florida after all!'

And with that she took her new computer, a wad of cash from my wallet, and left the Stark sound studio.

She was crying as she did it, but I didn't care.

Or I told myself I didn't, anyway. She was just a kid. A jealous kid. What did she know about anything? She was just mad about the Gabriel thing, and the fact that I wouldn't let her come to Lulu's party. She'd get over it. She'd have to. We were sisters. We fought all the time. We always got over it.

I wasn't turning into Nikki Howard. Sure, on the outside I looked like her. But on the inside, I was still me.

Wasn't I? I couldn't wait to get home and tear into my new Stark Quark so I could play *Realms*. Right?

Except . . .

Except it wasn't going to be that fun without Christopher to play against.

Frida left just as one of the costume assistants came in with my wings, fastened them on and escorted me down the long corridors to the backstage area. The rest of the girls were there, milling around. Kelley waved when she saw me and hurried over.

'Oh my God,' she said. Even though she was shouting, it was kind of hard to hear her with all the buzzing from the Stark investors. 'Can you believe this? They get their own private performance? Just because they've got stock in the company or something? This is ridiculous. Someone should complain.'

'Seriously,' I said. Except that I didn't mean it. The truth was, there was no instrument known to man small enough to measure how little I cared.

Maybe Frida was right. Maybe I *was* turning into Nikki. Maybe this was what happened to stunningly beautiful women. They just got to a point where they were so jaded about everything that nothing mattered any more. Their hearts turned hard as stone. Mine certainly felt like it. Or as heavy as stone anyway.

Up until Alessandro hissed, 'Ladies! We're on!' and we were lining up to begin, the techno music thumping so hard it seemed to have reached inside my heart and seized it and taken hold – *thump-thump-thump* – and Veronica turned around suddenly and pinched me. Hard.

'Ow!' I shrieked, rubbing my arm. Sorry, but no one whose heart was made of stone could be as sensitive to pain as I was. 'What did you do *that* for?'

'You know.' Her gaze blazed like twin lightning bolts.

'Why won't you quit emailing Justin? He doesn't like you like that any more. He's mine.'

'Email him?' I glared back at her. I had to shout to make sure she could hear me over the music. 'I didn't email anyone!'

'You're a liar.' Veronica shook her head, her silky blonde hair shimmering in the stage lights. 'He showed me the things you wrote. You're pathetic. You *miss* him. He's mine now.'

'I swear,' I said, 'I am not emailing your boyfriend. It's someone else—'

'How can you stand there, lying to my face?' Veronica wanted to know. 'Justin told me he broke it off and has been trying to ditch you, but you won't let it go.'

I glared at her angrily. 'I told you. I don't know what you're talking about. I haven't been emailing Justin. It's some other girl using my name. Which isn't my problem. Now, you better pay attention to what you're doing, or you're going to be late onstage. And don't pull that feather thing again because next time I'll speak to Mr Stark about it and he'll boot you out of here. That I'll guarantee.'

Something very much like fear flickered across Veronica's face and I realized I'd finally gotten the upper hand in our relationship. It was sad that I'd had to invoke the name of Brandon's dad to do it, but what choice did I have really? The girl was trying to kill me, and for something I didn't even do. Some wacko was trying to steal her boyfriend and was using my name to do it. How was that my fault?

Looking scared – until her stage face fell into place like

a mask – Veronica sailed out on to the runway. I stood there for a few seconds, waiting for my cue – the 'Nikki' song – and wondering how everything had gotten so complicated. My life before the accident hadn't been so great, it was true . . . I'd been in love with a guy who hadn't known I was alive. Now that guy had finally realized he loved me back. The only problem was, he thought I was dead, but I couldn't tell him I wasn't. And he wouldn't like the me I was now anyway, because I represented pretty much everything he hated.

Meanwhile, so did a bunch of other people. Hate me, I mean.

It was hard, being a teenage supermodel in the twenty-first century.

Then I heard it.

'The thing of it is, girl . . . in spite of it all . . . I really do think . . . I love you.'

The problem was, it was the wrong guy singing it.

And as I moved out on to the stage – carefully putting one six-inch heel in front of the other and giving my all to my sassy catwalk strut, a knowing, catlike smile plastered across my face as the Stark investors cheered – I knew my heart hadn't actually been turned to stone.

Because it hurt.

It hurt a lot.

Nineteen

Steven wasn't in the mood for a party.

Neither was I actually. I mean, Steven hadn't spent the night before at the Stark Angel dress rehearsal and investor after-party, signing autographs and posing for photos with Stark Enterprises executives, pretending to be *so thrilled* to be there.

Nor had he woken up the next day and dragged himself to school for his remaining finals, or slunk around to the teachers whose exams he'd missed the day before, begging them to let him reschedule.

I was the only one who appeared to care about having missed any exams. Christopher didn't even bother to show up to school the next day. I had no idea where he was. Probably still with Felix in the basement, hatching their evil revenge plot against Stark.

Which didn't appear to be working, because as far as I could tell, Stark Enterprises showed every sign of still going strong.

Frida, who I passed in the hallway, stuck up her nose at me and carried on walking. So I had no idea if her teachers were allowing her to retake the finals she'd missed when she'd followed me out to Brooklyn. Mine weren't so keen on the idea. I got a lot of, 'Miss Howard, do you realize how much of this semester you've missed already? We here at

Tribeca Alternative are willing to be flexible with students who have special schedules, but you're going to have to make up your mind. Do you want a modelling career, or do you want an education?'

Um . . . how about both?

But I understood. I took my Fs on the finals where the teachers were totally unwilling to compromise and let me do extra work to make up for missing the final exam or project.

Such as Public Speaking. Well, Mr Greer always did think a bit too highly of himself for a guy who slept through class every day.

In some cases, the F wouldn't affect my total grade in the class too badly. I'd still end up making a C or a B. But in others . . .

Well, let's just say it was a good thing I had my modelling career to fall back on if I didn't make it into college.

I knew not everybody was going to think this was such a good thing. My parents, for instance, weren't going to be so thrilled when they heard about it . . . if I ever told them, that is. They had no way to find out about Nikki Howard's grades, not being related to her – nor would the school have notified them that she'd skipped school yesterday.

Frida, however, was another matter. She'd gotten into some pretty big trouble for leaving school and missing her exams. TAHS had notified Mom about both, as I found out when I'd called Mom and Dad to check in – stung by Frida's rebuke that I cared more about my 'new family' than I did about my old one.

Mom had been frantic about Frida's skipping . . . until I told her she'd been with me at the Stark Angel fashion-show rehearsal.

'What?' Mom sounded stunned. 'With *you*?'

'She was just worried about me,' I said. 'We had a little fight. She saw me leaving school and she didn't know why, and so she followed me. I was going to a rehearsal at the Stark studios . . . she was with me the whole time.' This part, at least, wasn't technically a lie.

'So you skipped school too,' Mom said. Now she sounded more bitter than stunned.

'It was work, Mom,' I said. Technically, this wasn't a lie either. 'Don't be too hard on Frida. She really thought she was doing the right thing.'

Mom sighed. 'You're both getting coal in your stocking this year,' she said. She didn't sound like she was joking either.

So Frida hadn't told Mom where she'd been – chasing me to Brooklyn. What was Frida up to? Why hadn't she told Mom and Dad where she'd been? What was going on with her? Why was she so mad at me? Surely she couldn't really believe I was taking on the personality that went with my donor body, forgetting my real family in place of Nikki's. It was true sometimes – especially when a guy was kissing me – I felt as if I were losing control over Nikki.

But forsake Frida and Mom and Dad for Nikki's family? No. It was just that they needed me right now. And I was in a position where I could help them.

Besides, I owed them. Didn't I? Who else was going to help them, if I didn't?

When I got home from school that day, I found Steven – still not in the mood for a party – looking pleased with himself.

'Come with me,' he said, and guided me towards the music-system unit.

'What?' I asked, unwinding my scarf as Cosabella jumped excitedly against my legs. 'You didn't get us a present, did you? You didn't have to . . .' My voice trailed off as I saw what Steven slid back the unit doors to show me. It was sat next to our CD player, a black box with a lot of knobs on it.

'Oh,' I said, 'that's so nice. But. I think we already have one.' I didn't know what it was. But we had one of everything. 'I'm sure yours is better though,' I said, to make him not feel bad.

'You don't have one of these,' Steven assured me with a chuckle. 'It's an acoustic noise generator. And don't ask where I got it, because you're better off not knowing. It works by injecting noise on all the frequencies on which you might be being bugged. In your case –' He pointed upwards.

I cocked my head. 'But . . . I can't hear anything.'

'Right,' Steven said. 'That's the point. You're not sup-posed to know it's here. And neither will they. All they're going to know is that they can't hear you any more. They'll probably send someone in to try to find out why.' He closed the unit doors again. 'But they won't be able to figure it out. They'll never have seen one of those before. It's for military use only.'

I stared at him. 'Which is why I'm not supposed to ask where you got it,' I said. 'Right?'

'Right,' he said. 'Or ask where I got this.' He passed me a small black hand-held device, not much bigger than my bug detector.

'It's a portable audio jammer,' he said in response to my inquisitive look. 'It only operates on two frequencies, but it will stop any surveillance microphones operating within a distance of a hundred and fifty feet of you from picking up normal conversation. And sound-lessly.'

I looked down at the sleek black device in my hand. I was touched.

'This is so nice of you, Steven,' I said, feeling my eyes grow moist. I'd been paranoid for so long about Stark overhearing my every word. And now, suddenly, I didn't have to be. And it had all happened so fast. 'But I . . . I didn't get you anything.'

'What?' Steven looked incredulous. 'Yes you did. This was the least I could do.'

I shook my head. I couldn't believe I was getting teary-eyed. Then again, I always had been a big geek. I guess this was proof that what Frida had accused me of wasn't true – I *wasn't* turning into Nikki Howard after all. I'm pretty sure she wouldn't have been impressed by gifts of an acoustic noise generator and an audio jammer. 'What do you mean?'

'The TV stations who ran interviews with you say they've had hundreds of calls,' Steven said. 'All from people who think they've seen Mom.'

'Are any of them credible sightings?' Lulu, using some of her *Law & Order* jargon, came into the loft suddenly. She was helping Katerina with the caterers, who'd begun arriving in advance of her party.

'No.' Steven hastily moved away from the music-system unit. 'Not yet. But I have a feeling we're getting close.'

'Fantastic!' Lulu smiled brilliantly at him, then pointed an imperious finger at a guy carrying a carved-out pumpkin in which some kind of liquid was going to be poured. 'No! Katerina, where does that go?'

'Here!' Katerina took over, looking ready to physically move the guy holding the pumpkin, if not the gourd itself.

'So it's OK with you,' I asked, looking nervously at Nikki's brother, 'that I did all those interviews?'

'OK with me?' Steven shook his head. 'We should have thought of it sooner. But is it going to get you in trouble with – ?'

He raised his gaze to the ceiling, where the performer from Cirque du Soleil, wearing very little except a nude-coloured bra, a pair of panties and a long red scarf, was testing out a newly installed trapeze with her weight. Not far from the trapeze were the round holes in the ceiling I'd noticed a few weeks earlier. Steven wasn't avoiding the word Stark for fear of being overheard by my employer . . .

not any more, thanks to his gifts. He just didn't want to bring it up in front of Lulu while she was in such a party mood.

'I don't know,' I said with a shrug. 'I guess we'll see.'

'I can't believe all the fuss she's going to for this,' Steven said, looking at Lulu as she flitted from one table to another, making last minute adjustments. She had already changed into her party finery, a poofy-skirted black cocktail gown. She looked like one of her favourite movie characters, Holly Golightly, from *Breakfast at Tiffany's*. All she needed was a long cigarette holder.

'It's important to her,' I explained. 'She doesn't have any family. Her friends are her family.' I looked at him. 'You're part of that family too now.'

'I am?' He looked a bit startled. I was pretty sure he didn't fully comprehend what I meant – at least so far as Lulu having an enormous crush on him went. I highly doubted it had occurred to Steven Howard that Lulu Collins, of all people, thought he was hot. He just didn't have a high enough opinion of himself. The two of them had had a huge struggle over his outfit for the party. He'd wanted to wear his normal clothes – T-shirt and jeans – and Lulu had wanted him to wear an ensemble she'd put together for him at Barneys. Lulu had won in the end, by pouting.

But Steven looked as uncomfortable as a jock at a Comic-Con. Not that he looked bad – exactly the opposite. I just wasn't used to seeing him resemble such a typical New Yorker, in a striped button-down shirt with dark-rinse jeans, and a fitted jacket with frayed stitching that I know had to have cost at least a thousand dollars.

I doubted Steven knew that, however.

'Nikki, people are *coming* soon,' Lulu cried when she saw me sitting on the couch, petting Cosy and talking to Steven. 'Are you going to change or what? I mean, you're not wearing that, are you?'

I was still in my school clothes, having been too exhausted to slip into something else.

'I'm changing,' I said. 'I'm changing.' I slunk off to my bedroom to find something to wear, relieved to be out of the way of Katerina and the party caterers. Cosabella looked relieved too, and hopped into her little basket to curl up and go to sleep.

In Nikki's closet was an endless supply of couture, most of it still with the price tags attached. I never had to go shopping, because stylists just gave Nikki things to wear right off the racks from the shoots I went to. I found a slinky black evening gown, made of some kind of sparkly material, that tied with a halter around the neck. It was cold outside, but inside the loft it was hot, because Lulu had a blaze going full blast in the fireplace. She'd turn the air conditioning on and open every window to combat the body heat from all the guests later . . . we'd had a few gatherings in the past. I took off my clothes and slithered into the dress, which was the kind you couldn't wear with underwear or the lines would show, then spent half an hour messing around with my make-up. I was never the type to care about make-up before, but it was very soothing if, for instance, you were upset about a guy – say, a guy like Christopher – to screw around in the mirror, trying to give yourself a smoky eye, while waiting for him to call, and telling yourself it would be a really, really bad idea to call him.

I mean, after all, Christopher prefers a dead girl. What did I want to hang out with a guy like that for anyway? Right?

I suppose I had zero chance of that relationship ever working out . . . which was just as well, I guess. No guy needed to tangle with someone as messed up as me. Christopher was better off without me. Maybe I should just step aside and let McKayla Donofrio have him, that lactose-intolerant, National Merit Scholarship-winning, Business Club-founding, tortoiseshell-headband-wearing little cow.

My eyes ended up looking more haunted than smoky. I could see I'd put on too much liner, and had to start over. By the time I came out of my bedroom, it was late, and the first guests – the early ones, Lulu had assured me, were always wannabes and losers – had already arrived. I used the opportunity to grab some food – no need to worry about getting it while it was still hot, since Katerina, in the kitchen, was supervising the caterers to make sure everything stayed exactly the temperature at which it was supposed to be served all night – so I wouldn't faint with hunger later on when it all ran out.

Meanwhile, DJ Drama had arrived and was setting up. I went over to chat with him. He seemed shy. Or maybe he was just uninterested in anything a seventeen-year-old girl stuffing her face with sushi had to say. Above our heads, while we chatted, the Cirque du Soleil performer was doing unbelievable contortions, an intense look of concentration on her face. I wondered what it would be like to be her. Better, I figured, than it was to be me. The loft kept filling up with more and more people, some of whom I recognized from the pages of Lulu's copies of *Vogue* and Frida's copies of *Us Weekly*, and some of whom I'd never seen before. DJ Drama got the music pulsing and was soon too busy to speak to me – but that was OK, because Nikki's friends had started crowding around me, telling me how great I looked and leading me towards the bar, where they'd all begun ordering some of the exotic drinks the astrologist bartenders were mixing.

I couldn't help it. I started having fun. OK, my life was a shambles. The guy I loved didn't love me back. The mother of the body my brain had been transplanted into was missing. And I'd flunked half my finals because I'd missed them.

But it was hard not to have a good time when there was so much good music, good food and happy people around.

Even Steven, I saw, wasn't having a bad time. I spotted him dancing with Lulu – if you could call what he was doing dancing. Mainly, he was standing still while Lulu cavorted all around him like a crazy wild woman.

That's when he happened to catch my eye. He saw me staring. And he looked towards the ceiling. Not like he was glancing at the Cirque du Soleil performer. But like he was saying, *Can you believe this?* But also, he was smiling. So his glance towards the ceiling was sort of saying, *I know, right? This is crazy . . . but it's kind of fun too.*

And that's when I realized maybe things weren't quite so bad. At least I had a connection with someone who thought about things the same way I did.

It was just surprising that it was Nikki's brother Steven.

Maybe, I thought to myself, Frida was right. Just a little bit. Not the part where she'd accused me of turning into Nikki Howard, but the part where she'd implied I'd found a new family. Maybe, like Lulu, I was making a new family . . . one that included my old family.

But that wasn't as surprising as what happened next. And that was that the crowd parted a little and I saw something I never in a million years expected to see.

And that was a member of my old family – my sister Frida – dancing with Brandon Stark.

I had no idea what she was doing there. Clearly she'd invited herself, since I certainly hadn't given her the OK to be there.

Worse, she was wearing a tiny dress – no bigger than two handkerchiefs sewn together (I might be exaggerating, but not really) – and gyrating her hips like she thought she was Miley Cyrus or someone. That was not cool. It was so not cool, that I was stalking over to give her a piece of my mind when I heard a familiar voice say, 'Nikki,' and I turned round.

There wasn't a person in the world who could have

distracted me at that moment from wanting to kill my sister. Not a single person. Except the second-to-last person I'd expected to see at that party, after my little sister:

Christopher.

What was *he* doing there? I had never invited him. How could I, now that he'd gone to the dark side?

And I had already given him everything he had asked for. What more could he possibly want from me?

Then I glanced into his face, and my shock gave way to concern . . . Christopher looked white as a sheet. What was the matter?

Then it hit me: Oh God. Felix had been arrested. I knew it. Just knew it. They'd overheard us in Christopher's apartment. Of course they had. I hadn't had the audio jammer then.

And they'd be coming for Christopher next. He was on the run. And he'd come to me for help.

And in that minute I knew – as much as I'd told myself I didn't care about Christopher any more, as much as I told myself McKayla Donofrio could have him – I'd been lying to myself. I loved him. I always would. I'd do whatever I had to do to hide him from the cops. Even if he never, ever gave me the time of day.

Because that's what you did for people you loved. Even people who didn't love you back.

'Can I talk to you for a minute?' Christopher asked me. He had to raise his voice almost to a shout to be heard above the pounding music.

'What's going on?' I asked him, fear clutching my

throat. It was a different kind of fear than I'd felt for Frida when I'd seen her in her handkerchief dress, dancing with Brandon. That had been more like annoyance, really. I knew she couldn't really get into trouble when Lauren Conrad was dancing in front of a camera crew right beside her. 'Is—'

Christopher seemed to have read my thoughts. He shook his head.

'Everything's fine,' he said. 'Well, I mean, relatively. I'm probably going to flunk out of school. But other than that. And I'm sorry to crash your party like this. I just really need to talk to you. Look, can we go somewhere a little quieter? Where's your room?'

'It's over there,' I said, pointing.

'Good.' Christopher reached out and wrapped his hand around my wrist. The next thing I knew, he was pulling me through the crowded loft towards the door to my room. He didn't seem to care how many people he bumped into along the way – caterers serving drinks, models from the Stark Angel fashion show whose numbers Brandon had evidently gotten and summoned to come along, fashionistas, Karl the doorman, improbably dancing with Katerina, both of them having had too much to drink. He evidently just wanted to get where it was quieter, and get there as soon as he possibly could.

And when we were in my empty bedroom, he dropped my hand and turned to face me. He didn't even bother turning on a light, just settled for the glow from the city that shone in from the floor-to-ceiling windows.

234

I stood there looking at him, a little out of breath from how quickly he'd pulled me in there. It was a lot quieter in my room. The music was still thumping unbelievably loudly outside, but at least you could hear yourself think. The building, having once been a police precinct, had decent enough soundproofing from room to room. I guess the old-time cop higher-ups hadn't wanted to be able to hear the prisoners scream as they were being tortured back in their prison cells.

'So what's so important,' I asked him, 'that you couldn't tell me out there?'

And the next thing I knew, without uttering a single word, he was reaching out, cupping both my cheeks with his hands, and tilting my face until it was just inches from his.

And then he was kissing me.

Christopher Maloney was kissing me.

It wasn't a possessive kiss or a greedy kiss. He didn't smash his lips up against mine the way some guys – OK, Brandon – did when they got a chance to kiss Nikki Howard, like they wanted to own her or drive themselves up against her or whatever.

It was a sweet kiss. It was almost . . . well, if I didn't know better, I'd have said it was a loving kiss.

But Christopher didn't love Nikki Howard. Christopher loved Em Watts.

Still, I felt his kiss from my lips all the way down to my painfully throbbing – in my too-tight Jimmy Choo shoes – toes. My lips were tingling as if they'd been stung by a thousand tiny bees. Or been slathered in a ton of Lip Venom.

My God, was all I could think. Christopher was kissing me. Christopher Maloney was kissing me.

And the thing was, even though people always say dreams never stand up to the reality, this totally did. Christopher kissing me felt exactly as I'd always imagined it would – as warm and as right and as electric as I'd dreamed – when I'd been idiotic enough to dream of Christopher Maloney kissing me, before the accident, before I'd given up all my dreams. Because after the accident, of course, there'd been no point in dreaming . . . none of those dreams had a chance of ever coming true.

But now . . . now. The dream I'd fantasized about most often as I'd sat in Public Speaking was coming true right in front of me. Not only was Christopher kissing me, but – because my legs appeared to have given out from the shock of it all – he was lifting me up . . . no, really, he had scooped an arm up under my collapsing knees and was *lifting me up* – and carrying me towards the bed.

Wait – was this really happening?

Except that it had to be. Because I could feel the metal rivets from his leather jacket biting into my skin through the thin material of my dress. Surely I couldn't be dreaming *that*.

And I could feel the soft poofiness of my down comforter behind my back as he laid me down gently on top of it.

And then I could feel the hardness of his body as he, in

turn, lay down on top of me. Surely all these things had to be happening. I couldn't be imagining them, or the steady *thump-thump-thump* of the music from the next room, which seemed to be going exactly in time with the rapid *thump-thump-thump* of my heart . . .

Or the way his lips, so close to mine, murmured the word 'Em' before he kissed me again, this kiss so long and so hungry that I really couldn't have described it as sweet. Not this time. Not when every inch of skin in my body was so tingly and aware of every place it was in contact with his . . . not when suddenly I realized he was lying on top of me, with one leg between mine.

Not when all that was separating us was a few scraps of material and some leather.

And that was when it hit me, the word he'd said, that single syllable finally trickling down through my kiss-addled brain.

'*What* did you call me?' I asked, wrenching my lips away from his.

'I know,' he said. Since I'd pulled my head away, he couldn't reach my mouth. So he settled for kissing my neck. Needless to say, this was hugely distracting. It also felt really, really good. Better, even, than having my neck massaged.

His voice, when he spoke again, was a deep-throated growl, it was so rough with emotion. 'I know it's you, Em.'

'You *what*?' I was positive I was in some kind of dream now, and that I was going to wake up any minute, like I always did. Maybe this time I'd be at the bottom of the ocean in St John. Maybe I'd never really left there after all, and everything that had happened after that was just one long, McKayla Donofrio-filled nightmare.

'Your file,' Christopher murmured against my neck. 'I read it. The Stark Institute for Neurology and Neurosurgery didn't do its due diligence when selecting an offshore IT consultancy.'

OK. *That* didn't sound like part of a dream . . . or something I'd imagine.

'What?' I said intelligently.

'Stark cut corners,' Christopher said. His lips were still on my throat. 'Not a wise move when it comes to your network.'

Wait a minute . . .

'I'm surprised no one's found out about those brain transplants they've been doing before now.' Christopher's voice was still a low, gravelly rasp. 'It's really just a matter of time before the press discovers what they've been up to.'

Wait. Christopher knew? He *knew*?

'It's not . . . I don't know what you're talking about,' I said. Even as I was saying it, I thought, confusedly, *No, wait . . . the acoustic noise generator. Stark can't overhear me any more. I can tell him. I can tell him the truth now.*

But old habits die hard.

'Em.' Christopher's lips travelled up my neck to my mouth again. 'It's all right. I know. I know you couldn't tell me. I know you tried. But I'm here now. Everything's going to be all right. You know I always loved you.'

It was fantastic, what his mouth was doing to me. The things he was saying were even more amazing. It was everything I had ever wanted. It was all just incredible.

'You always loved me?' I echoed.

'Of course I did.' Christopher looked down at me. His expression, which moments before had been supremely confident, now seemed confused. 'You know that. I mean, you saw what a mess I was after your funeral. Em, when you died . . . it nearly tore me apart. Now that I've found out you are alive, I can't even describe to you—'

I didn't know why I couldn't just lie there and enjoy what was happening to me. I didn't know why I couldn't just accept what he was saying and forget that he'd never said he loved me back when I had that snaggle tooth and didn't look like the goddess that I do now. I mean, I was still the person on the inside then that I am now. So what did it matter?

Except . . .

It mattered.

I pushed him away from me. He moved, seemingly dazed by what I was doing, then watched as I wriggled out from beneath him, rolled off the bed – careful not to step on Cosabella, who'd come trotting over to see what was going on – then went to one of the windows and wedged it open, letting in the sound of the traffic below, as well as a blast of fresh winter air.

I knew there was no danger of us being overheard by Stark. Not any more. I just needed some air to help me think.

'So if you loved me so much,' I turned around to demand, *why didn't you ever try to kiss me when I was in my old body?*'

'Oh my God,' Christopher said in a different voice, more like his normal one, no longer deep and gravelly, blinking at me from the bed. Even he couldn't believe what was happening. 'Are you seriously going there? *Now?*'

'Yeah,' I said, 'I am. I mean, you never even noticed I existed until I died. Except as someone to play *Journeyquest* with. You never noticed me as a *girl*. I don't think it's unreasonable that I ask for some kind of explanation for that. And just what do you mean *Everything's going to be all right?* How is everything going to be all right? You're going to sweep in and take care of everything because you're some big man and I'm just a delicate little girl and I can't handle the situation? I can assure you, Christopher, I'm handling the situation.'

'Oh yeah,' Christopher said, sitting up. 'First you get your head cracked open with a plasma-screen TV. Then you get your brain transplanted into a supermodel's body. And now you're working for an evil corporation. You're doing a great job so far, Em.'

As great as it felt to hear him calling me Em again — as transporting an experience as that was — I wanted to smack him across the head for his sarcasm.

'Oh,' I said, 'you're one to talk, with your stupid idea to hack into Stark Enterprises. Like that's going to work.'

'As a matter of fact, it *is* working. I found out the truth about you, didn't I? And at least I had an idea,' Christopher said. 'What's your plan? Throw a party and invite Lauren Conrad and DJ Drama?'

I crossed back over to the bed until I was standing in front of him. 'The party wasn't my idea. And lately I've been slightly preoccupied trying to find Nikki Howard's missing mom.'

'Did it ever occur to you,' Christopher asked, ignoring me, 'that those two things might be connected?'

I threw him a startled look.

'What are you talking about?'

'Nikki's mom disappearing,' Christopher said, 'and what happened to you.'

I stared at him. This was something I too had considered. But I'd never thought anyone but me would take the notion seriously. Well, me and Steven.

'I'm sorry,' I said. 'But I think you had one too many Lychee-tinis.'

'I didn't have any,' Christopher said, looking devious, the way he used to when we were younger and we'd try to pool our money and buy games marked 'adult only' from Kim's Video down on St Mark's Place. 'Maybe Nikki's mom found out something she wasn't supposed to know. And have you ever considered the fact that maybe Nikki did too?'

'Nikki?' I tilted my head to look at him in the dim half-light that was streaming in through the massive windows. 'You think Nikki – what are you *talking* about, Christopher?'

'I'm saying there are no accidents, Em.' His blue eyes searched my face intently. 'Does anyone really know what happened to Nikki that day? She went down and never got back up again. Stark says it was an aneurysm . . . but how do we know? Felix and I checked everywhere, but we couldn't find a medical file on her . . . only the one for you.'

I opened my mouth. It seemed so strange to be having this conversation in my room with Christopher, of all people. I'd missed him so much, and now here he was, and finally, finally, what I'd never thought could happen was happening . . .

And we were having a fight.

'Of course we don't know the truth about what happened to Nikki that day,' Christopher went on before I had a chance to speak. 'Maybe we never will. We have to accept Stark's word for it.'

I shook my head. 'What are you saying? That she didn't have an aneurysm? Christopher, that's insane.'

Except that Steven had said the exact same thing.

Christopher shrugged. 'There are no accidents. Nikki was the Face of Stark. They invested millions in her. She was too important for them to lose. As you know only too well. Especially with them distributing this massive roll-out of PCs with this new software, and the new version of *Journeyquest*. But they didn't hire her for her brains, did they?'

I bristled. 'Modelling isn't as easy as everyone thinks,' I snapped. 'It's really hard work. You try pretending you're comfortable in a pair of skintight leather trousers under a bunch of hot lights for hours on end—'

'Look, Stark Enterprises . . . that whole organization is out of control . . .' Christopher's gaze on me was unsympathetic. I guess anyone's would be. Getting paid thousands of dollars to stand in a pair of leather trousers under some hot lights for a few hours wasn't *that* big a sacrifice. You do tend to lose your perspective pretty quickly after a while. '. . . unsecured wireless systems, the whole network totally misconfigured. It just makes you wonder.'

I thought about the computer I'd found in Nikki's bedroom when I'd first arrived. It had been infected with spyware. So, when I'd checked it, had Lulu's. I hadn't unpacked the new PC that Robert Stark had just given me from its box yet, but who knew what might be wrong with it.

'You don't think . . .' I could barely breathe.

'I don't know what to think,' Christopher said. 'Except that there's something going on. Something they don't want anyone to know. Something I think Nikki – and now maybe her mom – found out about. And Stark tried to shut both of them up. And you were in the wrong place at the wrong time.'

'Wait a minute.' I felt cold, and not just because the wind was blowing in from the open window. 'You think Stark *killed* Nikki? Because she knew something she wasn't supposed to?'

'They didn't kill her, did they?' Christopher smiled at me grimly. 'Because she's standing right in front of me.'

I shivered. 'You know what I mean.'

'I know exactly what you mean,' he said. 'And in answer to your question, I think it's possible . . . even likely, that they had her brain conveniently removed.'

'My God,' I breathed.

It was so weird to be talking to Christopher again. Not that I hadn't talked to him lately. I had, obviously. But he hadn't known it was me. Now he did . . . he'd even touched me, knowing it was me. And he wanted to touch me again, I could tell, from the way his hand kept lifting and then at the last minute he'd sweep his fingers through his hair or mess with the comforter on my bed instead.

I knew how he felt. But I wasn't going to go rushing into anything. I had too many questions . . . the first of which he still hadn't answered.

'But you think Nikki's mom is alive,' I said. 'That's what Felix told Steven.'

'There's no reason to think she's dead,' Christopher said.

'So where is she?' I asked.

'Out there,' he said, nodding towards the bright city lights shining beyond my open window. 'No one can just disappear forever. It's really hard. Even when they give people in witness protection programmes new identities, they feel compelled to reach out to friends they knew before, at the risk of their own lives. It's force of habit. Everyone messes up eventually. You did it, with the dinosaur stickers. I was just too stupid to get it.'

I felt myself blushing. I still couldn't believe I'd done that.

And now his words triggered a memory deep in the back of my brain. *It's force of habit. Everyone messes up eventually.*

Only what? What was I thinking of?

'The thing is,' Christopher said, reaching out to take my hand. 'You're right. I was a jerk before. A jerk not to see what a great thing we had. I guess I just didn't know it until you were gone. And then . . . seriously, Em, part of me died too. All I could think about after that was getting revenge on Stark—'

'But now that you know the truth,' I said, pulling my hand gently from his, 'you see that you can't. You can't do anything to them, Christopher. Because they've got my family in a stranglehold. And if what happened gets made public, Stark will take it out on my parents.'

'We'll figure it out,' Christopher said. He stood up and put both hands on my bare shoulders. 'I told you. I'll take care of everything.'

I wanted so badly to believe him. It would have been bliss to have allowed myself to relax and let him do just that. As he pulled me towards him and laid the gentlest kiss on my forehead, I inhaled the scent of his leather jacket, felt the heat radiating from his strong body. It felt so nice, just for that minute or two, to have his arms around me and to feel his heart beating against mine. For the first time in what seemed like the longest time, I knew I was protected and warm and not – well, *alone*.

Then a cold wind swept in from the open window, sending shivers up and down my spine.

And then a second later, the door to my room burst open, and a very male, very surprised voice said, 'Nikki?'

And I turned my head and saw Brandon standing there, staring at us in the half-light.

Twenty

'Brandon,' I cried, leaping away from Christopher as if his embrace had scorched me.

Don't ask me what instinct made me do this. But something told me being seen in the arms of another man would not sit well with Nikki's ex.

I needn't have worried, however. Brandon was wasted. He stood, wavering a little, in the doorway, squinting into my darkened room as if he couldn't see very well. I was more glad than ever that Christopher and I hadn't turned on the lights.

'Uh,' Brandon said, 'Nikki? Yeah, you better come . . .'

'Why?' I asked, adjusting my halter top where I thought it might have slipped a little.

'Some girl said to get you.' Brandon was squinting at Christopher now, trying to see if he recognized him in the half-light from the window. Which, since Christopher had never graced the pages of TMZ.com, Brandon surely didn't. 'Some girl named Frida? She's sick or something.'

I was out of the room like a shot.

'Where?' I demanded in a tight voice. 'Where is she?'

But Brandon just shrugged. He was so out of it, he had no idea where he was.

Out in the main part of the loft, the party was in full tilt – it was everything Lulu could ever have hoped for.

There were so many gyrating bodies dancing – and sweating – in time to the music you could hardly see from one end of the room to the other. Overhead, the girl on the trapeze had ditched her long red scarf. The music was so loud it seemed to pulse through my chest. I wondered if the other tenants in the building would call the cops – then I realized Lulu had foreseen this problem by inviting all the other tenants . . . I could have sworn I saw the guy who lived on the floor below us dancing with someone who looked a lot like Perez Hilton. Lulu, obviously, was a genius. It wouldn't surprise me if the cops themselves turned out to be here somewhere, dancing.

But I couldn't find Frida. Looking for her in that packed room of sweaty bodies was a nightmare. I had to shove past Moschino-clad guest after Moschino-clad guest, murmuring, 'Excuse me,' again and again. And of course half of them – the male half – one after another, would reach out to grab my arm, crying, 'Nikki! Stay and dance! Come on, don't be a drag!'

'I can't,' I'd say regretfully. 'I'm looking for someone.'

'Me, I hope,' some of the guys would leer.

'Oh, ha ha,' I'd say. 'Sorry. But I'll be back in a minute.'

'You better!'

It wasn't pretty.

The truth was, I felt guilty. I never should have let Frida out of my sight in the first place. If it had been anyone but Christopher, I never would have. Of course, I'd explicitly forbidden Frida from attending this party. Then again . . . I should have known she'd show up anyway. Frida'd always done precisely what I – or Mom and Dad – had asked her not to. Didn't all little sisters, intent on proving they were just as 'good' as their big sisters? It was no surprise she was in trouble somewhere.

And when I found her, I knew what her excuse was going to be too: 'But you're here, Em. Why can't I be? Just because you're older . . . it's not fair!'

I stumbled across Lulu before I found Frida. Lulu was dancing with Steven, and she looked as if she was having the time of her life. Steven didn't look as if he was having a half-bad time either. But Lulu's face was the one that was transported with joy. It brightened even more when she saw me, her dark eyes, rimmed with mascara that had gotten smudgy with perspiration, widening to their limits as she let go of Steven and hurried over to grasp my arm, standing up on tiptoes to whisper in my ear, 'Oh, Nikki! Can you believe it? Everyone showed up! Everyone! This is the best party ever! And can you believe it? Steven . . . your brother? He's a Libra!'

I blinked down at her. 'That's . . . that's amazing,' I said.

'No, you don't understand,' she said, shaking me a little. 'My astrologer. She said I'm supposed to end up with a *Libra!*'

'Oh,' I said, 'that's great. Have you seen Frida?'

Lulu's smile immediately vanished. 'Frida's here? I thought you told her she couldn't come.' Her gaze flicked to someone behind me. 'Oh, hi, Christopher.'

I turned my head. He'd followed me, of course. All

those guys I'd thought I'd managed to put off with my bold assertiveness had actually been put off by a supervillain's menacing glare. Great.

'Hey,' he said. Then he pointed. 'Isn't that her over there, with that Gabriel Luna guy?'

I turned my head and saw Frida — or someone who looked like Frida, in her handkerchief dress — leaning perilously close to the open windows, with Gabriel Luna's arms around her shoulders. What was he *doing*? Knowing the depths of Frida's crush on him, whatever it was, I instantly assumed it was something inappropriate.

'Hold on,' I said, and stalked towards the two of them, ready to shove Gabriel out of the window, if necessary, that's how huge my murderous rage towards him for taking advantage of my little sister was.

But when I got closer, I saw what was actually happening. Frida was retching out of the window, which was tilted open, into the flower box — mercifully empty this time of year — and Gabriel was holding on to her as convulsive spasms clutched her body. He looked up as I approached and said, raising his voice to be heard above the pounding music, 'She's a bit young to handle an open bar, I think.'

Frida reached up with a trembling fist to wipe her mouth. I saw a caterer walking by with tray of canapés, and so I grabbed a handful of napkins from it and passed her those instead. Frida accepted them gratefully.

'He said it was fruit punch,' she said weakly as she sat back on her heels and looked up at us with big, mournful eyes.

'Who said it was fruit punch?' I asked her, picking up some of the extra napkins from the pile and dabbing at her face where she'd missed.

'He did.' She pointed an indignant finger at a group of people dancing nearby. 'Justin Bay.'

I turned my head and looked where she was pointing. Sure enough, Justin Bay, star of the movie version of *Journeyquest* (which sucked), stood nearby, swivelling his hips against some slinky looking model types (not his girlfriend Veronica), all of whom were wearing even less clothing than Frida, and even higher heels.

Lulu, who'd walked up behind me with with Steven, followed the direction of my gaze and gasped.

'Who invited *him*?' she demanded, looking furious.

'Half the people here,' Steven said, 'have invitations they printed off the Internet, according to the bouncers at the door. They did their best to screen, but after a while it was too hard to tell the fakes from the real invites. There's paparazzi all up and down the street, as well,' Steven went on. 'Your party may go down in the history books . . . not the least for violating every fire code in Manhattan.'

'It wasn't really fruit punch,' Frida said sadly. 'Was it?'

I couldn't look away from Justin. There was just something about him – not the skintight black silk shirt he was wearing, or the multiple gold chains – that made it impossible for me to think about anything else.

No one can just disappear forever . . . Even when they give people in witness protection programmes new identities, they feel compelled to reach out to friends they knew before, at the risk of their own lives. It's force of habit. Everyone messes up eventually. You did it, with the dinosaur stickers. I was just too stupid to get it.

Oh my God. Of *course.*

It didn't seem possible. It was ridiculous. It was beyond insane.

But then . . . didn't that apply to everything that had happened to me so far?

I elbowed my way to where Justin was dancing and laid a hand on his arm. He opened his eyes to snake-like half slits and then slowed down his gyrating when he recognized me.

'Oh,' he said, with a lazy smile. 'Hey, there, Nik.'

'Justin,' I said without smiling. 'I need to see your cellphone.'

'Now that's a new one.' He looked over his shoulder at the models he was semi-humping and started to laugh. They were all as wasted as he was, and started laughing too, none of them pausing in their dancing. 'I've heard some crazy come-ons in my day, but I need to see your *cellphone* has to take the cake.'

In a flash, Christopher was at my left shoulder. 'Show it to her.'

'Now.' And Gabriel was at my right.

Justin, realizing something serious might be going on, finally stopped dancing. His eyes widened to normal size.

'Whoa,' he said. 'What's with the third degree? I'm just dancing.'

'You'll be lying in a pool of your own blood if you don't hand your cellphone over to my sister,' Steven advised him from behind me.

Neither Christopher nor Gabriel nor Steven could have had any idea why I was so anxious to see Justin Bay's cellphone. But the fact that they were willing to wipe the floor with him merely on my say-so was warming my heart. It really was.

'Fine.' Justin reached into a pocket of his tight striped suit trousers and pulled out a silver flip phone, which he tossed in my direction. 'I don't know what you want it for anyway. You email me enough as it is.'

I nodded, feeling triumphant. 'That's what I thought,' I said, scrolling through Justin's messages.

'You still email him?' Lulu stared at me. 'Oh my God, I thought you gave up on that loser, like, months ago.'

'Hardly,' Justin said with a sneer. 'She's still begging for it. Bad.'

Christopher stepped forward and, in a smooth motion, wrapped Justin in a headlock. It was a startling development that caused Frida's jaw to drop. I have to admit, I was shocked myself. Christopher had never been the most physical of guys back in his pre-supervillain days.

But now I suppose he had the forces of evil propelling him.

'Jesus,' Justin croaked. The models he'd been dancing with, so skinny they looked like pieces of Slim Jim, pranced backwards a little, eager to get out of the danger-zone, in case there was bloodshed. They didn't want their D&G outfits messed up. 'Let go of me, man! Do you know who my father is?'

'Apologize,' Christopher said. He'd evidently squeezed, since Justin began making choking noises.

'Sorry,' Justin said, gagging. 'Don't bruise the face, man. I'm starting an Ang Lee film after the New Year.'

I scrolled until I found a message with NikkiH as the sender, then read the extremely flowery email I found there.

It didn't make any sense.

But then, neither had the dinosaur stickers.

'Can Felix trace an email?' I asked Christopher.

'Of course,' Christopher said.

'Tell me where to send this so he can figure out where it came from.'

Christopher did. I pressed *forward*, and sent the message from 'Nikki' to Felix, with a note asking him to trace its origin.

'Oh,' I said, looking up when I was done. 'You can let go of him now.'

Christopher released Justin, who staggered around a bit, holding on to his neck.

'Christ,' he said. 'Have you lost your mind? What was *that* all about?'

'I don't know.' Gabriel seemed quite calm. 'But this is for lying to the little girl about the punch.'

And he slammed his fist into Justin's stomach – really hard, judging by the way Justin doubled over, then

254

collapsed on to the floor, gasping like a goldfish that had leaped from its bowl.

Steven, standing beside Lulu, glanced from Justin to Gabriel to Christopher and then back again. Then he said, with a grin, 'You know, I had my doubts at first. But this is turning out to be a really great party.'

'I don't understand any of this,' Frida said, looking upset as she stared down at Justin, who was beginning to recover himself – with the help of the models who'd come tottering over to his rescue. 'What's going on? Why did you need to look at Justin Bay's cellphone? What is Christopher even doing here?'

'That's a very good question for you,' I said, eyeing her severely. 'And what have you got on? Where did you get a dress like that? If it can even be called a dress.'

'I came to support Lulu,' Frida said, pouting. 'I know how much this party means to her. I didn't want to let her down—'

Lulu looked touched. 'Aw,' she said, 'isn't that sweet? Really, Nikki, you can't be mad at her for that.'

'Yeah, I can,' I said. 'I told her she wasn't invited, and you were there when I did it, remember, Lulu? I don't think there's anything sweet about it.'

'I think you're being a bit harsh,' Gabriel said. To my utter astonishment, he plucked off his jacket – an ultra-expensive one with frayed edges, just like Steven's – and put it over Frida's bare shoulders, since she was shivering a little from the breeze that was seeping in through the open window she was still standing in front of. 'She's learned her lesson, don't you think?'

'Yeah,' Frida said, clutching the collar of the jacket closed and gazing up at Gabriel with, literally, what looked like stars in her eyes. But then I realized they were reflections of the special party halogens Lulu had installed. 'I've learned my lesson.'

Lulu elbowed me, giggling, but I didn't see what was so funny really. My little sister was crushing on Gabriel Luna – something she'd been doing for months now – and it was inappropriate. He was too old for her, and he was only encouraging her with this behaviour, knocking out idiots like Justin Bay.

And OK, yeah, that had been pretty badass. But hello. That didn't mean Gabriel could just go around giving his coat to my sister. My *little* sister, who wasn't even supposed to be here, let alone dating at her age.

'This is probably Felix,' Christopher said, and reached into the pocket of his leather jacket for his cellphone, which had just let off Dragon Battle Cry. When he glanced at the screen, he nodded and picked up. 'What have you got?' he asked.

He nodded a few more times. Then he looked at me. His blue-eyed gaze was like a laser pointer, it was so sharp. I could feel it all up and down my spine.

And not in a good way.

I couldn't read the thoughts behind the gaze. But I sensed trouble.

Christopher pressed End and put away the phone. Then,

that impenetrable blue-eyed gaze still on me, he asked, 'Can I have a word with you – in private?'

But Steven put his foot down.

'No,' he said. He didn't say it angrily. He said it quite calmly as a matter of fact.

Though that 'No' came out as forcefully as a king's.

'Anything you have to say to her involving all this, you can say to me,' Steven said. 'I'm her brother, remember?'

He wasn't really my brother – which we all knew (well, maybe not Gabriel).

And yet, in those few seconds, it seemed that he truly was my brother. Christopher certainly didn't seem to question it.

'Right,' he said to Steven. 'Well, here's what Felix found out. He traced the email to a computer with an IP address in Westchester.'

I gaped at him. 'Westchester? That's just, like, twenty miles from here.'

'Right. And it belongs to a doctor. His name is Jonathan Fong.'

Lulu made a face. 'Why would a doctor be sending emails to Justin Bay, pretending to be Nikki Howard? What kind of sick perv is he, anyway?'

'That's not the real question,' Christopher said. 'The real question is, who does Doctor Jonathan Fong work for?'

I stared at him. Even though the party was still in full swing behind us, and it was boiling hot in the apartment, I felt cold as ice all of a sudden.

'No,' was all I said.

Twenty-one

In the end, five of us – not counting Cosabella – ended up going to Westchester. And one of us was unconscious.

It wasn't nice or fair to use Brandon Stark that way. But we needed his limo. How else were we going to get to Dr Fong's house? No taxi would take us some place so far away, and the trains had stopped running until morning. Christopher said his Aunt Jackie would probably let us borrow her minivan, but that meant schlepping all the way out to Brooklyn to pick it up first, not to mention explaining why we needed it.

Whereas there was Brandon, passed out on my couch from too many Lychee-tinis.

At least we took him with us. Even if we did tell Tom, his driver, to run inside to get some Pepto for him at the deli – then, while he was gone, Steven slipped behind the wheel and drove off with us all inside.

The hard part to explain – at least to Gabriel – was why he couldn't come along. He had no idea where we were going (except to Westchester), or why. But he wanted to come with us. When I thanked him for his help with Frida and said, 'Well, we have to go on an important errand now. I guess we'll see you later,' he'd said, 'That's nice. I'll help you,' and held all doors as Christopher and Steven dragged a semi-conscious Brandon through them.

And because he wouldn't leave, of course neither would Frida. Finally I took him by the arm and whispered, 'Please... will you do me a huge favour and take her home? She's too young to be out this late, and I'm afraid something will happen to her if I try to send her home alone. You saw what happened at the party. Will you see that she gets home to her parents safely? It's only a few blocks away.'

Gabriel agreed – but only when I said we'd wait for him. And of course when Frida found out she'd be riding – alone – in a cab with Gabriel Luna, she was more than willing to go with him. She whispered to me as we hugged goodbye, 'I'm sorry I said such bitchy things to you the other day. I didn't mean any of them. You're an awesome big sister actually. And thanks for these.' She pointed to her earlobes, into which, I saw, she'd slipped the diamond studs I'd gotten for her.

'You were supposed to wait to open those on Christmas morning,' I said, feeling dismayed. 'Now what will you have to look forward to?'

'Seeing you,' she said, and kissed me goodbye, then took Gabriel's arm and disappeared with him down Centre Street.

But of course we had no intention of waiting for Gabriel to come back. Steven pulled out and started towards the highway at once, anxious to get to Dr Fong's as soon as possible. Not that he – or any of us – had any idea what to expect when we got there. Out of all of them, I think I was the only one who kept thinking *Dinosaur stickers*. Those emails still didn't make sense . . .

But neither had those dinosaur stickers I'd given to Christopher – at least, not to him at the time. Seen out of context, they had to have been so random, like those emails Justin kept getting, allegedly from me.

Christopher's words kept reverberating through my head, *'No one can just disappear forever . . . they feel compelled to reach out to friends they knew before . . . It's force of habit. Everyone messes up eventually.'*

But who was messing up with those text messages? Maybe it was only a mean-spirited prank (except . . . how could some random kid have gotten Justin Bay's private number?). Maybe it was nothing. Maybe this whole thing was just a wild goose chase.

But maybe it wasn't.

The problem was, once we left Manhattan and got to Westchester, Christopher wouldn't let Steven use the limo's GPS to find the address we were looking for.

'Are you kidding?' he said. 'Stark will point every satellite they've got right at us. The cops'll pull us over in five seconds.'

Lulu looked excited. 'Are we actually doing something *against the law*?' she asked.

Christopher gave her a sarcastic look. 'We just stole a limo,' he said.

'Well,' I said. 'Technically, we only borrowed it.' I glanced at the sleeping Brandon, stretched out on the side seat, dozing like an angel in a tux. He was wearing a red velvet Santa hat. 'The owner's still inside, right?'

'Here,' Christopher said, pulling up a map on his iPhone,

and showing the screen to Steven. 'You've got another two miles to go on his road.'

'Thanks,' Steven said. The winding countryish road we were on, dotted with large mansiony house after large mansiony house, seemed virtually deserted this time of night. Snow came down in light fluffy flakes, not enough to stick yet, but enough to be beautiful. I was still glad I'd thought to kick off my Jimmy Choo heels and replace them with a pair of Marc Jacobs boots. Steven had the heat up in the limo, but even so, my leather jacket didn't seem like it would provide much warmth when I got out of the car. Maybe that's because I still had on my halter-top evening gown. At least I had Cosabella draped across my thighs for warmth.

'I still don't get where we're going,' Lulu said from where she sat, next to Steven. Lulu was wearing Tom's chauffeur cap, which he'd left in the car. It went very rakishly with her bleached-blonde pageboy. 'But I guess that's the adventure of it! It's like a scavenger hunt! Isn't Nikki fantastic? She always knows the best way to make a party fun!'

I couldn't tell if Lulu was just trying to make herself feel better, or if she really didn't understand that something serious was going on. She still seemed to be on cloud nine about her discovery that she and Steven were astrologically compatible, according to her astrologist.

And then Christopher said, 'It should be the next driveway.'

And Steven turned down a long driveway walled on

either side by low round stones piled one on top of the other, with a sloping yard and nice trees, bare-branched this time of year. Because the snow clouds were hanging so low, the lights from the city reflected up against them, so it wasn't hard to see the house, even though it was nighttime. It was an old-fashioned red-brick Colonial, with black shutters and a single electric imitation candle in each window.

I remembered reading somewhere that women put those candles in their windows during war time, to guide loved ones home. Now people had started doing it during the holiday season, as well. Who was Dr Fong guiding home? I wondered.

Steven pulled all the way down the driveway until it made a circular loop to the front door. Then he stopped the car and turned off the engine.

'Well,' Lulu asked, turning around to peer at us from the front seat, the chauffeur's cap jauntily askew. 'What now?'

I looked up at the house through the tinted windows of the limo. It wasn't an intimidatingly huge mansion like some of the other houses we'd driven past, but it wasn't small either. It looked almost aggressively normal – the kind of house you'd drive by and never think twice about, never wonder who lived there, never think to yourself, Gee, that's the kind of house I'd like to have some day. It was just . . . *there*.

It was silent in the car, except for Brandon's gentle snoring.

I lifted Cosabella, who was still spread out across my lap, and crawled across Christopher's legs for the car door.

'What – ?' Christopher sounded alarmed. 'Wait for me.'

'And me,' Steven said, getting out.

'Me too,' Lulu said.

Soon I was leading a little parade up to Dr Fong's front door – everyone from inside the limo but Brandon, who hadn't stirred. It was incredibly cold out – so cold my nostrils felt as if they would freeze together if I inhaled too deeply. The air smelt pleasantly of woodsmoke. It was silent – absolutely still – in Dr Fong's neighbourhood, except for the sound our footsteps made as we walked up the icy pathway to his front door.

Once there, I lifted the heavy brass knocker and let it fall two or three times. The sound it made seemed so loud in the snowy stillness, I was afraid it might wake some of his neighbours.

After a minute, when there was no reaction, Lulu said, 'N-no one is home.' Her teeth were chattering from the cold. 'Let's g-go back to the car. At least it's warm there.'

I ignored her. Instead, I reached up and lifted the knocker and let it fall again.

This time, a light turned on above our heads. I heard footsteps inside the house. Then the door opened to reveal a middle-aged man in a bathrobe, peering out at us sleepily. When he saw my face, his eyes widened perceptibly.

'Hi,' I said.

Dr Fong started to shake his head. 'No,' he said. That's all. Just a single word.

But there was a world of fear in it.

And he started to close the door.

But Steven was too quick for him. He inserted his foot between the door and the jamb so it was impossible for Dr Fong to close it.

Then he said, 'We've come a long way. We just want to come inside for a little while and have a word with you.'

'No,' Dr Fong said again. He still looked terrified. 'I think you must have the wrong house. I don't know you—'

'Uh,' Christopher said, moving to stand behind Steven. 'Actually, I think you know Nikki Howard – or should I say Em Watts – pretty well. Or aren't you one of the surgeons who worked on her brain transplant at the Stark Institute for Neurology and Neurosurgery a few months ago? See, I read her medical file, and I know all about it. So, unless you want me to release that file to the press, you'd better let us in.'

Dr Fong, looking like someone was holding a knife to his throat – which, I guess in a way, we were – thought about it for a minute, then finally took a step back, and let us in. We filed into a foyer that was decorated in New England chic, dark polished wood and portraits of duck-hunting dogs. Cosabella sniffed around politely but curiously.

'This isn't a game, you know,' Dr Fong said resentfully when we were all inside and he'd shut the door behind us. 'They'll kill you if they find out you know. They've killed before. How do you think I got into this mess?'

Hearing those words coming from such a mild-looking doctor, standing in a red plaid bathrobe in the dark stillness of his old-fashioned hallway, chilled me in a way the cold outside never could have.

If it chilled me, it had an even more startling effect on Lulu, who really had no idea what she'd been getting herself into, climbing into Brandon Stark's limo back on Centre Street in Manhattan. She grew very still – and very sombre. Hearing you might be killed definitely destroyed whatever kind of party mood you might have been in. I could attest to that.

'Why don't we sit down so you can tell us about it?' Steven suggested in the same calm voice he'd used before. Apparently he was used to dealing with hysterical brain surgeons.

Dr Fong did as he asked, but it was obvious it was only because he was cornered, not because he wanted to. He padded in his slippers into the living room, a square room decorated, again, with New England sparseness, where apparently a fire had been burning earlier in the evening. It had gone out, but the smell of burning wood lingered pleasantly in the air. He turned on a single lamp on a table by the window, but only after he'd made sure to close every set of curtains in the room, glancing out each window in a paranoid manner to make sure there were no other cars on the driveway but ours.

'You're sure you weren't followed?' he demanded.

Christopher and I exchanged glances. I had actually been paying attention to this, paranoid as this made me seem.

'Yes,' I said. 'And no, we weren't.'

'You couldn't have picked a less obtrusive vehicle?' Dr Fong demanded. 'You think a stretch limo won't be noticed around here?'

'We didn't have a choice,' I said, taken aback.

Dr Fong looked around – at Lulu, still in her chauffeur cap and poofy-skirted party dress, perched on the edge of a Chippendale chair; Steven standing tense and at attention by the foyer door, as if expecting Stark to burst in at any moment; and Christopher and I standing by the dead hearth, Cosabella sitting at our feet. He looked so totally confused in his pyjamas and robe, with his black hair sticking up a little in the middle. It was clear from his expression he wasn't very impressed by what he saw.

'Is there,' I asked, because the thought had just occurred to me, 'a Mrs Fong?'

Dr Fong looked scornful. 'No,' he said. 'No, my mother doesn't live with me.'

I'd meant did he have a wife, but I guess that answered my question anyway.

'Why,' Christopher demanded, cutting straight to the chase, 'is an ex-boyfriend of Nikki Howard's getting emails from someone using a computer in this house?'

Dr Fong suddenly buried his face in his hands. Then he turned and marched over to a small secretaire, opened it, took out a cut-crystal decanter of whisky, and poured himself a glass with shaking fingers.

Then he downed the entire contents of the glass in one go. And poured himself another.

This one he carried over to the couch, on to which he

sank down next to Cosabella, who'd helped herself to the comfiest seat in the house. When he turned to face us, I was shocked to see he'd gone as white as the sails on the picture of the ship hanging on the wall above his head.

'Who else knows about this?' he asked.

'No one,' I said, glancing over at Steven. 'I mean, except everyone in this room. And the person who traced the email to here.'

'Will he tell anyone?' Doctor Fong asked, raising the glass to his lips with trembling fingers.

'No,' I said. I crossed the room to sink into an armchair across from the couch where Dr Fong was sitting. 'Dr Fong. What is going on?'

Dr Fong didn't say anything for a moment. He just stared into the amber depths of his drink. When he finally did speak, it was to ask, 'Do you know what the Hippocratic oath is?'

Lulu looked blank. Steven still looked like he wanted someone to come bursting in through the door so he could karate chop them or something.

Finally, Christopher said, 'Yeah. It's something all doctors have to swear before they can begin practising medicine.'

'First,' I said, 'do no harm.'

'That's right,' Dr Fong said. 'At the Stark Institute, that's what we tell ourselves we're doing. No harm. We're transplanting brains from horribly deformed bodies that otherwise wouldn't survive into healthy bodies belonging to brain-dead donors so that our patients have another chance at life. That's what happened to you.' He looked up at me. 'I've been working at the Stark Institute for ten years, and I've never for a moment questioned the morality of what we do there. Until the day of your accident.'

His gaze flitted around the room, looking from Steven to Christopher to me.

'What happened that day?' I asked, my voice rough. I coughed to clear it.

'I was only assisting,' Dr Fong said, his gaze looking far away. 'Doctor Holcombe was in charge of your case. Nikki Howard was far too important to be handled by anyone but him. Normally I run the teaching wing of the Institute—'

'Teaching wing?' I interrupted.

'Yes, of course,' Dr Fong said. 'The demand for transplants is so high that there's a waiting list. But it's several years long, and some patients can't – or don't want to – wait. So for a fee, surgeons from around the world can come to the Institute and we'll train them to perform the surgery themselves. We allow them to practise on donor bodies—'

'Donor *bodies*?' I was horrified. Christopher threw me an annoyed look for interrupting again, but I couldn't help it. Donor bodies?

'Oh, we have quite a lot of *them*,' Dr Fong explained. 'All sorts of individuals who've been declared legally brain dead and who've donated their bodies to science. Sadly, there's no shortage of individuals in vegetative states thanks to accidents and, quite often, drug and alcohol overdoses. What we don't have, of course, are viable

268

brains to put in them, and that's what patients like you provide—'

I held up a hand, too sickened to hear more. 'Never mind,' I said. 'Go on.'

'Well,' Dr Fong said. 'Like I was saying, obviously Doctor Holcombe and Doctor Higgins were the main surgeons on your case. But there was something . . . odd about your surgery. I was told by Doctor Holcombe that Nikki Howard had had a family history of genetic brain defects and that was what killed her.'

I saw Lulu look more confused than ever. When no one else, however, reacted to Dr Fong's reference to the fact that I was dead, when there I was, clearly alive, she didn't say anything.

'After he was done stitching you up, I did something I'd never do, under ordinary circumstances,' Dr Fong went on. 'I went to examine the brain he'd removed. I've always been interested in brain anomalies, and I wanted to see what Nikki Howard's was.'

Somewhere upstairs, I heard a door open and close, and then some thumping sounds. Someone was walking around above our heads. Dr Fong, however, didn't appear to notice.

'But Nikki Howard hadn't any brain anomaly. Hers was perfect. There was no defect. The aneurysm Doctor Holcombe claimed she had suffered? The whole reason for her death and this emergency transplant in the first place? It hadn't happened. She was completely healthy.'

I looked over at Christopher. He had said there were

no accidents. 'Does anyone really know what happened to Nikki that day?' he'd asked. *She went down and never got back up again. Stark says it was an aneurysm . . . but how do we know?*

And now we had our answer. It hadn't been an accident. He looked back at me, smugly satisfied that he'd been right.

'Then . . . what did they do to her,' I asked him, 'to make her pass out like that?'

'We may never know,' Dr Fong said. 'Once the surgery was over, I wasn't allowed near the body – Nikki's body – any more. I was only supposed to handle the medical waste.'

Lulu inhaled, looking horrified. 'Nikki's . . . brain?'

He threw her an appraising look, as if she'd suddenly struck him as a lot more intelligent than he'd previously given her credit for.

'That's right,' he said. 'I was the one charged with disposing of it.'

'But,' Steven said, 'you took an oath.'

'Do no harm,' I murmured.

'Why?' Steven asked. He looked as horrified as Lulu. 'Why would anyone remove a perfectly healthy brain from a girl's body?'

'I think I can tell you why,' Christopher said.

But at that moment there was thumping from the staircase – a familiar skittering sound that caused Cosabella to perk up her ears alertly.

And the next thing I knew, she'd begun barking . . . and

those barks were met by answering yips as two miniature poodles exactly like her – only one was black, the other cocoa-coloured – came bursting into the room. They rushed towards Cosy, who leaped down from the chair and tore over to them, her tail whipping back and forth excitedly, as she greeted what appeared to be two long-lost friends.

'Harry! Winston!' An older woman in a terry-cloth robe hurried into the room after the dogs, clapping her hands. 'Down! Down!'

Even though her hair was plastered to her head from sleep, and she didn't have any make-up on, I recognized her. Before Steven broke his stance by the doorway and cried in astonishment, 'Mom?' I knew who she was.

Dee Dee Howard. Nikki Howard's mom was living in Dr Fong's house.

The thing was, I'd sort of known it. From the moment I'd put two and two together and I'd realized what those email messages Veronica had told me about really meant. Why else would she have left behind her business and everything else she knew, if it hadn't been to be with something – or someone – she loved a billion times more?

'Steven!' she cried when she saw him. She reached out to him joyously. He was so much bigger than she was that he had to hunch down to let her take him into her arms. His expression was one of incredulity. 'I didn't know you were here!'

He seemed dazed. 'Mom,' he said as she hugged him.

'I've been looking for you. Everyone's been worried sick – Leanne, Mary Beth. Didn't you see the recent news reports on TV?

'Oh,' Mrs Howard said. 'I'm so sorry, honey. Yes, we saw those. But we assumed it was Stark, trying to trick me. I never thought it was really *you*.' She glanced over at me. Then froze. 'Oh. Oh my,' she said as her eyes filled with tears. Her gaze swept over me with what appeared to be a mix of horror and fascination. 'I . . . I don't know what to say. You . . . you look just like . . .'

She couldn't go on. She didn't have to. I knew who she thought I looked just like.

The thing was, I knew I didn't just look like that person. I *was* that person. I mean, in a way.

Christopher came over to me then and laid a hand on my shoulder. It was a supportive gesture and I couldn't have been more grateful for it.

'This must be very hard for you,' Christopher said gently to Mrs Howard.

'It's . . .' Steven's mother shook her head. Her Southern accent was much more pronounced than her son's. But it was pleasant, like her slightly faded good looks. 'I'm sorry. I don't mean to stare. You just look so much like her.'

Because I *am* her, I wanted to say. Or at least, I'm inhabiting her body.

'It's all right,' I said instead. At my feet, Cosabella was still having a joyous reunion with her cousins – or brothers, for all I knew – Harry and Winston, happily cavorting on

Dr Fong's rug. I decided to change the subject. 'So you've been here the whole time?'

'Oh, yes,' Mrs Howard said. She had slipped her hand into Steven's, and was happily holding his arm. 'Dr Fong called me and explained the situation. He told me how important it was not to leave a trail that Stark could trace. I came right away. I'm so sorry to have worried you, honey,' she said to Steven. 'But I didn't dare check in with Leanne, you know how she gossips. And Mary Beth's just hopeless. But you're here now, and that's all that matters. Oh, I've got so many things to tell you! How are you? Oh, I'm so glad you're home!'

Steven looked torn between wanting to laugh and to cry. I knew the feeling. Home. He was as far from home as he could be.

And yet, he was in her arms. So wasn't he, in fact, home?

From the chair where Lulu had sunk down, I heard a sound. When I glanced over, I saw her twirling a curl of her blonde pageboy nervously. When she saw that almost everyone in the room was looking at her, she jumped, and said apologetically, 'Sorry! I just . . .' She looked wan and delicate in the dim light of Dr Fong's living room. 'I don't get it. What are we doing here?'

'We're here to find her,' I said, nodding towards Mrs Howard. 'But the real story is why she's here. Right, Doctor?'

Dr Fong sighed. He didn't want to talk about this. He didn't want to talk about it at all.

'I needed her help. I took an oath,' he said wearily. 'They told me to throw Nikki's brain away. But to do that when there was nothing wrong with it . . . that would have been murder. I owe a lot to Stark Enterprises. But I'll not be party to killing an innocent woman.'

'So . . . if you didn't dispose of Nikki's brain,' Steven said, looking confused, 'what did you do with it?'

As if on cue, a side door opened and a young woman I'd never seen before, of average height and average weight, with auburn hair that was neither curly nor straight, came into the room wincing as if she'd just woken up, even though the lamplight wasn't particularly bright.

'God,' she was complaining, 'could you guys make any more noise? Some people are still trying to sleep, you know.'

Then she seemed to realize that there were more people in the room than just Dr Fong and Mrs Howard, and her eyes widened a bit.

It was only when she came to stand beside me and looked at me properly that she fully reacted, however. Colour rushed into her full, slightly cherubic face, and her eyes, which were green, flashed.

In a second flat, she'd lifted her hand and brought it right across my face with as much force as she could.

That's right. She'd slapped me.

'*You bitch*,' Nikki Howard said.

Twenty-two

Mrs Howard and Steven jumped in to separate us before things got really bad. I mean, Nikki tried to go to town on me – or I guess I should say, on her old body – as she began hitting and pinching me, pulling at my hair. Dr Fong shouted at me that I couldn't hit Nikki back – after I tried to do so, entirely in self-defence – because her recovery hadn't been as speedy as mine, and she hadn't bounced back as quickly from her surgery as I had from mine. Nikki hadn't had the incredible technology of the Stark Institute for Neurology and Neurosurgery to help her with her rehabilitation the way I had – only her mother's tender care and whatever help Dr Fong could give her when he got home from work. Apparently, Nikki wasn't a hundred per cent yet, like I was.

'But she's still well enough to be emailing her ex-boyfriends,' I pointed out snarkily. I'm sorry, but that slap had hurt. And the subsequent pinches hadn't felt too good either.

Mrs Howard threw Nikki an accusing look. She'd been pretty angry with her over the slap and subsequent attack on me, yelling, 'Nicolette Elizabeth Howard! You quit hitting that girl right now, you hear me!' It was the first time anyone had ever called me by my full name.

Only she hadn't been addressing me.

'Look at her, Mom,' Nikki had shouted in reply as Mrs Howard had dragged her daughter from me. 'Just look at her! That's *my* dress! And my new Marc Jacobs boots! And look how she's making up my eyes. They look awful!'

But Mrs Howard wasn't willing to put up with any crap from her daughter, despite her delicate state of health. 'Nikki, you apologize,' she said. 'You know that's no way to behave. Especially in someone else's home.'

Nikki, looking truculent, jutted out her lower lip and sneered. 'Sorry.'

That, apparently, was all the apology I was to get for my throbbing cheek.

Mrs Howard, however, came over to me and put an arm around my shoulders and said, 'I'm so sorry, honey.' Honey. Just like she'd called Steven. Her arm felt soft and comforting. When she looked at me, I saw that there wasn't any flicker in her gaze, unlike my own mother's. The look Mrs Howard gave me was strong and steady and compassionate. 'This has been really hard on her. But I want to thank you. Thank you . . . for bringing me my son.'

And then she'd kissed me on the cheek Nikki had slapped.

And I know it had just been Nikki's body reacting. But I'd felt comforted in a way I hadn't really felt with my own mom in ages.

Which was weird.

Now Nikki's mother turned an outraged look on her

daughter and said, 'Nikki, what are you doing, emailing people? I told you, you can surf the Net, but no emailing!'

Sitting on the couch where Steven had pinned her, scowling at all of us, Nikki pouted. 'Well, what else am I supposed to do all day? You can only watch so many episodes of *Flavor Flav*. I'm so bored!'

'Of course you are, sweetie,' Lulu said, going to sit on the couch beside her, and stroking her arm. She was trying to calm her old friend down – not that it seemed to be doing much good. Nikki didn't look any more thrilled to see Lulu than she did to see me. 'I can't believe they've been keeping you cooped up in here. But I'm sure they'll let you out soon.'

'To do what?' Nikki demanded churlishly. 'Work at the Gap? Look at me. I'm ugly and my hair is stupid. What are you wearing, anyway? You look weird.'

Lulu touched her chauffeur's cap. 'I think it's cute,' she said defensively. 'I think *you* look cute. Red hair suits you. And there's *lots* of things you can do. This man saved you from being dead. Aren't you glad about not being dead?'

'No,' Nikki said. She turned her attention to Cosabella. 'Cosy.' She snapped her fingers at the dog, who was still wrestling with the other dogs. 'Cosy!' She leaned back, frustrated. 'God, this sucks. Even my own dog likes this one better.' She sneered at me. I was apparently *this one*.

'Hon, I told you. We'll get you a new dog,' Mrs Howard said. She looked tired, and not just because it was the middle of the night. It seemed as if this was a conversation they'd had numerous times before. 'The important thing is that we don't let Stark find out you're still alive. You have to stop emailing people. Doctor Fong has gone to so much trouble for you.'

'Yeah,' I said. I looked from Nikki to Dr Fong. 'How come I didn't see you in the recovery ward at the Institute when I was there?'

Dr Fong seemed even more tired than Mrs Howard. 'In order to save Nikki's life,' he explained, 'I was forced to employ subterfuge. I used her brain in one of our demonstration surgeries for some foreign surgeons, with the assistance of some of my colleagues. They didn't, of course, know where the healthy brain we were using had come from. The donor body Nikki has now belonged to a young woman – a drunk driver – who had gone into a vegetative state due to a vehicular accident.'

Nikki rolled her eyes. 'Right,' she said, when I glanced at her. 'You get the supermodel's body. I get the drunk-driver's body.'

'At least you're alive, Nikki,' her big brother said.

Nikki made a face. 'Oh, stay out of it, Steven.'

'Once the surgery was successfully completed,' Dr Fong went on, 'in order to keep Nikki from asking any questions that might arouse suspicion when she woke, it was necessary to have her transferred immediately, while she was still in her coma, from the Institute – I forged documents stating she was being transferred to another hospital closer to the brain transplant's home. But really, I had her transported here, and bribed the ambulance attendants to keep quiet

278

about it. Her mother was the one who did most of her nursing.'

'The question is why Stark tried to kill her in the first place,' Christopher said.

'Yeah,' Nikki said, looking at Christopher appraisingly. She evidently liked what she saw, since she flipped some of her red hair back flirtatiously. Well, what girl wouldn't like Christopher? Especially one who'd been cooped up in the house as long as she had. Although if she made a move towards him, I'd be forced to break her nose. 'Why would Stark want to kill me after everything I've done for them? I mean, just because I overheard them talking about that stupid game—'

Christopher's interest sharpened. 'What game?'

'That computer game,' Nikki said. 'The new one. Travelquest or whatever.'

'*Journeyquest*,' I corrected her. 'You mean the new version, *Realms*?'

'Right,' Nikki said. She dropped the flirtatiousness for a look of mystery. 'I mean, I *might* have overheard something about that . . . Something Robert Stark wouldn't want getting out. At least, that's what he said when I brought it up.'

Christopher and I exchanged glances. Uh-oh.

Even Lulu knew enough to know this was bad. She took her hand away from Nikki's arm.

'Nikki,' she said with a gasp, 'did you *tell* Mr Stark you knew this secret?'

'Sure,' Nikki said, with a shrug. 'I wanted to see how

much it would be worth to him for me to keep quiet about it. And it turned out, it was worth quite a bit . . .' She laughed delightedly at the memory of it. Then her face darkened as she stared at me. 'Except you're the one enjoying the money now, aren't you? What have you been spending it on? It better be good.'

'What money?' I asked, genuinely bewildered. 'I don't know what you're talking about—'

But I had a very bad feeling about it . . . a feeling that, I could tell, was shared by the rest of the room, if the uneasy expressions everyone was wearing were any indication.

'The *money*,' Nikki went on, 'that Stark promised to pay me to keep my mouth shut about Stark Quark! I never got to see a dime of it. I had the accident right after that.'

Dr Fong, who clearly hadn't heard any of this before, sank his head into his hands and groaned.

I glanced at Christopher, who said with a knowing smile, 'Told you. There are no accidents.'

I swallowed. Hard. He *had* said that. But he didn't have to look so smug about it. This was a girl's life we were talking about. A girl who used to walk around in the body I was currently inhabiting, living in the loft I currently lived in . . . a girl whose dog no longer recognized her.

It was so sad. I wanted to cry just looking at her, sitting there on the couch, so proud of herself for something that had, in the end, ruined her life.

No . . . *ended* that life.

'Oh, *Nikki*,' Mrs Howard said with a groan, covering her mouth with both her hands.

Her son, however, had a lot more to say about it than just his sister's name.

'Has it occurred to you, Nikki,' Steven demanded sharply, 'that Stark might just have tried to have you killed instead of paying you? What you did was blackmail.'

Nikki rolled her eyes. 'God, Steven, you were always so dramatic. It's just a stupid video game.'

'It's a billion dollar line of software,' Christopher corrected her. 'And even if you were the Face of Stark, you were replaceable.' He nodded at me. 'See? They replaced you. With her.'

Nikki stared at me. As she did so, her lower lip started to tremble, just a tiny bit. It was all starting to sink in. Finally.

'They chose the software over you,' Christopher went on brutally. So brutally, I wanted to shout at him to stop. Just stop. This was all too much. I was so tired. I wanted to crawl into bed and go to sleep and make it all go away. Except that I couldn't, of course. 'Or at least they meant to. Doctor Fong saved your life.'

For the first time, Nikki began to look scared. She glanced at me, and then at Christopher. Finally, she looked at Lulu.

'You guys found me,' she said, 'because of an email? An email I sent to Justin?'

'Yes, sweetie,' Lulu said gently, taking her hand. 'Your mom is right. You have to be more careful.'

'Yeah,' Christopher said. 'And what we need to know is . . . have you sent any more emails to anyone else?

Because – in case you haven't already guessed – your location can be traced that way.'

Nikki chewed her lower lip. 'Just a couple,' she said in a meek voice. She seemed really frightened now. 'But not to anyone who matters.'

'Who, Nikki?' Mrs Howard asked. She sounded as frightened as her daughter. 'Just tell us who.'

'Just to . . . to . . . Brandon Stark,' Nikki said.

My heart sank. Brandon. Of course. Of course she'd email Brandon. They'd been a couple before the accident.

No wonder Brandon seemed to have such mixed-up ideas about me. He was getting emails from someone named NikkiH telling him how much she missed him. Then he was seeing me, in the flesh . . . and it didn't help that sometimes I did flirt with him, a little . . .

OK, a lot.

Great. And he was outside, in the limo. The last thing we needed was Brandon bursting in here, realizing Nikki Howard – the *real* Nikki Howard, the one his father thought he had had killed – was still alive.

'Excuse me,' I said in a tight voice.

I leaped up from the chair I'd been sitting in, hurried out of the room and stepped into the foyer. I knew I wasn't the only one freaking out over the fact that we'd led the son of the man responsible for this entire mess to Dr Fong's very door. I needed to go and check on Brandon. I was just reaching for the handle to the front door when something hard and rough wrapped around my throat, and suddenly I found myself pressed against the wall, all the breath knocked out of me from the impact.

And looming in front of me was Brandon Stark, five o'clock shadow standing out sharply all along his jaw. With his right arm, he was pushing me by the throat against one of Dr Fong's duck portraits.

'Don't say a word,' Brandon hissed. 'If you scream or make any noise at all, I swear I'll tell my dad exactly where he can find the real Nikki Howard.'

Twenty-three

I clamped my mouth shut. The truth was, I'd been about to let out a shriek to wake the dead.

Brandon's warning caused me to think twice about that, though. Also, because he was pressing so hard on my throat, I couldn't have made a sound if I wanted to. Besides, I wasn't sure he actually wanted a reply.

'So,' he went on, 'brain transplant? That's what happened to you? Not this amnesia bull you've been feeding me and everyone else?'

I remembered how, back in St John, his fingers had touched the scar on the back of my head. That must have been the first clue that all was not as I kept assuring him it was.

I nodded mutely, wondering how I was going to get out of this. Christopher, I knew, could have no idea anything was wrong. None of them would. Not until I didn't come back for a while. *Would* I be back? I wondered. This was a side of Brandon I'd never seen before. It was a side that scared me witless.

'Yeah. That actually explains a lot,' he said. He moved one thumb down my jaw line. Creepy was not a strong enough word to describe how it felt. I'd always thought Brandon was dumb. But it turned out I'd been wrong.

'You changed,' he went on, 'but I could never put my

finger on how, exactly. Until today. I mean, obviously there was the Stark-is-evil crap. But the old Nikki –' The old Nikki. I wondered how she'd feel about being called that – 'had been spewing crap about how she knew something about Stark Quark for ages. I just never listened. Now I know I should have . . .'

My heart thumped. Oh God. We were so dead. Brandon was going to tell. He was going to tell his dad everything. There had to be a way out of this, there just had to be. What did Brandon want? What could I give him to shut him up about this?

'The problem is, she was an amateur,' Brandon went on. 'You all are. You don't know my dad. He doesn't care about anyone or anything . . . except Stark. The only way to hurt him is through his company. Whatever she knows about Stark Quark, if it's worth killing Nikki Howard for – and then giving her a brain transplant to keep her image alive – it's worth knowing. Believe me. And I want in.'

I opened my mouth. I was in such shock, I didn't remember to be quiet, like he'd asked. This was the last thing I'd expected him to say – that he wanted in.

'But—' I croaked.

'No,' Brandon said, and laid a hand over my lips. 'Shh. I know that's what she was doing – blackmailing him. But obviously she wasn't going about it the right way. She didn't know just how powerful the information she had was. I'm going to do it right. I'm going to get her to tell me what she knows – and she will, because she's obviously still got the hots for me, since she keeps emailing me. And then you're going to get your personal geek squad back there to tell me what the hell she's talking about. And then they'll figure out what we can do with that information to hurt my dad. And then I'm going to blackmail him myself.'

I looked up at him like he was crazy. Only the thing was, I didn't really believe for a minute he was. Crazy, I mean. Not at all.

And that was the scary part.

'Why should I help you?' I demanded.

'Because,' he said very simply, 'if you don't, I'll tell my dad where the real Nikki Howard is. And I'll tell him about the doctor too.' He ran a strand of my long blonde hair through his fingers, testing its silkiness. 'OK? Now, you're going to go in there and tell them that you found me awake and that you've told me the whole story because I'm such a great guy, and that I'm on your side.'

My jaw dropped. He smiled as he tugged on the curl of hair he held.

'And if you tell them that I'm making you do it, I'll tell my father about the girl. And one last thing,' he said, moving his arm so it was no longer pressing against my neck, but wrapped around my shoulders. 'No more messing around with that guy in there, that one I found you with in your bedroom. You and I are together now. Understand?'

I felt myself turning bright red. So he *had* seen me with Christopher . . .

'I'm tired of this little cat-and-mouse game of yours, emailing me and then avoiding me,' he went on.

'That wasn't me emailing you,' I said, feeling sick

to my stomach. Because it *had* been me kissing him in St John . . . oh, how I wished now I had never listened to Lulu. 'It was Nikki. The real Nikki.'

'Right,' Brandon said, looking bored with the conversation. 'What's your name again? Your real name?'

'Em,' I said. My voice was rough from where he'd been pressing against my larynx with his arm. 'Emerson.'

'OK,' Brandon said, 'Emerson.' Then he laughed. 'The truth is, I don't really care what your name is. You can be sweet when you want to. Unlike the old Nikki. Only you're not stupid like she was. So remember what I said. You're mine now.' He squeezed my shoulders, hard. 'No more of that other guy, the one in the leather jacket, who seems so into you. Just me. Understand?'

I nodded. What choice did I have?

He lifted his arm, so I could move again, keeping one hand firmly wrapped around my arm.

But even though I could move physically, I felt paralysed mentally and emotionally. What had just happened? Was this really Brandon, the guy who had jumped into the water in St John to save me from drowning? He'd put his arm around my neck there too, but to tow me to the boat to save me, not to press me to a wall and threaten me. How could he be so drastically different than I'd remembered him? Was the Brandon who'd complained to me so often about his distant father really the same one who was now preparing to participate in blackmail – not to mention forcing me to become his girlfriend against my will?

I had thought Christopher had turned into a super-villain, but it turned out I didn't even know what a supervillain was. Brandon was the supervillain of all super-villains. He had embraced evil in a way Christopher, I was quite certain, couldn't even begin to contemplate.

Numb, I moved away from him, leaving the foyer and turning back towards the living room, just as Christopher was turning to Mrs Howard to say, his voice so even and measured it sent chills up my spine, and not just because I'd basically been dealing with a human snake seconds ago, 'The fact is, it's just not safe for you here any more. You and Nikki have to go.'

'Not without me they don't,' Steven said.

Mrs Howard sounded nervous. 'Oh, Steven . . . But do you really think – are we really in that much danger of being found out?'

I wanted to shout, *You already have been*! But I kept my mouth shut.

'If we could trace those emails, it's pretty likely someone from Stark could, if they found out about them,' Christopher said. 'It's safer that all of you get out of here.'

'But where will you go?' It was Lulu who spoke up. 'You can't hide from Stark's people forever. They're everywhere.'

Yeah. She had no idea.

It was at that moment Brandon propelled me forward with the grip he was keeping on my arm. I stepped into the living room without glancing behind me to show I was being followed.

'Was Brandon still sleeping like a baby?' Lulu wanted to know.

'Um . . .' I said, 'not exactly.'

Which was when Brandon loped into the room behind me, causing everyone to freeze with alarm before they realized who it was.

'Relax,' Brandon said with a big smile and a wide-open gesture with his hands. 'Nikki – or Em, as I guess her name is really – filled me in on the whole thing.'

I saw Christopher and Steven throw me startled glances, filled with surprise and even rebuke.

What could I do? I knew both guys could have taken Brandon down physically.

But short of killing him, how could they have kept him from telling his dad what he'd overheard once he'd recovered? He knew where Dr Fong lived, and probably knew Christopher's last name too. I couldn't let him go to his father with what he knew. I couldn't! He'd agreed to play along . . . as long as I met his conditions.

I just wished I'd never been stupid enough to have kissed him in the first place. Obviously that had only been playing with fire. Why had I mistaken him for a mere drunken playboy for so long? I should have known that, like his father, there was a scheming businessman underneath that handsome facade that would stop at nothing to get what he wanted . . . which in Brandon's case was revenge on Stark.

Not at all unlike Christopher. Only Brandon wanted revenge on one particular Stark, not the whole company.

'I don't want any of you to worry about a thing,' Brandon said in a soothing tone. 'I've got it all under control. First of all, as you know, I'm no friend of my father. Secondly, Nikki, Mrs Howard and Steven . . . I've got it all figured out. My limo outside can take you to a private plane that's waiting on the tarmac at Teterboro. It can fly you all to my summer house in South Carolina. You'll be completely safe there.'

Nikki, who'd been sitting on the couch gaping up at Brandon like an angel had suddenly burst into the room, looked as if she'd become transported with joy. Her face beaming, she leaped up and threw her arms around him. 'Oh, Brandon,' she cried, 'I *knew* you'd come through for us! I *knew* it!'

Brandon gamely hugged her back. Behind him, Steven stared at me, as if to say, *Who* is *this guy? What's going on?*

I gave him a queasy smile that I meant to be reassuring. But I'm not sure it did the trick.

'Well, Mr Stark,' Mrs Howard said, glancing at me as uneasily as her son had. 'That's awfully . . . kind. But you're sure your father won't find out?'

'Robert?' Brandon laughed humourlessly. 'No way. He's too busy with the Stark Quark roll-out to have the slightest idea what's going on. Besides which, as I said, it's my house. Dad doesn't even know about it. You'll love it. Six bedrooms, six baths, plenty of room for all of you, including the dogs.' He looked down at the poodles fondly. Any guy who liked dogs that much couldn't be all bad, right? OK, wrong. 'And we're in luck, since Em has agreed to come with us –' He wrapped an arm around my waist and drew me towards him, anchoring me to his side in a grip I could attest was much tighter than it appeared – 'to spend the holidays.'

I couldn't even look at Christopher. I knew the hurt and disappointment I'd see in his eyes would be more than I could bear. My heart was breaking enough as it was.

'Well,' Brandon said to Nikki, 'go and get packed. We don't have much time. The plane is fuelling up now.' Nikki let go of Brandon with a squeal and darted out of the room to go and get her things. 'Mrs Howard,' Brandon went on, 'how about you? Can you be ready soon?'

She looked like a woman in a daze. She'd been through a lot in the past few months – she'd been through a lot in the past few *hours*. But all she said was, 'Yes. Yes, I think so.'

She called to her dogs and started up the stairs. Steven was the first to turn towards Brandon after both women were gone.

'I'm sorry,' he began tersely, 'but we're just supposed to *trust* you? Your father is Robert Stark. It's because of him we're in this situation in the first place.'

'Oh, I totally get where you're coming from,' Brandon said. 'But remember, I hate my father.'

'It's true,' Lulu said, speaking up from the couch with a squeak. 'He does hate his father. He says it all the time. Even when he's not drunk.'

'And I can't believe,' Brandon went on, not taking offence at Lulu's remark, 'that he would do this. I'm happy to do whatever I can to try to help you and make things right. I've ordered a local cab for you, Lulu, and your friend –' He nodded at Christopher – 'to take you back into Manhattan. It should be here any minute. I'm really sorry for this whole mess. If there's anything else I can do . . . well, you only have to ask.'

'*Mess?*' Christopher stepped forward. I had to look at him now, even though I didn't want to. He wore an expression of murderous rage. And the same look of hurt I'd seen in his eyes from before. 'You're calling this a *mess*? Your father had a girl murdered – or tried to – and another girl's brain transferred into her body, and you call that a *mess*?'

Brandon barely glanced at him. 'Look, buddy,' he said out of the corner of his mouth. 'I'm doing the best I can, all right? I'm trying to get them to safety, and keep the doctor from losing his job . . . and his life. One step at a time, OK? You try growing up with a guy like Robert Stark as a father. It's not easy.'

Christopher was breathing so hard, he was practically panting. He glanced over at me, standing anchored to Brandon's waist. 'You're not actually going with this clown, are you, Em?'

'Um,' I said. This was something I didn't really feel emotionally able to handle at the moment. Besides, while my heart was busy breaking, my mind was busy racing. There might – might – be a way out of this, if everyone just played along. Including Christopher. 'Do we have to discuss this right now?'

'Yeah.' Christopher's voice was as icy cold as the air outside. 'Right now would be good, actually.'

'I think you heard the lady.' Brandon's voice was as cold as Christopher's. 'She said not now.'

Lulu, looking nervous, had stood up. 'What about Steven and Nikki's – I mean, Em's – things?' she wanted to know. 'They're still at our place in Manhattan.'

'It's all right,' Steven said. 'I can buy new things.'

'I'll send them,' Lulu said. 'I don't mind.' The look she flung him was full of emotion, but Steven didn't appear to notice. He was still regarding Brandon suspiciously.

'They might trace the package,' Christopher said. He seemed as if he was in a bad mood. And that was putting it mildly. 'Em,' he went on, 'I *really* need to talk to you.'

'There'll be plenty of time for talking,' Brandon said, releasing me and going to one of the windows and lifting the curtain to look out, 'once we get the Howards to safety. What we really don't want right now is my father or any of his people getting here before we get them out.'

Lulu looked alarmed. 'Could that happen? Do they know we're here?'

'There's a vehicle tracking system on all the Stark limos,' Brandon said casually. 'If my driver reported the limo stolen – and I imagine he probably did –'

Steven let out a swear word. I pressed both my hands to my face. I couldn't believe none of us had thought of that.

'Oh, don't worry,' Brandon said, seeing our expressions. 'I already called to let them know I'm all right. But I'm sure if any of them was paying attention, they'd have to be wondering what I was doing at the home of a surgeon with the Stark Institute for Neurology and Neurosurgery . . .'

Dr Fong looked more miserable than ever, seeming to curl in on himself. I felt a pang for him. He'd only, after all, been trying to do the right thing.

Hadn't we all though?

'Oh,' Brandon said, still peering out the window, 'here comes the cab.'

I saw Lulu turn and, as if she couldn't hold it in any longer, throw herself against Steven, wrapping her arms around his neck in as passionate an embrace as I'd ever seen . . . so passionate the chauffeur's cap got knocked clean off.

To say Steven looked surprised would have been an understatement. But not in a bad way. His arms even went around her before he realized what he was doing. Then he broke the embrace with a firm, 'Now, Lulu,' looking both pleased and disturbed at the same time, if such a thing was possible.

'I can't help it,' I was close enough to hear Lulu whisper. 'I'm going to miss you. Promise me you'll call me somehow. Only if it's safe though.'

'I'll try,' Steven replied. He reached up and wiped some of her tears away with his thumb. 'You take care of yourself. Don't spend all your time practising your coq au vin.'

Lulu laughed tearfully and let him go.

She came up to me and laid a hand on my wrist. Her eyes were as big and tear-filled as I'd ever seen.

'Nikki – I mean, Em,' she said. 'Are you sure you're all right?'

'I'm fine,' I said.

'So . . .' She looked confused. 'I guess it wasn't a spirit transfer after all?'

'No,' I said with a little laugh.

'But . . . you're going with them? Why?' Lulu wanted to know. 'What about Frida?'

'I can't tell you why,' I said, my pulse pounding suddenly. I couldn't tell her, of course . . . that a psychopathic billionaire's son seemed to think he was in love with me, and was blackmailing me into doing it. 'And you can't tell Frida, OK? You know this can't go any further than this room. This is serious. Lives are at stake. I'll just tell Frida I went away for the holidays with –' I glanced over at Brandon, who'd dropped the window curtain and was watching us, a tiny smile on his lips. A chill went up and down my spine that had nothing to do with the fact that the fire in the room had gone out so long ago – 'my boyfriend.'

The tears in Lulu's eyes spilled over. 'Your *boyfriend*? But what about . . .' Her gaze strayed towards Christopher.

I reached out and hugged her. Her body felt so slight. 'I know,' I whispered miserably. Over her shoulder, I looked at Christopher, whose expression was inscrutable.

'Take care of her,' I said to him, indicating Lulu.

To my relief, he nodded.

There was some clattering on the stairs, and suddenly the dogs appeared, followed by Nikki and her mom, each holding an overnight bag.

'I think we're ready,' Mrs Howard announced. She had changed into outdoor clothes and applied some make-up, as well as doing to her hair. She actually looked good now, and much more recognizably like the attractive woman in the photos Steven had emailed to all the news shows. It was obvious where Nikki had got her good looks.

Nikki, on the other hand, was still applying her make-up. Her hair was a work in progress as well, half flat-ironed and half wavy. She seemed irritated at having been hurried along. She still wore the clothes she'd slept in.

'Great,' Brandon said, ignoring the yapping dogs at his feet and the mascara wand in Nikki's hand. He strode to the front door and yanked it open, letting in a rush of bitterly cold air. 'Let's go then . . .'

I kept my head down, my hair tumbling over my face as much to protect it from the biting cold as to keep from having to see what was going on around me as I stepped through the new-fallen snow, which was still coming down steadily. I didn't want to have to look at Christopher's face . . . I didn't want to have to answer his questions . . . not with the lies I'd have to tell, since Brandon would be nearby, listening.

I especially didn't want to have to say goodbye. Not when I'd finally managed to get him back after so long.

But it turned out I didn't have a choice. Because just as I was about to follow Nikki into the limo, a hard hand closed around my arm, and Christopher's voice said, 'Em.'

I closed my eyes before turning round and prayed for strength. When I opened them again I saw Brandon standing on the other side of the limo, looking right at me. He was smiling. He said, 'I think your little friend wants to speak to you.'

I hated him then. I'd never hated anyone as much as I hated him at that moment.

And I swore that when this was all over – if it ever ended – I'd find some way to get back at him, the same way he was trying to get back at his dad.

I turned my head, flipping my blonde hair out of the way so I could see.

And there was Christopher, looking down at me, his breath coming out in white puffs in the chilly air. His cheeks were pink, like they always were when the temperature dipped below freezing.

But his blue eyes were blazing.

'Em, what are you doing?' he demanded. 'Why are you going with them?'

'I have to,' I said, looking everywhere but into those burning eyes.

'Why?' Christopher asked. 'They'll be all right. Steven's with them.'

'Because,' I said. I looked at some lavender clouds in the sky. Anywhere but Christopher's face. 'Brandon asked me to.'

'*Brandon* asked you to?' Christopher's voice rose incredulously. 'Who the hell cares what Brandon Stark wants?'

'Uh, I believe she might,' Brandon said from across the top of the car. 'Tell him, Em.'

'Tell me what?' Christopher asked.

'Tell him,' Brandon repeated. He drummed the top of the limo in time with the words. 'About us.'

'Us,' Christopher repeated. I saw his head swivel towards me. Since I couldn't look at his face, I only heard the disbelief in his voice. I didn't see it in his expression. 'There's an *us* with you and Brandon? When did this happen?'

I knew what I had to do. Brandon had spelled it out back in Dr Fong's foyer simply enough for a child to understand. I had no choice. I had to do it, because the Howards were my family now, and I had to protect them, same as I would my real parents. Family wasn't just the people who'd raised you. Family wasn't just the people who had the same blood as you coursing through their veins.

Family was people who needed you. Family was people who had nothing when you had everything.

You had to do what was right by them. You had to, even if doing so broke your heart.

Besides, I could do this. I could find out what Nikki knew about Stark before Brandon found out, and use that information against him to get out of this, turn this whole thing around, and get Christopher back. Somehow. Right?

But until then . . . I had to play the game.

'I've been going out with him for a while,' I told Christopher. Each word felt like a stab wound. 'I tried to tell you before.' I lifted my head and looked him in the eye. 'I mean, if you had made a move back when I was alive,

298

maybe things might have been different. But you waited too long – you waited until I was someone else. Until I was *with* someone else.'

I wasn't sure where all this was coming from. But it wasn't feigned for Brandon's benefit. It was real emotion, and it was welling up from deep inside me. And it was accompanied by real tears that were spilling out, hot and fast, as well.

'What are you talking about?' Christopher asked, his voice cracking.

'Maybe if you had just liked me the way I was before,' I went on brutally. 'But you didn't. And now it's too late.'

I could see that every word I'd said, which had felt to me like a knife wound, had hit him like a fist. The red had gone from his cheeks. He looked pale as the snow on the sloping yard all around us.

'So,' I said. I don't know why I kept going. Maybe because of that picture. That picture of me he'd kept in his room. I just couldn't get it out of my head. I couldn't believe he'd kept it. I couldn't believe he'd loved me all this time, the same way I'd loved him. And now I had to make him stop loving me, because I didn't want him to do anything stupid that might get him hurt. 'I'm with Brandon now. I . . . I love Brandon. And I'm going with him. So . . . Goodbye. Goodbye, Christopher.'

And I ducked into the limo before Christopher could say another word – and before I took another look at his face – climbing inside to sit between Nikki and her mom. Mrs Howard looked over at me with some concern, as

Cosabella leaped up on to my lap, and asked, 'Honey . . . are you all right?'

'I'm fine,' I said, wiping away my tears with the backs of my fists. 'Sorry about that.'

'God,' Nikki said. She was still working on her eyelashes with the mascara wand. 'And everyone said *I* was bad.'

This didn't exactly make me want to cry any less hard. In the driver's seat I saw Steven adjust the rear-view mirror so he could see me in it. He looked at me . . . but he didn't say anything. Not a word. He just looked. It was as if, in that moment, we shared a secret.

Just what that secret was, I had no idea.

But I knew, in the battle that was coming, I had an ally in Steven Howard.

But I guess I'd always known that, really. I just needed to figure out a way to let him know what was happening . . . before it was too late.

'All right,' Brandon said cheerfully, climbing into the limo behind me. 'Are we all set?' And without waiting for an answer, he closed the car door . . . and in that sound, I felt as if I was hearing the end of the world. Or at least the end of all my hopes and dreams. Not that I'd had that many, at least not recently.

'God,' Nikki said with relish, 'I've *missed* limos.'

'Stark Travel is the way to go,' Brandon said. And he reached into a side cooler and pulled out a bottle. 'Champagne, anyone? Oh, sorry, not you, Steven. But we'll fill you up when we get there. Do you know how to get to Teterboro Airport? No, of course you don't. Here, let me tell you. Better not programme it into the GPS, we're trying to keep this whole trip on the down low . . .'

And he crawled up towards the front to talk to Steven about how to get to where we were going.

And while the limo slowly began moving down the driveway, I shifted in my seat to look back through the tinted windows. I saw Dr Fong turn away and close his front door, his long journey finally over.

I saw Lulu waiting by the taxi, the wind tugging at her poofy black skirt, and making it swell out like a bell.

And I saw Christopher, standing in the exact spot where I'd left him, staring after us – after me. He appeared smaller and smaller the further we drove away.

I stared at him until finally I couldn't see him any more, because the tears coming from my eyes made it impossible to see anything at all.

Coming soon . . .

runaway

The final book in the **airhead** *trilogy*

By **meg cabot**

*Where can you hide
when everyone knows your name?*

Emerson Watts is on the run: from school, from work, from her family, from her friends, from herself . . .

She's still in shock over the fact that the girl whose life she was forced to take over when her brain was transplanted into her body is alive – alive and furious with her for stealing what she claims was rightfully hers . . .

Now Brandon Stark is intent on finding out what that girl's secret was, and using it to get revenge on his father. But that's not all Brandon wants to use . . . he's not above using Em to trick Nikki into revealing that secret, and to help him secure his place as head of Stark Enterprises once and for all.

But Brandon's not the only one who wants vengeance. Christopher might just want to get even with Em for being with Brandon now.

With everyone she loves furious with her for something she can't explain, and nothing but the live Stark Angel fashion show on New Year's Eve to look forward to, Em's reached the end of her rope . . . what's the point of even going on?

But when she discovers the truth about Nikki's secret, she knows there's only one person she can turn to.

Will Christopher be able to put aside his personal feelings and help her expose her employer to the world? Is it even fair to get Christopher involved – since if he agrees, there's every chance that Stark Enterprises will try to have them both killed – this time permanently?

Maybe it would be better for Em to just keep on running . . .

JINX

Meg Cabot

Does Jinx have bad luck – or special powers?

Misfortune has followed Jean Honeychurch all her life – which is why everyone calls her Jinx. And now her parents have shipped her off to New York to stay with relatives – including her sophisticated cousin, Tory – until the trouble she's caused back home dies down.

Could she even be . . . a WITCH?

Tory is far too cool to bother with Jinx – until Jinx's chronic bad luck wreaks havoc in Tory's perfect life. Only then does Jinx discover that beneath Tory's big-city glamour lies a world of hatred and revenge. Now it seems that the jinx that's driven Jean crazy may just be the only thing that can save her life . . .

MEG CABOT

Avalon High, Ellie's new school, is pretty much what she'd expected. There's Lance, the hunky footballer; Jennifer, the cute cheerleader; Marco, the troublemaker. And then there's Will – the most gorgeous guy Ellie's ever met. She can hardly believe he likes HER.

When Will says he thinks he's met Ellie before, things start getting a little weird. A feeling that grows as Ellie discovers the strange bonds that entwine Will, Lance, Jen, Marco – and herself.

As darkness turns to danger, can Ellie stop the horrific chain of events that threatens to engulf them all . . .

HOW TO BE
Popular

Meg Cabot

Do you want to be popular?

Everyone wants to be popular – and Steph Landry wants it more than most. Steph's been the least popular girl in class ever since she spilt that red Super Big Gulp over Lauren Moffat's white D&G miniskirt five years ago.

Does being popular matter?

It matters very much – to Steph. That's why this year she's got a plan to get in with the It Crowd in no time flat. Her secret weapon: an old book called – what else? – *How to Be Popular*.

But don't forget the most important thing about popularity!

It's easy to become popular. It's a lot less easy staying that way.

Ten out of Ten

Princess Amelia Mignonette Grimaldi
Thermopolis Renaldo (Mia)

invites you to an exclusive event to celebrate her
18th birthday and the FABULOUS last ever
instalment of The Princess Diaries

Dress code: Glamorous and gorgeous. Tiaras optional.
And, Lana Weinberger, don't forget your underwear!

Etiquette: No curtsying. No paps. No kissing Prince William.

Mia's princess training is almost over. She can climb out of
a limo as elegantly as any European heir presumptive. Even
Grandmere approves of her practically perfect boyfriend, J.P.
So this is the final instalment, the very end, the last EVER
entry in The Princess Diaries. After all, Mia's about to turn
eighteen – it's time to leave childish things behind. Like:

1. Lying.
2. Therapy with Dr Knutz – Mia's so ready to move
   on!
3. Being Albert Einstein High's last and only
   unicorn*.
4. Thinking about Michael Moscovitz. I mean, come
   ON. He's in Japan. And, besides, Mia is TOTALLY
   in love with J.P.
5. Michael who?

* You have *so* got to read the book!

A selected list of titles available from
Macmillan Children's Books

The prices shown below are correct at the time of going to press. However, Macmillan Publishers reserves the right to show new retail prices on covers, which may differ from those previously advertised.

Meg Cabot

All American Girl	978-0-330-41555-2	£5.99
All American Girl: Ready or Not	978-0-330-43834-6	£5.99
Airhead	978-0-330-45382-0	£5.99
Avalon High	978-0-330-44687-7	£5.99
Teen Idol	978-0-330-43300-6	£5.99
How to Be Popular	978-0-330-44406-4	£5.99
Tommy Sullivan Is a Freak	978-0-330-44407-1	£5.99
Jinx	978-0-330-44201-5	£5.99

All Pan Macmillan titles can be ordered from our website, www.panmacmillan.com, or from your local bookshop and are also available by post from:

Bookpost, PO Box 29, Douglas, Isle of Man IM99 1BQ

Credit cards accepted. For details:
Telephone: 01624 677237
Fax: 01624 670923
Email: bookshop@enterprise.net
www.bookpost.co.uk

Free postage and packing in the United Kingdom